## ANOTHER KIND OF JAIL

Johnson's face was working with excitement. "You said you had some whisky for me."

"Hold on for a minute."

"But I'm sick. You can see that I'm sick."

I left him alone and made a cursory search of the upstairs rooms. Only one other was occupied, a room containing a double bed that Johnson evidently shared with his wife. There was no painting under the mattress, nothing incriminating in the closet or chest of drawers, no evidence of any crime but that of poverty.

One narrow door at the end of the upstairs hallway was closed and padlocked. I stopped in front of it.

Johnson came up behind me. "That goes up to the attic. I don't have a key for it. Sarah's always afraid I'll fall down the stairs. Anyway, there isn't anything up there. Like me," he added foolishly, tapping the side of his head. "Nobody home upstairs."

He gave me a broad idiot smile. I gave him the half-pint of whisky. It was an ugly transaction, and I was glad to leave him. He closed the front door behind me like a trusty shutting himself into his prison. I locked the door.

# THE BLUE HAMMER
## ROSS MACDONALD

**BANTAM BOOKS**
TORONTO • NEW YORK • LONDON • SYDNEY • AUCKLAND

To William Campbell Gault

THE BLUE HAMMER
*A Bantam Book / published by arrangement with
Alfred A. Knopf, Inc.*

PRINTING HISTORY
*Knopf edition published May 1976
2nd printing . . . . . . May 1976
Bantam edition / July 1977*

| | |
|---|---|
| 2nd printing . . . . . . July 1977 | 6th printing . . December 1978 |
| 3rd printing . . . . . . July 1977 | 7th printing . . December 1979 |
| 4th printing . September 1977 | 8th printing . . December 1979 |
| 5th printing . . . . . . May 1978 | 9th printing . . . October 1984 |

*The title phrase is from a poem by Henri Coulette.*

*Bantam Books are published by Bantam Books, Inc. Its trade-
mark, consisting of the words "Bantam Books" and the por-
trayal of a rooster, is Registered in U.S. Patent and Trademark
Office and in other countries. Marca Registrada. Bantam
Books, Inc., 666 Fifth Avenue, New York, New York 10103.*

PRINTED IN THE UNITED STATES OF AMERICA

H    18 17 16 15 14 13 12 11 10 9

# I

I drove up to the house on a private road that widened at the summit into a parking apron. When I got out of my car I could look back over the city and see the towers of the mission and the courthouse half submerged in smog. The channel lay on the other side of the ridge, partly enclosed by its broken girdle of islands.

The only sound I could hear, apart from the hum of the freeway that I had just left, was the noise of a tennis ball being hit back and forth. The court was at the side of the house, enclosed by high wire mesh. A thick-bodied man in shorts and a linen hat was playing against an agile blond woman. Something about the trapped intensity of their game reminded me of prisoners in an exercise yard.

The man lost several points in a row and decided to notice my presence. Turning his back on the woman and the game, he came toward the fence.

"Are you Lew Archer?"

I said I was.

"You're late for our appointment."

"I had some trouble finding your road."

"You could have asked anybody in town. Everybody knows where Jack Biemeyer lives. Even the planes coming in use my home as a landmark."

I could see why. The house was a sprawling pile of white stucco and red tile, set on the highest point in Santa Teresa. The only things higher were the mountains standing behind the city and a red-tailed hawk circling in the bright October sky.

The woman came up behind Biemeyer. She looked

much younger than he did. Both her narrow blond head and her pared-down middle-aged body seemed to be hyperconscious of my eyes. Biemeyer didn't introduce us. I told her who I was.

"I'm Ruth Biemeyer. You must be thirsty, Mr. Archer. I know I am."

"We won't go into the hospitality routine," Biemeyer said. "This man is here on business."

"I know that. It was my picture that was stolen."

"I'll do the talking, Ruth, if you don't mind."

He took me into the house, his wife following us at a little distance. The air was pleasantly cool inside, though I could feel the weight of the structure surrounding and hanging over me. It was more like a public building than a house—the kind of place where you go to pay your taxes or get a divorce.

We trekked to the far side of a big central room. Biemeyer pointed at a white wall, empty except for a pair of hooks on which he said the picture had been hung.

I got out my notebook and ball-point pen. "When was it taken?"

"Yesterday."

"That was when I first noticed that it was missing," the woman said. "But I don't come into this room every day."

"Is the picture insured?"

"Not specifically," Biemeyer said. "Of course everything in the house is covered by some insurance."

"Just how valuable is the picture?"

"It's worth a couple of thousand, maybe."

"It's worth a lot more than that," the woman said. "Five or six times that, anyway. Chantry's prices have been appreciating."

"I didn't know you'd been keeping track of them," Biemeyer said in a suspicious tone. "Ten or twelve thousand? Is that what you paid for that picture?"

"I'm not telling you what I paid for it. I bought it with my own money."

"Did you have to do it without consulting me? I

thought you'd gotten over being hipped on the subject of Chantry."

She became very still. "That's an uncalled-for remark. I haven't seen Richard Chantry in thirty years. He had nothing to do with my purchase of the picture."

"I hear you saying so, anyway."

Ruth Biemeyer gave her husband a quick bright look, as if she had taken a point from him in a harder game than tennis. "You're jealous of a dead man."

He let out a mirthless laugh. "That's ridiculous on two counts. I know bloody well I'm not jealous, and I don't believe he's dead."

The Biemeyers were talking as though they had forgotten me, but I suspected they hadn't. I was an unwilling referee who let them speak out on their old trouble without the danger that it would lead to something more immediate, like violence. In spite of his age Biemeyer looked and talked like a violent man, and I was getting tired of my passive role.

"Who is Richard Chantry?"

The woman looked at me in surprise. "You mean you've never heard of him?"

"Most of the world's population have never heard of him," Biemeyer said.

"That simply isn't true. He was already famous before he disappeared, and he wasn't even out of his twenties."

Her tone was nostalgic and affectionate. I looked at her husband's face. It was red with anger, and his eyes were confused. I edged between them, facing his wife.

"Where did Richard Chantry disappear from?"

"From here," she said. "From Santa Teresa."

"Recently?"

"No. It was over twenty-five years ago. He simply decided to walk away from it all. He was in search of new horizons, as he said in his farewell statement."

"Did he make the statement to you, Mrs. Biemeyer?"

"Not to me, no. He left a letter that his wife made

public. I never saw Richard Chantry again after our early days in Arizona."

"It's not for want of trying," her husband said. "You wanted me to retire here because this was Chantry's town. You got me to build a house right next to his house."

"That isn't true, Jack. It was your idea to build here. I simply went along with it, and you know it."

His face lost its flush and became suddenly pale. There was a stricken look in his eyes, as he realized that his mind had slipped a notch.

"I don't know anything any more," he said in an old man's voice, and left the room.

His wife started after him and then turned back, pausing beside a window. Her face was hard with thought.

"My husband is a terribly jealous man."

"Is that why he sent for me?"

"He sent for you because I asked him to. I want my picture back. It's the only thing I have of Richard Chantry's."

I sat on the arm of a deep chair and reopened my notebook. "Describe it for me, will you?"

"It's a portrait of a youngish woman, rather conventionalized. The colors are simple and bright, Indian colors. She has yellow hair, a red and black serape. Richard was very much influenced by Indian art in his early period."

"Was this an early painting?"

"I don't really know. The man I bought it from couldn't date it."

"How do you know it's genuine?"

"I think I can tell by looking at it. And the dealer vouched for its authenticity. He was close to Richard back in the Arizona days. He only recently came here to Santa Teresa. His name is Paul Grimes."

"Do you have a photograph of the painting?"

"I haven't, but Mr. Grimes has. I'm sure he'd let you

have a look at it. He has a small gallery in the lower town."

"I better talk to him first. May I use your phone?"

She led me into a room where her husband was sitting at an old rolltop desk. The scarred oak sides of the desk contrasted with the fine teakwood paneling that lined the walls. Biemeyer didn't look around. He was studying an aerial photograph that hung above the desk. It was a picture of the biggest hole in the ground I'd ever seen.

He said with nostalgic pride, "That was my copper mine."

"I've always hated that picture," his wife said. "I wish you'd take it down."

"It bought you this house, Ruth."

"Lucky me. Do you mind if Mr. Archer uses the phone?"

"Yes. I do mind. There ought to be some place in a four-hundred-thousand-dollar building where a man can sit down in peace."

He got up abruptly and left the room.

# II

Ruth Biemeyer leaned on the doorframe, exhibiting the profile of her body. It wasn't young any longer, but tennis and possibly anger had kept it thin and taut.

"Is your husband always like this?"

"Not always. He's worried these days."

"About the missing picture?"

"That's part of it."

"What's the rest?"

"It may be connected with the picture, as a matter of

fact." She hesitated. "Our daughter, Doris, is an under-graduate at the university and it's brought her into con-tact with some people we wouldn't normally choose for her. You know how it is."

"How old is Doris?"

"Twenty. She's a sophomore."

"Living at home?"

"Unfortunately not. Doris moved out last month at the start of the fall semester. We got her an apartment in Academia Village on the edge of the campus. I wanted her to stay here, of course, but she said she had a right to her own life-style, just as Jack and I have a right to ours. She's always been very critical of Jack's drinking. Mine, too, if you want the exact truth."

"Is Doris into drugs?"

"I wouldn't say that. Not deeply, anyway." She was silent for a while, imagining her daughter's life, which seemed to frighten her. "I'm not too crazy about some of the people she goes around with."

"Anyone in particular?"

"There's a boy named Fred Johnson, whom she's brought to the house. Actually he's a pretty ancient boy; he must be at least thirty. He's one of those perpetual students who hang around the university because they like the atmosphere, or the pickings."

"Do you suspect he could have stolen your picture?"

"I wouldn't put it that strongly. But he is interested in art. He's a docent at the art museum, and taking college courses in that field. He was familiar with Richard Chantry's name, in fact he seemed quite knowledgeable about him."

"Wouldn't that be true of local art students in gen-eral?"

"I suppose so. But Fred Johnson showed unusual in-terest in the picture."

"Can you give me a description of Fred Johnson?"

"I can try."

I opened my notebook again and leaned on the roll-top desk. She sat in the swivel chair facing me.

"Color of hair?"

"Reddish blond. He wears his hair quite long. It's already thinning a bit on top. But he compensates for that with his mustache. He has one of those big bristly shoebrush mustaches. His teeth aren't very good. His nose is too long."

"What color are his eyes? Blue?"

"More greenish. It's his eyes that really bother me. He never looks straight at you, at least he didn't at me."

"Tall or short?"

"Medium size. Five foot nine, perhaps. Quite slender. On the whole he isn't bad-looking, if you like the type."

"And Doris does?"

"I'm afraid so. She likes Fred Johnson much too well to suit me."

"And Fred liked the missing picture?"

"He more than liked it. He was fascinated by it. He gave it a lot more attention than he gave my daughter. I sort of got the impression that he came here to visit the picture instead of her."

"Did he say anything about it?"

She hesitated. "He said something to the effect that it looked like one of Chantry's memory pictures. I asked him just what he meant. He said it was probably one of several Chantrys that hadn't been painted directly from a model, but from memory. He seemed to think that added to its rarity and its value."

"Did he mention its value?"

"He asked me how much I paid for it. I wouldn't tell him—that's my own little secret."

"I can keep a secret."

"So can I." She opened the top drawer of the rolltop desk and brought out a local telephone directory. "You wanted to call Paul Grimes, didn't you? Just don't try to get the price out of him, either. I've sworn him to secrecy."

I made a note of the dealer's number and his address in the lower town. Then I called the number. A woman's voice answered, faintly exotic, faintly guttural. She said that Grimes was busy with a client but would be free shortly. I gave her my name and said I would drop in later.

Ruth Biemeyer whispered urgently in my free ear, "Don't mention me to her."

I hung up. "Who is she?"

"I believe her name is Paola. She calls herself his secretary. I think their relationship may be more intimate than that."

"Where's her accent from?"

"Arizona. I believe she's part Indian."

I glanced up at the picture of the hole that Jack Biemeyer had made in the Arizona landscape. "This seems to be turning out to be an Arizona case. Didn't you say Richard Chantry came from there?"

"Yes, he did. We all did. But we all ended up here in California."

Her voice was flat, betraying no regret for the state she had left nor any particular pleasure with the state she lived in now. She sounded like a disappointed woman.

"Why did you come to California, Mrs. Biemeyer?"

"I suppose you're thinking about something my husband said. That this is Dick Chantry's town, or was, and that was why I wanted to settle here."

"Is that true?"

"I suppose there's some truth in it. Dick was the only good painter I ever knew really well. He taught me to see things. And I liked the idea of living in the place where he did his best work. He did it all in seven years, you know, and then he disappeared."

"When?"

"If you want the exact date of his departure, it was July 4, 1950."

"Are you sure he went of his own accord? He wasn't murdered, or kidnapped?"

"He couldn't have been. He left a letter to his wife, remember."

"Is she still in town?"

"Very much so. As a matter of fact you can see her house from our house. It's just across the barranca."

"Do you know her?"

"I used to know Francine quite well, when we were young. She and I were never close, though. I've hardly seen her at all since we moved here. Why?"

"I'd like to have a look at the letter her husband left behind."

"I have a copy. They sell photostats of it at the art museum."

She went and got the letter. It was framed in silver. She stood above me reading it to herself. Her lips moved as if she was repeating a litany.

She handed it over with some reluctance. It was typewritten except for the signature and dated July 4, 1950, at Santa Teresa.

Dear Francine,

This is a letter of farewell. It breaks my heart to leave you, but I must. We have often talked about my need to discover new horizons beyond which I may find the light that never was on sea or land. This lovely coast and its history have told me what they had to tell me, as Arizona once did.

But as in Arizona the history is shallow and recent, and cannot support the major work that I was born to do. I must seek elsewhere for other roots, a more profound and cavernous darkness, a more searching light. And like Gauguin I have decided that I must seek it alone. For it is not just the physical world I have to explore, but the mines and chambers of my own soul.

I take nothing with me but the clothes on my back, my talent, and my memory of you. Please remember me with affection, dear wife, dear friends, and wish me well. I only do what I was born to do.

Richard Chantry.

I handed the framed letter back to Ruth Biemeyer. She held it against her body. "It's beautiful, isn't it?"

"I'm not sure. Beauty is in the eye of the beholder. It must have come as quite a shock to Chantry's wife."

"She seems to have stood up to it very well."

"Have you ever discussed it with her?"

"No. I have not." I gathered from the sharpness of her tone that she and Mrs. Chantry were not friends. "But she seems to enjoy all that inherited fame. Not to mention the money he left her."

"Was Chantry suicidal? Did he ever talk about suicide?"

"No, of course not." But she added after a silence, "You must remember I knew Dick when he was very young. I was even younger. Actually I haven't seen him or talked to him for over thirty years. But I've got a very strong feeling that he's still alive."

She touched her breast, as if at least he was alive there. Droplets of sweat grew on her upper lip. She brushed them away with her hand.

"I'm afraid this is getting me down a little. All of a sudden the past rears up and smacks you. Just when I thought I finally had it under control. Does that ever happen to you?"

"Not so much in the daytime. At night, just before I go to sleep—"

"Aren't you married?" She was a quick woman.

"I was, about twenty-five years ago."

"Is your wife still alive?"

"I hope so."

"Haven't you tried to find out?"

"Not recently. I prefer to find out about other people's lives. Right now I'd like to talk to Mrs. Chantry."

"I don't see why that's necessary."

"Still I think I'll give it a try. She can help me fill in the background."

The woman's face stiffened with disapproval. "But all I want you to do is get my picture back."

"You also seem to want to tell me how to do it, Mrs. Biemeyer. I've tried to work that way with other clients, and it didn't turn out too well."

"Why do you want to talk to Francine Chantry? She isn't exactly a friend of ours, you know."

"And I'm only supposed to interview your friends?"

"I didn't mean that." She was silent for a moment. "You plan to talk to several people, do you?"

"As many as I have to. This case looks a bit more complex to me than it does to you. It may take me several days, and cost you several hundred dollars."

"Our credit is perfectly good."

"I don't doubt that. What I'm not certain of is your and your husband's intentions."

"Don't worry, I'll pay you if he doesn't."

She took me outside and showed me the Chantry house. It was a turreted neo-Spanish mansion with several outbuildings, including a large greenhouse. It lay far down the hill from where we stood, on the other side of a barranca that separated the two estates like a deep wound in the earth.

# III

I found my circuitous way to the bridge that crossed the barranca and parked in front of the Chantry house. A large hook-nosed man in a white silk shirt opened the door before I could knock. He stepped outside and shut the door behind him.

"What can I do for you?" He had the voice and look of a spoiled servant.

"I'd like to see Mrs. Chantry."

"She isn't here. I'll take a message for her if you want."

"I'd like to speak to her personally."

"What about?"

"I'll tell her, okay? If you'll tell me where she is."

"I guess she's at the museum. This is her day for that."

I decided to call on the dealer Paul Grimes first. I drove along the waterfront toward the lower town. There were white sails on the water, and gulls and terns in the air like their small flying counterparts. I stopped on impulse and checked in at a motel that faced the harbor.

The lower town was a blighted area standing above the waterfront about ten blocks deep. There were blighted men wandering along the main street or leaning against the fronts of the secondhand stores.

Paul Grimes's shop was a block off the main street between a liquor store and a soul-food restaurant. It wasn't impressive—no more than a dingy stucco storefront with what looked like living quarters above it. Inscribed across the front window in gilt was the legend *Paul Grimes—Paintings and Decorations*. I parked at the green curb in front of it.

A bell tinkled over the door as I went in. The interior had been disguised with painted plyboard screens and gray cloth hangings. A few tentative-looking pictures had been attached to them. On one side a dark woman in a loose multicolored costume sat behind a cheap desk and tried to look busy.

She had deep black eyes, prominent cheekbones, prominent breasts. Her long hair was unflecked black. She was very handsome, and quite young.

I told her my name. "Mr. Grimes is expecting me."

"I'm sorry, he had to go out."

"When will he be back?"

"He didn't say. I think he was going out of town on business."

"Are you his secretary?"

"You could call me that." Her smile was like the flash of a half-concealed knife. "You the man that called about a picture?"

"Yes."

"I can show you some pictures." She gestured toward

those on display. "Most of these are pretty abstract, but we have some representational ones in the back."

"Do you have any of Richard Chantry's paintings?"

"I don't think so. No."

"Mr. Grimes sold a Chantry painting to some people named Biemeyer. They told me he could show me a photograph of it."

"I wouldn't know about that."

She spread her hands in front of her, palms upward, and her loose sleeves fell away from her round brown arms. The light growth of hair on her arms looked like clinging smoke.

"Can you give me Mr. Grimes's home address?"

"He lives upstairs. He isn't in."

"When do you expect him back?"

"I wouldn't know. Sometimes he goes away for a week. He doesn't tell me where he's going, and I don't ask him."

I thanked her and went into the liquor store next door. The middle-aged black man behind the counter asked if he could help me.

"I hope so. Do you know Mr. Grimes?"

"Who?"

"Paul Grimes, the art dealer in the next building."

"Older man with a gray goatee?" He shaped a pointed beard with his fingers. "Wears a white sombrero?"

"That sounds like Mr. Grimes."

He shook his head. "Can't say I know him. I don't believe he drinks. Never does any business with me, anyway."

"What about his girl?"

"She came in for a six-pack once or twice. Paola, I think her name is. Has she got Indian blood, do you know?"

"I wouldn't be surprised."

"I thought so." The idea seemed to please him. "She's a sharp-looking chick. I don't know how a man his age holds on to a chick like that."

"Neither do I. I'd like to know when Mr. Grimes gets back here." I put two dollar bills on the counter between us and laid one of my cards on top of them. "Could I check back with you?"

"Why not?"

I drove up the main street to the chaste white building that housed the art museum. The young man at the turnstile said that Fred Johnson had left the building an hour or so before.

"Did you wish to see him about a personal matter? Or something connected with the museum?"

"I understand he's interested in the painter Richard Chantry."

His smile brightened. "We all are. Are you from out of town, sir?"

"Los Angeles."

"Have you seen our permanent Chantry collection?"

"Not yet."

"You came at a good time. Mrs. Chantry is here now. She gives us one afternoon a week."

He directed me through a room where a group of classical sculptures stood pale and serene, to a quite different kind of room. The first pictures I looked at resembled windows into an alternative world, like the windows that jungle travelers use to watch the animals at night. But the animals in Chantry's paintings seemed to be on the verge of becoming human. Or perhaps they were human beings devolving into animals.

A woman came into the room behind me and answered my unspoken question:

"These are known as the Creation pictures—the artist's imaginative conception of evolution. They represent his first great creative burst. He painted them in a period of six months, incredible as it may seem."

I turned to look at the woman. In spite of her conservative dark blue suit and her rather stilted patter, she gave an impression of rough strength. Her chastely trimmed graying hair seemed to glisten with vitality.

"Are you Mrs. Chantry?"

"Yes." She seemed pleased to be recognized. "I really shouldn't be here. I'm giving a party tonight. But it's hard for me to stay away from the museum on my day."

She led me to a farther wall on which was hung a series of figure studies of women. One of them stopped me. A young woman was sitting on a rock that was partly hidden, as she was, by a buffalo robe around her waist. Her fine breasts and shoulders were bare. Behind her and above her in the picture, the mounted head of a buffalo bull hung in space.

"He called it *Europa*," Mrs. Chantry said.

I turned to her. She was smiling. I looked again at the girl in the picture.

"Is that you?"

"In a sense. I used to model for Richard."

We looked at each other more sharply for a moment. She was about my age or a little younger, with *Europa*'s body holding firm under her blue suit. I wondered what kind of compulsion, what pride in her husband or in herself, made her serve as a museum guide to his pictures.

"Had you ever seen any of his paintings before? They seemed to take you by surprise."

"They did. They do."

"His work has that effect on most people seeing it for the first time. Tell me, what got you interested in it?"

I told her I was a private detective employed by the Biemeyers to investigate the theft of their picture. I wanted to get her reaction.

She went pale under her makeup. "The Biemeyers are ignorant people. That picture they bought from Paul Grimes is a fake. He offered it to me long before they saw it. I wouldn't touch it. It's an obvious imitation of a style that Richard abandoned long ago."

"How long ago?"

"About thirty years. It belonged to his Arizona period. Paul Grimes may have painted it himself."

"Does Grimes have that kind of a reputation?"

I'd asked her one question too many. "I can't discuss

his reputation with you, or anyone. He was Richard's friend and teacher in the Arizona days."

"But not a friend of yours?"

"I prefer not to go into that. Paul was helpful to my husband when it counted. But people change over the years. Everything changes." She looked around her, scanning her husband's paintings as if even they had become unfamiliar, like half-remembered dreams. "I try to guard my husband's reputation, keep the canon pure. All sorts of people try to cash in on his work."

"Would Fred Johnson be one of them?"

The question seemed to surprise her. She shook her head, setting her hair swinging like a flexible gray bell.

"Fred is fascinated by my husband's work. But I wouldn't say he's trying to cash in on it." She was silent for a moment. "Did Ruth Biemeyer accuse him of stealing her lousy picture?"

"His name came up."

"Well, it's nonsense. Even if he were dishonest, which he shows no signs of being, Fred has too much taste to be taken in by a poor imitation like that."

"I'd still like to talk to him. Do you happen to know where he lives?"

"I can find out." She went into the front office and came out a minute later. "Fred lives with his parents at 2024 Olive Street. Be nice to him. He's a sensitive young man, and a very great Chantry enthusiast."

I thanked her for the information. She thanked me for my interest in her husband. She seemed to be playing a complex role, part salesperson and part guardian of a shrine, and part something else. I couldn't help wondering if the undefinable part was an angry widowed sexuality.

# IV

The Johnson house was one of a block of three-story frame houses that appeared to date from the early years of the century. The olive trees that gave the street its name were even older. Their leaves looked like tarnished silver in the afternoon sunlight.

This part of the city was a mixed neighborhood of rooming houses and private residences, doctors' offices and houses half converted into offices. A large modern hospital, whose fenestration made it look like a giant honeycomb, rose in the middle of the area and seemed to have absorbed most of its energy.

The Johnson house was particularly run-down. Some of its boards were loose, and it needed paint. It stood like a gray and gabled ghost of a house in a yard choked with yellow grass and brown weeds.

I rattled the rusty screen door with my fist. The house seemed to stir into slow, reluctant life. I could hear lagging footsteps coming down the inside stairs.

A heavy old man opened the door and peered out at me through the screen. He had dirty gray hair and a short growth of moth-eaten gray beard. His voice was querulous.

"What's up?"

"I'd like to see Fred."

"I don't know if he's home. I've been sacked out." He leaned toward me, his face against the screen, and I could smell wine on his breath. "What do you want with Fred?"

"Just to talk to him."

His red little eyes scanned me up and down. "What do you want to talk to him about?"

"I'd prefer to tell Fred."

"You better tell me. My son is a busy young man. His time is worth money. Fred's got expertise"—he rolled the word on his tongue—"and that's worth more money."

The old man was probably out of wine, I thought, and getting ready to put the bite on me. A woman in a nurse's uniform came out from under the stairs. She carried herself with a certain clumsy authority, but her voice was small and girlish.

"I'll talk to the man, Gerard. You don't have to trouble your poor head with Fred's comings and goings."

She laid her open hand against the furred side of his face, peered sharply into his eyes like a diagnostician, and gave him a little slap of dismissal. He didn't argue with her but made his way back up the stairs.

"I'm Mrs. Johnson," she said to me. "Fred's mother."

She had gray-streaked black hair drawn back from a face whose history and meaning were obscured, like her husband's face, by an inert layer of flesh. Her heavy body was strictly girdled, though, and her white uniform was clean.

"Is Fred here?"

"I don't believe so." She looked past me into the street. "I don't see the car."

"When do you expect him back?"

"It's hard to say. Fred is a student at the university." She reported the fact as if it were the one great pride of her life. "They keep shifting his class hours around, and he works part-time besides at the art museum. They really depend on him there. Was it anything I could help you with?"

"It may be. Is it all right if I come in?"

"I'll come *out*," she said brightly. "The house isn't fit to be seen on the inside. Since I went back to full-time nursing, I haven't had the time to keep it up."

She removed a heavy key from the inside keyhole and used it to lock the door as she came out. It made me wonder if she kept her husband under lock and key when he had been drinking.

She led me off the porch and looked up at the peeling façade of the house. "It isn't fit to be seen on the outside, either. But I can't help that. The house belongs to the clinic—all these houses do—and they're planning to tear them down next year. This whole side of the street is going to be a parking lot." She sighed. "I don't know where we're going to go from here, with rents going up the way they are, and my husband no better than an invalid."

"I'm sorry to hear that."

"About Jerry, you mean? Yeah, I'm sorry, too. He used to be a fine strong man. But he had a nervous breakdown a while ago—it all goes back to the war— and he's never been the same since. And of course he has a drinking problem, too. So many of them do," she added meditatively.

I liked the woman's candor, even though it sounded slightly carnivorous. I wondered idly how it was that nurses so often ended up with invalid husbands.

"So what's your problem?" she said in a different tone.

"No problem. I'd simply like to talk to Fred."

"What about?"

"A picture."

"That's his field, all right. Fred can tell you anything you want to know about pictures." But she dropped the subject suddenly, as though it frightened her, and said in still a third voice, hesitant and low, "Is Fred in some kind of trouble?"

"I hope not, Mrs. Johnson."

"So do I. Fred is a good boy. He always has been. I ought to know, I'm his mother." She gave me a long dubious look. "Are you a policeman?"

I had been when I was younger, and apparently it

still showed to a cop-sensitive eye. But I had my story ready: "I'm a journalist. I'm thinking of doing a magazine piece on the artist Richard Chantry."

Her face and body tightened as if in response to a threat. "I see."

"I understand your son is an expert on Chantry."

"I wouldn't know about that," she said. "Fred is interested in a lot of different artists. He's going to make that his career."

"As a dealer?"

"That's what he'd like to be. But it takes capital. And we don't even own the house we live in."

She looked up at the tall gray house as if it were the source of all her trouble. From a window high up under the roof, her husband was watching us like a prisoner in a tower. She made a pushing gesture with her open hand, as if she were putting the shot. Johnson receded into the dimness.

"I'm haunted by the thought," she said, "that he'll tumble out of one of those windows. The poor man never got over his war injuries. Sometimes, when it takes him really bad, he falls right down on the floor. I keep wondering if I ought to put him back in the veterans' hospital. But I don't have the heart to. He's so much happier here with us. Fred and I would really miss him. And Fred is the kind of boy who needs a father."

Her words were full of feeling, but the voice in which she said them was emotionless. Her eyes were peering coldly into mine, assessing my reaction. I guessed that she was afraid for her son, trying in a hurry to put together a protective family nest.

"Where can I find Fred, do you know?"

"I *don't* know. He may be out on campus, or he could be down at the art museum, or anyplace in town. He's a very busy young man, and he keeps moving. He'll be taking his degree next spring, if all goes well. And it will."

She nodded emphatically several times. But there

seemed to be a stubborn hopelessness in the gesture, like a woman knocking her head against a wall.

As if in response, an old blue Ford sedan came down the street past the hospital. It slowed as it approached us, turning in toward the curb behind my car. The young man behind the wheel had long hair and a mustache, both reddish blond.

Out of the corner of my eye I saw Mrs. Johnson shake her head, once, in such a short arc that she hardly seemed to have moved. The young man's eyes flickered. Without having brought it to a full stop, he turned the Ford back in to the road, barely missing my left rear fender. The car accelerated sluggishly, leaving a trail of oil smoke on the air.

"Is that Fred, Mrs. Johnson?"

She answered after a brief hesitation: "That's Fred. I wondered where he thinks he's going."

"You signaled him not to stop."

"*I* did? You must be seeing things."

I left her standing there and followed the blue Ford. It caught a yellow light at the entrance to the freeway and turned off to the right in the direction of the university. I sat behind a long red light and watched the spoor of oil smoke dissipating, mixing with the general smog that overlay this part of the city.

When the light changed, I drove on out to the campus, where Fred's friend Doris Biemeyer lived.

# V

The university had been built on an elevated spur of land that jutted into the sea and was narrowed at its base by a tidal slough. Almost surrounded by water and softened by blue haze, it looked from the distance like a medieval fortress town.

Close up, the buildings shed this romantic aspect. They were half-heartedly modern, cubes and oblongs and slabs that looked as if their architect had spent his life designing business buildings. The parking attendant at the entrance told me that the student village was on the north side.

I followed a winding road along the edge of the campus, looking for Fred Johnson. There weren't many students in sight. Still the place seemed crowded and jumbled, like something thrown at a map in the hope that it would stick there.

Academia Village was even more haphazard than the campus proper. Loose dogs and loose students roamed the narrow streets in about equal numbers. The buildings ranged from hamburger stands and tiny cottages and duplexes to giant apartment buildings. The Sherbourne, where Doris Biemeyer lived, was one of the big ones. It was six stories high and occupied most of a block.

I found a parking place behind a camper painted to simulate a log cabin on wheels. No sign of the old blue Ford. I went into the Sherbourne and took an elevator to the third floor.

The building was fairly new but its interior smelled old and used. It was crowded with the odors of rapid generations, sweat and perfume and pot and spices. If there were human voices, they were drowned out by the music from several competing sources along the third-floor hallway, which sounded like the voices of the building's own multiple personality.

I had to knock several times on the door of Apartment 304. The girl who opened the door looked like a smaller version of her mother, prettier but vaguer and less sure of herself.

"Miss Biemeyer?"

"Yes?"

Her eyes looked past me at something just beyond my left shoulder. I sidestepped and looked behind me, half expecting to be hit. But there was nobody there.

"May I come in and talk to you for a minute?"

"I'm sorry. I'm meditating."

"What are you meditating about?"

"I don't really know." She giggled softly and touched the side of her head, where her light hair hung straight like raw silk. "It hasn't come together yet. It hasn't materialized, you know?"

She looked as though she hadn't quite materialized, herself. She had the kind of blondness you can almost see through. She swayed gently like a curtain at a window. Then she lost her balance and fell quite hard against the doorframe.

I took hold of both her arms and pulled her upright. Her hands were cold, and she seemed slightly dazed. I wondered what she had swallowed or sipped or imbibed.

With one arm around her shoulders, I propelled her into her living room. On its far side a screen door opened on a balcony. The room was almost as bare as a coolie's hut: a few plain chairs, a pallet on a metal frame, a card table, fiber mats. The only decoration was a large butterfly made of spangled red tissue paper on a wire skeleton. It was almost as big as she was, and it hung on a string from the central ceiling fixture and very slowly rotated.

She sat on one of the floor mats and looked up at the paper butterfly. Under the long cotton gown that seemed to be her only garment, she tried to arrange her legs and feet in the lotus position, and failed.

"Did you make the butterfly, Doris?"

She shook her head. "No. I don't make things. It was one of the decorations at the dance when I got out of boarding school. It was my mother's idea to hang it in here. I hate it." Her soft little voice seemed out of sync with the movements of her mouth. "I don't feel very well."

I went down on one knee beside her. "What have you been taking?"

"Just some pills to calm my nerves. They help me meditate." She began to struggle again with her feet and knees, trying to force them into position. The soles of her feet were dirty.

"What kind of pills?"

"The red ones. Just a couple. The trouble with me is I haven't eaten, not since sometime yesterday. Fred said he'd bring me something to eat from home, but I guess his mother won't let him. She doesn't like me—she wants Fred all to herself." The girl added in her gentle sibilant voice, "She can go to hell and copulate with spiders."

"What about your own mother, Doris?"

She let go of her feet. Her legs straightened out in front of her. She pulled her long dress down over them.

"What about her?" she said.

"If you need food or any kind of help, can't you get it from her?"

She shook her head with sudden startling violence. Her hair streamed over her eyes and mouth. She flung it back in an angry two-handed movement, like someone peeling off a rubber mask.

"I don't want her kind of help. She wants to take away my freedom—lock me up in a nursing home and throw away the key." She got up clumsily onto her knees, so that her blue eyes were on a level with mine. "Are you a shrink?"

"Not me."

"Are you sure? She threatened to turn the shrinks loose on me. I almost wish she would—I could tell them a thing or two." She nodded vengefully, chopping at the air with her soft chin.

"Like what?"

"Like the only thing they ever did in their lives was fight and argue. They built themselves that great big hideous house and all they ever did was fight in it. When they weren't giving each other the silent treatment."

"What were they fighting about?"

"A woman named Mildred—that was one of the things. But the basic thing was they didn't—they don't love each other, and they blamed each other for that. Also they blamed me, at least they acted that way. I don't remember much of what happened when I was a little girl. But one of the things I do remember is their yelling at each other over my head—yelling like crazy giants without any clothes on, with me in between them. And he was sticking out about a foot. She picked me up and took me into the bathroom and locked the door. He broke the door down with his shoulder. He went around with his arm in a sling for a long time after that. And," she added softly, "I've been going around with my mind in a sling."

"Downers won't cure that."

She narrowed her eyes and stuck out her lower lip like a stubborn child on the verge of tears. "Nobody asked you for your advice. You are a shrink, aren't you?" She sniffed. "I can smell the dirt on you, from people's dirty secrets."

I produced what felt from the inside like a lopsided smile. The girl was young and foolish, perhaps a little addled, by her own admission drugged. But she was young, and had clean hair. I hated to smell dirty to her.

I stood up and lightly hit my head on the paper butterfly. I went to the screen door and looked out across the balcony. Through the narrow gap between two apartment buildings I could see a strip of bright sea. A trimaran crossed it, running before a light wind.

The room seemed dim when I turned back to it, a transparent cube of shadow full of obscure life. The paper butterfly seemed to move in some sort of actual flight. The girl rose and stood swaying under it.

"Did my mother send you here?"

"Not exactly. I've talked to your mother."

"And I suppose she told you all the terrible things I've done. What a rotten egg I am. What a rotten ego." She giggled nervously.

"No. She is worried about you, though."

"About me and Fred?"

"I think so."

She nodded, and her head stayed down. "I'm worried about us, too, but not for the same reason. She thinks that Fred and I are lovers or something. But I don't seem to be able to relate to people. The closer I get to them, the colder I feel."

"Why?"

"They scare me. When he—when my father broke down the bathroom door, I climbed into the laundry hamper and pulled the lid down on top of me. I'll never forget the feeling it gave me, like I was dead and buried and safe forever."

"Safe?"

"They can't kill you after you're dead."

"What are you so afraid of, Doris?"

She looked up at me from under her light brows. "People."

"Do you feel that way about Fred?"

"No, I'm not afraid of him. He makes me terribly mad sometimes. He makes me want to—" She bit off the sentence. I could hear her teeth grind together.

"Makes you want to what?"

She hesitated, her face taut, listening to the secret life behind it. "Kill him, I was going to say. But I didn't really mean it. Anyway, what would be the use? Poor old Fred is dead and buried already, the way I am."

I felt an angry desire to disagree, to tell her that she was too pretty and young to be talking in that way. But she was a witness, and it was best not to argue with her.

"What happened to Fred?"

"A lot of things. He comes from a poor family and it took him half his life just to get where he is now, which is practically nowhere. His mother's some kind of a nurse, but she's fixated on her husband. He was crippled in the war and doesn't do much of anything. Fred was meant to be an artist or something like that, but I'm afraid he's never going to make it."

"Has Fred been in trouble?"

Her face closed. "I didn't say that."

"I thought you implied it."

"Maybe I did. Everybody's been in some kind of trouble."

"What kind has Fred been in?"

She shook her head. "I'm not going to tell you. You'd go back to my mother with it."

"No, I wouldn't."

"Yes, you would."

"You care about Fred, don't you?"

"I've got a right to care about somebody in this world. He's a nice boy—a nice man."

"Sure he is. Did the nice man steal the nice picture from your nice parents?"

"You don't have to get sarcastic."

"But I do sometimes. It comes from everybody being so nice. You haven't answered my question, Doris. Did Fred steal the picture?"

She shook her head. "It wasn't stolen."

"You mean it climbed down off the wall and walked away?"

"No. I don't mean that." Tears overflowed her eyes and ran down her face. "I took it."

"Why?"

"Fred told me—Fred asked me to."

"Did he give a reason?"

"He had a good reason."

"What reason?"

"He told me not to tell anybody."

"Did Fred keep the picture?"

"I guess he did. He hasn't brought it back yet."

"Did he say he was going to bring it back?"

"Yes, and he will, too. He wanted to make an examination of it, he said."

"An examination for what?"

"To see if it was genuine."

"Did he think it was a fake?"

"He wanted to find out."

"Did he have to steal it to do that?"

"He didn't steal it. I let him take it. And you're not very nice."

# VI

I was beginning to agree with her. I left her and walked down the stairs and out to my car. For over an hour, while the afternoon shadows of the buildings lengthened across me, I sat and watched the main entrance of the Sherbourne.

There was a natureburger place in a geodesic dome up the block, and now and then the uncertain wind brought me the smell of food. Eventually I went and had a natureburger. The atmosphere in the place was dim and inert. The bearded young customers made me think of early cave men waiting for the ice age to end.

I was back in my car when Fred Johnson finally came. He parked his blue Ford directly behind me and looked up and down the street. He went into the Sherbourne and took the elevator up. I took the stairs, fast. We met in the third-floor hallway. He was wearing a green suit and a wide yellow tie.

He tried to retreat into the elevator, but its door closed in his face and it started down. He turned to face me. He was pale and wide-eyed.

"What do you want?"

"The picture you took from the Biemeyers."

"What picture?"

"You know what picture. The Chantry."

"I didn't take it."

"Maybe not. But it came into your hands."

He looked past me down the hall toward the girl's room. "Did Doris tell you that?"

"We could leave Doris out of this. She's in enough trouble now, with her parents and with herself."

He nodded as if he understood and agreed. But his eyes had a separate life of their own, and were searching for a way out. He looked to me like one of those tired boys who go from youth to middle age without passing through manhood.

"Who are you, anyway?"

"I'm a private detective." I told him my name. "The Biemeyers hired me to reclaim their picture. Where is it, Fred?"

"I don't know."

He wagged his head despondently. As if I had taken hold of his head and squeezed it with my hands, clear drops of sweat stood out on his forehead.

"What happened to it, Fred?"

"I took it home, I admit that. I had no intention of stealing it. I only wanted to study it."

"When did you take it home?"

"Yesterday."

"Where is it now?"

"I don't know. Honestly. Somebody must have stolen it from my room."

"From the house on Olive Street?"

"Yes, sir. Somebody broke into the house and stole it

while I was sleeping. It was there when I went to bed and when I woke up it was gone."

"You must be a heavy sleeper."

"I guess I am."

"Or a heavy liar."

His slender body was shaken by a flurry of shame or anger. I thought he was going to take a swing at me, and I set myself for that. But he made a dash for the stairs. I was too slow to head him off. By the time I got down to the street, he was driving away in his old blue Ford.

I bought a natureburger in a paper bag and took the elevator back up to the third floor. Doris let me into her apartment, looking disappointed that it was me.

I handed her the sandwich. "Here's something to eat."

"I'm not hungry. Fred promised to bring me something, anyway."

"You better eat that. Fred may not be coming today."

"But he said he would."

"He may be in trouble, Doris, about that picture."

Her hand closed, squeezing the sandwich in the bag. "Are my parents trying to get him?"

"I wouldn't put it that strongly."

"You don't know my parents. They'll make him lose his job at the museum. He'll never become a college graduate. And all because he tried to do them a favor."

"I don't quite follow that."

She nodded her head emphatically. "He was trying to authenticate their painting. He wanted to examine the paint for age. If it was fresh paint, it would probably mean that it wasn't genuine."

"Wasn't a genuine Chantry?"

"That's correct. Fred thought when he first looked at it that it wasn't genuine. At least he wasn't sure. And he doesn't trust the man my parents bought it from."

"Grimes?"

"That's right. Fred said he has a bad reputation in art circles."

I wondered what kind of a reputation Fred was going to have, now that the picture had been stolen. But there was no use worrying the girl about it. The meaning of her face was still as diffuse as a cloud. I left her with her dilapidated sandwich and drove back down along the freeway to the lower town.

The door of Paul Grimes's shop was locked. I knocked and got no answer. I rattled the knob and raised my voice. No answer. Peering into the dim interior, I could see nothing but emptiness and shadows.

I went into the liquor store and asked the black man if he had seen Paola.

"She was out in front an hour or so ago, loading some pictures into her van. As a matter of fact, I helped her."

"What kind of pictures?"

"Framed pictures. Weird junk, gobs of color. I like a picture to look like something real. No wonder they couldn't sell 'em."

"How do you know they couldn't sell 'em?"

"It stands to reason. She said they were giving up on the shop."

"Was Paul Grimes with her—the man with the beard?"

"Nope, he didn't show. I haven't seen him since I saw you."

"Did Paola say where she was going?"

"I didn't ask. She took off in the direction of Montevista." He pointed southwest with his thumb.

"What kind of a van is she driving?"

"Old yellow Volkswagen. Is she in some kind of trouble?"

"No. I wanted to talk to her about a picture."

"To buy?"

"Maybe."

He looked at me incredulously. "You like that kind of stuff?"

"Sometimes."

"Too bad. If they knew they had a buyer, they might of stayed in business to accommodate you."

"They might. Will you sell me two half-pints of Tennessee whisky?"

"Why not a whole pint? It's cheaper that way."

"Two half-pints are better."

# VII

On my way uptown I stopped at the art museum, intending to ask for Fred. But the place was closed for the night.

I drove on up to Olive Street. Darkness had spread like a branching tree across the lawns and yards, and lights were coming on in the old houses. The hospital was a great pierced box of light. I parked near the gabled house where the Johnsons lived and made my way up its broken steps to the front door.

Fred's father must have been listening on the other side of the door. He spoke before I had a chance to knock: "Who is that?"

"Archer. I was here earlier today, looking for Fred."

"That's right. I remember." He sounded proud of the feat.

"May I come in and talk to you for a minute, Mr. Johnson?"

"Sorry, no can do. My wife locked the door."

"Where's the key?"

"Sarah took it with her to the hospital. She's afraid I'll go out in the street and get run over. But the fact is I'm completely sober. I'm so sober that it's making me physically sick. She's supposed to be a nurse, but little does she care." His voice was fogged with self-pity.

"Is there any way you can let me in? Through a window, maybe?"

"She'd crucify me."

"How would she know? I've got some whisky with me. Could you use a couple of snorts?"

His tone brightened. "Could I not. But how are you going to get in?"

"I have some keys."

It was a simple old lock, and the second key that I tried opened it. I closed the door behind me, moving into the cramped hallway with some difficulty. Johnson's thick body crowded mine. In the light of a dim overhead bulb, I could see that his face was working with excitement.

"You said you had some whisky for me."

"Hold on for a minute."

"But I'm sick. You can see that I'm sick."

I opened one of my half-pint bottles. He drained it in one continuous shuddering swallow, and licked the mouth of the empty bottle.

I felt like a pander. But the strong jolt of whisky didn't seem to bother him at all. Instead of making him drunker, it seemed to improve his diction and delivery.

"I used to drink Tennessee whisky in my palmy days. I drank Tennessee whisky and rode a Tennessee Walking Horse. That is Tennessee whisky, is it not?"

"You're right, Mr. Johnson."

"Just call me Jerry. I know a friend when I see one." He set down the empty bottle on the first step of the staircase, put his hand on my shoulder, and leaned his weight on it. "I won't forget this. What did you say your name was?"

"Archer."

"And what do you do for a living, Mr. Archer?"

"I'm a private investigator." I opened my wallet and showed Johnson a photostat of my state license. "Some people in town hired me to trace a painting that they lost. It's a portrait of a woman, probably by a well-known local painter named Richard Chantry. You've heard of him, I suppose."

He scowled with concentration. "I can't say I have. You should take it up with my son Fred. That's his department."

"I already have. Fred took the picture and brought it home."

"Here?"

"So he told me this afternoon."

"I don't believe it. Fred wouldn't do a thing like that. He's a good boy, he always has been. He never stole anything in his life. The people at the art museum trust him. Everybody trusts him."

I interrupted Johnson's alcoholic flow of words: "He claims he didn't steal it. He said he brought it home to make some tests on it."

"What kind of tests are you talking about?"

"I'm not sure. According to Fred, his idea was to find out how old the picture was. The artist who was supposed to have painted it disappeared a long time ago."

"Who was that?"

"Richard Chantry."

"Yeah, I guess I have heard of him. They've got a lot of his pictures in the museum." He rubbed his gray scalp as if to warm his memory. "Isn't he supposed to be dead?"

"Dead or missing. One way or the other, he's been gone for twenty-five years. If the paint on the picture is comparatively fresh, he probably didn't paint it."

"Sorry, I don't quite follow that."

"It doesn't matter. The point is that Fred brought the picture here, and he says it was stolen from his room last night. Do you know anything about that?"

"Hell, no." His whole face wrinkled as if old age had fallen on him suddenly. "You think I took it?"

"I don't mean that at all."

"I hope not. Fred would kill me if I touched any of

his sacred things. I'm not even supposed to go into his room."

"What I'm trying to find out—did Fred say anything about a painting being stolen from his room last night?"

"Not that I know of."

"Did you see him this morning?"

"I certainly did. I dished up his porridge for him."

"And he didn't mention the missing painting?"

"No, sir. Not to me."

"I'd like to take a look at Fred's room. Would it be possible?"

The suggestion seemed to frighten him. "I don't know. I don't think so. *She* hates to have anybody in her house. She'd even like to get rid of me if she could."

"Didn't you say she's gone to the hospital?"

"That's right, she went to work."

"Then how would she know?"

"I don't know *how* she knows, but she always does. I guess she worms it out of me or something. It's *hard* on me, hard on my nerves." He giggled shamefacedly. "You wouldn't have any more of that Tennessee walking whisky?"

I got out the other half-pint and showed it to him. He reached for it. I held it away from him.

"Let's go upstairs, Jerry. Then I'll leave this with you." I put it back in my pocket.

"I don't know."

He glanced up the stairs as if his wife might be there listening. She wasn't, of course, but her invisible presence seemed to fill the house. Johnson was trembling with fear of her, or with desire for the whisky.

The desire won out. He switched on a light and led me up the stairs. The second floor was in much poorer condition than the first. The ancient paper on the walls was discolored and peeling. The carpetless floor was splintered. A panel was missing from one of the bedroom doors, and had been replaced with the side of a cardboard carton.

I had seen worse houses in the slums and barrios,

places that looked as if a full-scale infantry battle had passed through them. The Johnsons' house was the scene of a less obvious disaster. But it suddenly seemed quite possible to me that the house had hatched a crime; perhaps Fred had stolen the picture in the hope of improving his life.

I felt a certain sympathy for Fred. It would be hard to come back to this house from the Biemeyers' house, or from the art museum.

Johnson opened the door with the missing panel and switched on a light that hung by a cord from the ceiling.

"This is Fred's little room."

It contained an iron single bed covered with a U.S. Army blanket, a bureau, a torn canvas deck chair, a bookcase almost full of books, and in one corner by the blinded window an old kitchen table with various tools arranged on it, hammers and shears and saws of varying sizes, sewing equipment, pots of glue and paint.

The light over the bed was still swinging back and forth, its reflection climbing the walls alternately. For a moment, I had the feeling that the whole house was rocking on its foundations. I reached up and held the light still. There were pictures on the walls, modern classics like Monet and Modigliani, most of them cheap reproductions that looked as though they had been clipped from magazines. I opened the closet door. It contained a jacket and a couple of shirts on hangers, and a pair of shiny black boots. For a man in his early thirties, Fred had very few possessions.

I went through the bureau drawers, which contained some underwear and handkerchiefs and socks and a high school senior class picture for the year 1961. I couldn't find Fred in the picture.

"This is him," Johnson said at my shoulder. He pointed out a teen-age boy's face that from this distance in time looked touchingly hopeful.

I looked over the books in the bookcase. Most of them were paperbacks on art and culture and technology. There were a few books about psychiatry and psychoanalysis. The only ones I had read myself were *The Psychopathology of Everyday Life* and *Gandhi's Truth*—unusual background reading for a thief, if that's what Fred was.

I turned to Johnson. "Could someone have gotten into the house and taken the picture from this room?"

He lifted his heavy shoulders and dropped them. "I guess anything is possible. *I* didn't hear anybody. But then I generally sleep the sleep of the dead."

"You didn't take the picture yourself, Jerry?"

"No, sir." He shook his head violently. "I know enough not to mess with Fred's stuff. I may be an old nothing man but I wouldn't steal from my own boy. He's the only one of us with any future, in this house."

"Just the three of you live here—you and Fred and Mrs. Johnson?"

"That's correct. We had roomers at one time, but that was long ago."

"Then what happened to the picture Fred brought home?"

Johnson lowered his head and swung it from side to side like a sick old bull. "I never saw the picture. You don't understand how it is with me. I spent six, seven years after the war in a veterans' hospital. Most of the time I was in a daze, most of the time I still am. The days go by, and half the time I don't know what day it is and I don't want to. I'm a sick man. Now why don't you leave me alone?"

I left him alone and made a cursory search of the upstairs rooms. Only one other was occupied, a room containing a double bed that Johnson evidently shared with his wife. There was no painting under the mattress, nothing incriminating in the closet or chest of drawers, no evidence of any crime but that of poverty.

One narrow door at the end of the upstairs hallway was closed and padlocked. I stopped in front of it.

Johnson came up behind me. "That goes up to the attic. I don't have a key for it. Sarah's always afraid I'll fall down the stairs. Anyway, there isn't anything up there. Like me," he added foolishly, tapping the side of his head. "Nobody home upstairs."

He gave me a broad idiot smile. I gave him the other half-pint. It was an ugly transaction, and I was glad to leave him. He closed the front door behind me like a trusty shutting himself into his own prison. I locked the door.

# VIII

I left my car where it was and walked toward the hospital. I hoped to get some further information about Fred from Mrs. Johnson. The night was almost fully dark, the streetlights scattered sparsely among the trees. On the sidewalk ahead of me I noticed a spillage of oil drops that became more frequent as I moved along.

I dipped my finger in one of the spilled drops and held it up to the light. It had a reddish tinge. It didn't smell like oil.

On the grass beside the sidewalk ahead of me someone was snoring. It was a man lying face down. I ran to him and got down on my knees beside him. The back of his head was dark and lustrous with blood. I moved him just enough to look at his face. It was bloody, too.

He groaned and tried to raise himself in a sad and helpless parody of a push-up, then fell on his face again. I turned his head to one side so that he could breathe more freely.

He opened one eye and said, "Chantry? Leave me alone."

Then he relapsed into his broken-faced snuffling. I could see that he was very badly hurt. I left him and ran to the emergency entrance of the hospital.

Seven or eight adults and children were waiting inside on collapsible chairs. A harassed young nurse behind a counter was manning it like a barricade.

I said, "There's an injured man just up the street."

"So bring him in."

"I can't. He needs an ambulance."

"How far up the street?"

"Next block."

"There's no ambulance here. If you want to call one, that's a public phone in the corner there. Do you have a dime?"

She gave me a number to call. In less than five minutes an ambulance pulled up outside. I got in with the driver and directed him to the bleeding man in the grass.

His snoring was less regular now, and less loud. The ambulance attendant turned a flashlight on him. I took a closer look. He was a man of sixty or so, with a pointed gray beard and a lot of bloody gray hair. He looked like a dying sea lion, and his snoring sounded like a sea lion's distant barking.

"Do you know him, sir?"

I was thinking that he fitted the liquor-store proprietor's description of the art dealer Paul Grimes.

I said, "No. I've never seen him before."

The ambulance men lifted him gently onto a stretcher and drove him to the emergency entrance. I rode along and was there when they carried him out. He raised himself on his arms, almost overturning the stretcher, and looked at me from his blind broken glistening face.

He said, "I know you, you bastard."

He fell back and lay still. The ambulance men rushed him into the hospital. I waited outside for the inevitable police.

They came in an unmarked car, a pair of youngish detective-sergeants wearing light summery clothes and dark wintry faces. One went into the hospital, and the other, a Sergeant Leverett, stayed with me.

"You know the injured man?"

"I never saw him before. I found him on the street."

"How did you happen to call an ambulance for him?"

"It seemed like the logical thing to do."

"Why didn't you call us?"

"I knew somebody would."

Leverett reddened slightly. "You sound like a smart bastard. Who in hell are you, anyway?"

I swallowed my anger and told him that I was a private detective doing a job for the Biemeyers. Leverett knew the name and it altered his voice and manner.

"May I see your identification?"

I showed it to him. He asked me to stick around, if I would be so good. I promised that I would.

Interpreting my promise loosely, I wandered back into the next block and found the place on the sidewalk where the drippings of blood had started. They were already drying in the warm air.

Parked at the adjacent curb was an old black convertible with a ragged top. Its key was in the ignition. A square white envelope was stuck between the black plastic seat and the back cushion. On the shelf behind the seat were a pile of smallish oil paintings and a white sombrero.

I turned on the dashboard light and examined the square envelope. It was an invitation to cocktails addressed to Mr. Paul Grimes, on Mrs. Richard Chantry's stationery, and signed "Francine Chantry." The party was tonight at eight o'clock.

I looked at my watch: just past eight. Then I examined the stack of paintings behind the seat. Two of them were framed in old-fashioned gilt, the rest unframed. They didn't resemble any of the Chantrys I had seen.

They didn't look like much of anything. There were a few seascapes and beach scenes, which looked like minor accidents, and a small portrait of a woman, which looked like a major one. But I didn't entirely trust my eye or my judgment.

I took one of the seascapes and put it in the trunk of

my own car. Then I started back toward the hospital.

Leverett and the other detective-sergeant met me on the way. They were accompanied by a captain of detectives named Mackendrick, a heavy powerful-looking middle-aged man in a crumpled blue suit that went with his crumpled face. He told me that the man I had found was dead. I told him who the man probably was.

Mackendrick absorbed my information quickly and made a few scrawlings in a black notebook. He was particularly interested in the fact that Grimes had mentioned Richard Chantry before he died.

"I remember Chantry," he said. "I was a rookie when he pulled his big disappearance."

"You think he disappeared deliberately?"

"Sure. There was plenty of evidence of that."

He didn't tell me what the evidence was. I didn't tell him where I was going.

# IX

I drove through the lower town, past Grimes's lightless and uninhabited little building. I could taste the salty tang of the sea long before I got to it, and feel its cool breath. A seaside park stretched along the shore for more than a mile. Below it waves foamed on the beach, preternaturally white against the darkness. There were pairs of lovers here and there in the grass instead of dead men, and that was good.

Channel Road ascended a cliff that overlooked and partly enclosed the harbor. Suddenly I was looking down at its masts. The road climbed away over the shoulder of the cliff, wound past a Coast Guard colony, and skirted a deep barranca that opened out onto the

sea. Beyond the barranca was the hill on which the Biemeyers' house stood.

Mrs. Chantry's house was perched between the barranca and the water. It was built of stone and stucco,
with many arches and several turrets. There was a
glass-roofed greenhouse on one side, and between me
and the house was a walled flagstone parking area holding about twenty cars. A white-coated attendant came
up to the side of my car and offered to park it for me.

A uniformed black maid greeted me pleasantly at the
open front door. She didn't ask me for my invitation or
any identification. She didn't even allow herself to notice that I wasn't wearing party clothes or a party look
on my face.

Piano music drew me past her into a central room of
the house, a wide high room that rose two stories to the
roof. A woman with short black hair was playing
"Someone to Watch Over Me" on a grand piano that
was dwarfed by the room. A couple of dozen men and
women stood around in party clothes with drinks. It
looked like a scene recovered from the past, somehow
less real than the oil paintings hanging on the walls.

Mrs. Chantry came toward me from the far end of
the room. She was wearing a blue evening dress with a
lot of skirt and not much top, which displayed her arms
and shoulders. She didn't seem to recognize me at first,
but then she lifted both her hands in a gesture of happy
surprise.

"How good of you to come. I was hoping I'd mentioned my little party to you, and I'm so glad I did. It's
Mr. Marsh, isn't it?" Her eyes were watching me carefully. I couldn't tell if she liked me or was afraid of me.

"Archer," I said. "Lew Archer."

"Of course. I never could remember names. If you
don't mind, I'll let Betty Jo Siddon introduce you to my
other guests."

Betty Jo Siddon was a level-eyed brunette of about
thirty. She was well-shaped but rather awkward in her
movements, as if she weren't quite at home in the

world. She said she was covering the party for the local paper, and clearly wondered what I was doing there. I didn't tell her. She didn't ask.

She introduced me to Colonel Aspinwall, an elderly man with an English accent, an English suit, and a young English wife who looked me over and found me socially undesirable. To Dr. Ian Innes, a cigar-chomping thick-jowled man, whose surgical eyes seemed to be examining me for symptoms. To Mrs. Innes, who was pale and tense and fluttering, like a patient. To Jeremy Rader, the artist, tall and hairy and jovial in the last late flush of his youth. To Molly Rader, a statuesque brunette of about thirty-nine, who was the most beautiful thing I'd seen in weeks. To Jackie Pratt, a spare little long-haired man in a narrow dark suit, who looked like a juvenile character out of Dickens but on second glance had to be fifty, at least. To the two young women with Jackie, who had the looks and the conversation of models. To Ralph Sandman and Larry Fallon, who wore black silk jackets and ruffled white shirts, and appeared to comprise a pair. And to Arthur Planter, an art collector so well known that I had heard of him.

Betty Jo turned to me when we had finished our rounds. "Would you like a drink?"

"Not really."

She looked at me more closely. "Are you feeling all right? You look a little peaked."

I caught it from a dead man I just found on Olive Street. What I said was, "I don't believe I've eaten for a while."

"Of course. You look hungry."

"I *am* hungry. I've had a big day."

She took me into the dining room. Its wide uncurtained windows looked out over the sea. The room was uncertainly lit by the tall candles on the refectory table.

Standing behind the table with the air of a proprietor was the large dark hook-nosed man, whom the girl addressed as Rico, I had met on my earlier visit. He cut some slices off a baked ham and made me a sandwich with which he offered me wine. I asked for beer instead, if he didn't mind. He strutted toward the back of the house, grumbling.

"Is he a servant?"

Betty Jo answered me with deliberate vagueness: "More or less." She changed the subject. "A big day doing what?"

"I'm a private detective. I was working."

"Policeman was one of the thoughts that occurred to me. Are you on a case?"

"More or less."

"How exciting." She squeezed my arm. "Does it have to do with the picture the Biemeyers had stolen?"

"You're very well informed."

"I try to be. I don't intend to write a social column for the rest of my life. Actually I heard about the missing picture in the newsroom this morning. I understand it's a conventionalized picture of a woman."

"So I've been told. I haven't seen it. What else was the newsroom saying?"

"That the picture was probably a fake. Is it?"

"The Biemeyers don't think so. But Mrs. Chantry does."

"If Francine says it's a fake, it probably is. I think she knows by heart every painting her husband did. Not that he did so many—fewer than a hundred altogether. His high period only lasted seven years. And then he disappeared. Or something."

"What do you mean, 'Or something'?"

"Some old-timers in town here think he was murdered. But that's pure speculation, so far as I can find out."

"Murdered by whom?"

She gave me a quick bright probing look. "Francine Chantry. You won't quote me, will you?"

"You wouldn't have said it if you thought I would. Why Francine?"

"He disappeared so suddenly. People always suspect the spouse, don't they?"

"Sometimes with good reason," I said. "Are you professionally interested in the Chantry disappearance?"

"I'd like to write about it, if that's what you mean."

"That's what I mean. I'll make a deal with you."

She gave me another of her probing looks, this one edged with sexual suspicion. "Oh?"

"I don't mean that. I mean this. I'll give you a hot tip on the Chantry case. You tell me what you find out."

"How hot?"

"This hot."

I told her about the dead man at the hospital. Her eyes became narrower and brighter. She pushed out her lips like a woman expecting to be kissed, but kissing was not what was on her mind.

"That's hot enough."

Rico came back into the room carrying a foaming glass.

"It took me a long time," he said in a complaining tone. "The beer wasn't cold. Nobody else drinks beer. I had to chill it."

"Thanks very much."

I took the cold glass from his hand and offered it to Betty Jo.

She smiled and declined. "I have to work tonight. Will you forgive me if I run off now?"

I advised her to talk to Mackendrick. She said she would, and went out the back door. Right away I found myself missing her.

I ate my ham sandwich and drank my beer. Then I went back into the room where the music was. The woman at the piano was playing a show tune with heavy-handed professional assurance. Mrs. Chantry, who was talking with Arthur Planter, caught my eye and detached herself from him.

"What happened to Betty Jo? I hope you didn't do away with her."

She meant the remark to be light, but neither of us smiled.

"Miss Siddon had to leave."

Mrs. Chantry's eyes became even more unsmiling. "She didn't tell me that she was going to leave. I hope she gives my party proper coverage—we're raising money for the art museum."

"I'm sure she will."

"Did she tell you where she was going?"

"To the hospital. There's been a murder. Paul Grimes was killed."

Her face opened, almost as if I'd accused her, then closed against the notion. She was quiet but internally active, rearranging her face from the inside. She drew me into the dining room, reacted to the presence of Rico, and took me into a small sitting room.

She closed the door and faced me in front of a dead and empty fireplace. "How do you know Paul Grimes was murdered?"

"I found him dying."

"Where?"

"Near the hospital. He may have been trying to get there for treatment, but he died before he made it. He was very badly smashed up around the head and face."

The woman took a deep breath. She was still very handsome, in a cold silvery way, but the life seemed to have gone out of her face. Her eyes had enlarged and darkened.

"Could it have been an accident, Mr. Archer?"

"No. I think he was murdered. So do the police."

"Who is in charge of the case, do you know?"

"Captain Mackendrick."

"Good." She gave an abrupt little nod. "He knew my husband."

"How does your husband come into this? I don't understand."

"It's inevitable that he should. Paul Grimes was close to Richard at one time. His death is bound to stir up all the old stories."

"What old stories?"

"We don't have time for them now. Perhaps another day." Her hand came out and encircled my wrist, like a bracelet of ice. "I'm going to ask you to do something for me, Mr. Archer. Two things. Please don't tell Captain Mackendrick or anyone else what I said to you about poor dear Paul today. He was a good friend to Richard, to me as well. I was angry when I said what I did. I shouldn't have said it, and I'm terribly sorry."

She released my wrist and leaned on the back of a straight chair. Her voice was veering up and down the scale, but her eyes were steady and intense. I could almost feel them tangibly on my face. But I didn't really believe in her sudden kindly feeling for Paul Grimes, and I wondered what had happened between them in the past.

As if the past had slugged her from behind, she sat down rather suddenly on the chair.

She made her second request in a wan voice, "Will you get me a drink, please?"

"Water?"

"Yes, water."

I brought her a glassful from the dining room. Her hands were shaking. Holding the glass in both hands, she sipped at the water and then drank it down and thanked me.

"I don't know why I'm thanking you. You've ruined my party."

"I'm sorry. But it really wasn't me. Whoever killed Paul Grimes ruined your party. I'm just the flunky who brought the bad tidings and gets put to death."

She glanced up at my face. "You're quite an intelligent man."

"Do you want to talk to me?"

"I thought I had been."

"I mean really talk."

She shook her head. "I have guests in the house."

"They'll do all right on their own, as long as the drinks hold out."

"I really can't." She rose to leave the room.

I said, "Wasn't Paul Grimes supposed to be one of your guests tonight?"

"Certainly not."

"He was carrying an invitation to your party. Didn't you send it to him?"

She turned to face me, leaning on the door. "I may have. I sent out quite a few invitations. Some were sent out by other members of my committee."

"But you must know whether Paul Grimes was invited."

"I don't think he was."

"But you're not sure?"

"That's right."

"Has he ever been here to your house?"

"Not to my knowledge. I don't understand what you're trying to prove."

"I'm trying to get some idea of your relationship with Grimes."

"There wasn't any."

"Good or bad, I mean. This afternoon you practically accused him of faking the Biemeyers' painting. Tonight you invite him to your party."

"The invitations went out early last week."

"You admit that you sent him one."

"I may have. I probably did. What I said to you this afternoon about Paul wasn't intended for the record. I confess he gets on my nerves."

"He won't any more."

"I know that. I'm sorry. I'm sorry he's been killed." She hung her pretty gray head. "And I did send him that invitation. I was hoping for a reconciliation. We hadn't been friends for some time. I thought he might respond to a show of warmth on my part."

She looked at me from under the wings of her hair. Her eyes were cold and watchful. I didn't believe what she was telling me, and it must have showed.

She said with renewed insistence, "I hate to lose friends, particularly friends of my husband's. There are fewer and fewer survivors of the Arizona days, and Paul was one of them. He was with us when Richard made his first great breakthrough. Paul really made it possible, you know. But he never succeeded in making his own breakthrough."

"Were there hard feelings between them?"

"Between my husband and Paul? Certainly not. Paul was one of Richard's teachers. He took great pride in Richard's accomplishment."

"How did your husband feel about Paul?"

"He was grateful to him. They were always good friends, as long as Richard was with us." She gave me a long and doubting look. "I don't know where this is leading."

"Neither do I, Mrs. Chantry."

"Then what's the purpose of it? You're wasting my time and your own."

"I don't think so. Tell me, is your husband still alive?"

She shook her head. "I can't answer that. I don't know. I honestly don't know."

"How long is it since you've seen him?"

"He left in the summer of 1950. I haven't seen him since then."

"Were there indications that something had happened to him?"

"On the contrary. He wrote me a wonderful letter. If you'd like to see it—"

"I've seen it. As far as you know, then, he's still alive."

"I hope and pray he is. I believe he is."

"Have you heard from him since he took off?"

"Never."

"Do you expect to?"

"I don't know." She turned her head to one side, the cords of her white neck taut. "This is painful for me."

"I'm sorry."

"Then why are you doing it?"

"I'm trying to find out if there's any possibility that your husband killed Paul Grimes."

"That's an absurd idea. Absurd and obscene."

"Grimes didn't seem to think so. He spoke Chantry's name before he died."

She didn't quite faint, but she seemed to come close to it. She turned white under her makeup, and might have fallen. I held her by the upper arms. Her flesh was as smooth as marble, and almost as cold.

Rico opened the door and shouldered his way in. I realized how big he was. The small room hardly contained him.

"What goes on?"

"Nothing," the woman said. "Please go away, Rico."

"Is he bothering you?"

"No, he's not. But I want both of you to go away. Please."

"You heard her," Rico said to me.

"So did you. Mrs. Chantry and I have something to discuss." I turned to her. "Don't you want to know what Grimes said?"

"I suppose I have to. Rico, do you mind leaving us alone now? It's perfectly all right."

It wasn't all right with Rico. He gave me a black scowl that at the same time managed to look hurt, like the scowl of a little boy who has been told to stand in the corner. He was a big good-looking man, if you liked the dark florid type. I couldn't help wondering if Mrs. Chantry did.

"Please, Rico." She sounded like the mistress of a barely controllable watchdog or a jealous stud.

The big man moved sideways out of the room. I closed the door behind him.

Mrs. Chantry turned to me. "Rico's been with me a long time. He was devoted to my husband. When Richard left, he transferred his allegiance to me."

"Of course," I said.

She colored faintly, but didn't pursue the subject.

"You were going to tell me what Paul Grimes said to you before he died."

"So I was. He thought I was your husband, apparently. He said: 'Chantry? Leave me alone.' Later he said: 'I know you, you bastard.' It naturally gave me the idea that it may have been your husband who beat him to death."

She dropped her hands from her face, which looked pale and sick. "That's impossible. Richard was a gentle person. Paul Grimes was his good friend."

"Do I resemble your husband?"

"No. Richard was much younger—" She caught herself. "But of course he'd be a great deal older now, wouldn't he?"

"We all are. Twenty-five years older."

"Yes." She bowed her head as if she suddenly felt the weight of the years. "But Richard didn't look at all like you. Perhaps there's some similarity of voices."

"But Grimes called me Chantry before I spoke. I never did say anything to him directly."

"What does that prove? Please go away now, won't you? This has been very hard. And I have to go out there again."

She went back into the dining room. After a minute or two I followed her. She and Rico were standing by the candlelit table with their heads close together, talking in intimate low tones.

I felt like an intruder and moved over to the windows. Through them I could see the harbor in the distance. Its masts and cordage resembled a bleached winter grove stripped of leaves and gauntly beautiful. The candle flames reflected in the windows seemed to flicker like St. Elmo's fire around the distant masts.

# X

I went out to the big front room. The art expert Arthur Planter was standing with his back to the room, in front of one of the paintings on the wall. When I spoke to him, he didn't turn or answer me, but his tall narrow body stiffened a little.

I repeated his name. "Mr. Planter?"

He turned unwillingly from the picture, which was a head-and-shoulders portrait of a man. "What can I do for you, sir?"

"I'm a private detective—"

"Really?" The pale narrow eyes in his thin face were looking at me without interest.

"Did you know Paul Grimes?"

"I wouldn't say I *know* him. I've done some business with him, a very little." He pursed his lips as if the memory had a bitter taste.

"You won't do any more," I said, hoping to shock him into communication. "He was murdered earlier this evening."

"Am I a suspect?" His voice was dry and bored.

"Hardly. Some paintings were found in his car. Would you be willing to look at one of them?"

"With what end in view?"

"Identification, maybe."

"I suppose so," he said wearily. "Though I'd much rather look at this." He indicated the picture of the man on the wall.

"Who is it?"

"You mean you don't know? It's Richard Chantry—his only major self-portrait."

I gave the picture a closer look. The head was a little like a lion's head, with rumpled tawny hair, a full beard partly masking an almost feminine mouth, deep eyes the color of emeralds. It seemed to radiate force.

"Did you know him?" I said to Planter.

"Indeed I did. I was one of his discoverers, in a sense."

"Do you believe he's still alive?"

"I don't know. I earnestly hope he is. But if he is alive, and if he's painting, he's keeping his work to himself."

"Why would he take off the way he did?"

"I don't know," Planter repeated. "I think he was a man who lived in phases, like the moon. Perhaps he came to the end of this phase." Planter looked around a little contemptuously at the other people in the crowded room. "This painting you want me to look at, is it a Chantry?"

"I wouldn't know. Maybe you can tell me."

I led him out to my car and showed him in my headlights the small seascape I had taken from Paul Grimes's convertible. He lifted it out of my hands with delicate care, as if he were showing me how to handle a painting.

But what he said was, "I'm afraid it's pretty bad. It's certainly not a Chantry, if that's your question."

"Do you have any idea who might have painted it?"

He considered the question. "It could be the work of Jacob Whitmore. If so, it's very early Whitmore—purely and clumsily representational. I'm afraid poor Jacob's career recapitulated the history of modern art a generation or so late. He'd worked his way up to surrealism and was beginning to discover symbolism, when he died."

"When did he die?"

"Yesterday." Planter seemed to take pleasure in giving me this mild shock. "I understood he went for a dip in the sea off Sycamore Point and had a heart attack." He looked down musingly at the picture in his hands. "I wonder what Paul Grimes thought he could do with this. A good painter's prices will often go up at his death. But Jacob Whitmore was not a good painter."

"Does his work resemble Chantry's?"

"No. It does not." Planter's eyes probed at my face. "Why?"

"I've heard that Paul Grimes may not have been above selling fake Chantrys."

"I see. Well, he'd have had a difficult time selling this as a Chantry. It isn't even a passable Whitmore. As you can see for yourself, it's no more than half finished." Planter added with elaborate cruel wit, "He took his revenge on the sea in advance by painting it badly."

I looked at the blurred and swirling blues and greens in the unfinished seascape. However bad the painting was, it seemed to be given some depth and meaning by the fact that the painter had died in that sea.

"Did you say he lived at Sycamore Point?"

"Yes. That's on the beach north of the campus."

"Did he have any family?"

"He had a girl," Planter said. "As a matter of fact, she called me up today. She wanted me to come and look at the paintings he left behind. She's selling them off cheap, I understand. Frankly I wouldn't buy them at any price."

He handed the picture back to me and told me how to find the place. I got into my car and drove northward past the university to Sycamore Point.

The girl that Jacob Whitmore had left behind was a mournful blonde in a rather late stage of girlhood. She lived in one of half a dozen cottages and cabins that sprawled across the sandy base of the point. She held her door almost completely closed and peered at me through the crack as if I might be bringing a second disaster.

"What do you want?"

"I'm interested in pictures."

"A lot of them are gone. I've been selling them off.

Jake drowned yesterday—I suppose you know that. He left me without a sou."

Her voice was dark with sorrow and resentment. The darkness appeared to have seeped up from her mind into the roots of her hair. She looked past me out to sea where the barely visible waves were rolling in like measured installments of eternity.

"May I come in and look?"

"I guess so. Sure."

She opened the door and swung it shut behind me against the wind. The room smelled of the sea, of wine and pot and mildew. The furniture was sparse and broken-down. It looked like a house that had barely survived a battle—an earlier stage of the same desultory battle against poverty and failure that had passed through the Johnson house on Olive Street.

The woman went into an inner room and emerged with a stack of unframed paintings in her arms. She set them down on the warped rattan table.

"These'll cost you ten apiece, or forty-five for five of them. Jake used to get more for his paintings at the Saturday art show on Santa Teresa beach. A while ago, he sold one of them to a dealer for a good price. But I can't afford to wait."

"Was Paul Grimes the dealer?"

"That's right." She looked at me with some suspicion. "Are you a dealer, too?"

"No."

"But you know Paul Grimes?"

"Slightly."

"Is he honest?"

"I don't know. Why?"

"*I* don't think he is. He put on quite an act about how much he liked Jake's work. He was going to publicize it on a big scale and make our fortune. I thought that Jake's big dream had come true at last. The dealers would be knocking on our door, Jake's prices would skyrocket. But Grimes bought two measly pictures and that was that. One of them wasn't even Jake's—it was somebody else's."

"Who painted the other picture?"

"I don't know. Jake didn't discuss his business with me. I think he took the picture on consignment from one of his friends on the beach."

"Can you describe the picture?"

"It was a picture of a woman—maybe a portrait, maybe imaginary. She was a beautiful woman, with hair the same color as mine." She touched her own bleached hair; the action seemed to arouse her fear or suspicion. "Why is everybody so interested in that picture? Was it worth a lot?"

"I don't know."

"I think it was. Jake wouldn't tell me what he got for it, but I know we've been living on the money for the last couple of months. The money ran out yesterday. And so," she added in a toneless voice, "did Jake."

She turned away and spread out the unframed paintings on the table. Most of them were unfinished-looking small seascapes like the one in my car that I'd shown to Arthur Planter. The drowned man had clearly been obsessed by the sea, and I couldn't help wondering if his drowning had been entirely accidental.

I said, "Were you suggesting that Jake drowned himself?"

"No, I was not." She changed the subject abruptly: "I'll give you all five of them for forty dollars. The canvases alone are worth that much. You know that if you're a painter."

"I'm not a painter."

"I sometimes wonder if Jake was. He painted for over thirty years and ended up with nothing to show for it but this." The gesture of her hand took in the paintings on the table, the house and its history, Jake's death. "Nothing but this and me."

She smiled, or grimaced with half of her face. Her eyes remained cold as a sea bird's, peering down into the roiled and cloudy past.

She caught me watching her and recoiled from the look on my face. "I'm not as bad as you think I am," she said. "If you want to know why I'm selling these things, I want to buy him a coffin. I don't want the county to bury him in one of those pine boxes. And I don't want to leave him lying in the basement of the county hospital."

"Okay, I'll take the five pictures."

I handed her two twenties, wondering if I'd ever get the money back from Biemeyer.

She took it with some distaste and held it. "That wasn't a sales pitch. You don't have to buy them just because you know why I need the money."

"I need the pictures."

"What for? *Are* you a dealer?"

"Not exactly."

"That means you are. I knew you weren't a painter."

"How did you know?"

"I've lived with a painter for the last ten years." She moved the position of her hips, resting her weight against the corner of the table. "You don't look like a painter or talk like one. You don't have a painter's eyes. You don't smell like a painter."

"What do I smell like?"

"A cop, maybe. I thought when Paul Grimes bought those two pictures from Jake that maybe there was something funny about them. Is there?"

"I don't know."

"Then why are you buying these?"

"Because Paul Grimes bought the others."

"You mean if he put out money for them, they must be worth something?"

"I'd certainly like to know why he wanted them."

"So would I," she said. "Why do *you* want the pictures?"

"Because Paul Grimes wanted them."

"You mean you do everything he does?"

"I hope not everything."

She gave me her cold half-smile and nodded. "Yeah,

I heard he's slightly crooked on occasion. I shouldn't say that, though. I've got nothing against him. And his daughter's kind of a friend of mine."

"Paola? Is she his daughter?"

"Yeah. You know her?"

"We've met. How do you happen to know her?"

"I met her at a party in the barrio. She told me her mother was part Spanish and part Indian. Paola's a beautiful woman, don't you think? I love those Spanish types."

She hunched her shoulders and rubbed her palms together as if she were warming herself at Paola's heat.

I drove back to Santa Teresa and paid a visit to the morgue in the basement of the hospital. A young deputy coroner named Henry Purvis, whom I knew, told me that Jacob Whitmore had drowned while swimming. He pulled out a drawer and showed me the blue body with its massive hairy head and shrunken sex. I walked out of the cold room shivering.

# XI

As if he were feeling lonely, the deputy coroner, Purvis, followed me into the anteroom, letting the heavy metal door swing shut behind him. He was almost as hairy as the dead man, and almost young enough to be his son.

I said, "Is there any official doubt that Whitmore died by accident?"

"I don't think so. He was getting too old for the kind of surf they have at Sycamore Point. The coroner put it down as an accident. He hasn't even ordered an autopsy."

"I think he should, Henry."

"Do you have a reason?"

"Whitmore and Grimes had a business connection. It's probably not a coincidence that they're in here together. Of course there'll be an autopsy on Grimes, won't there?"

Purvis nodded. "It's set for first thing in the morning. But I did a preliminary examination, and I can tell them what the probable results will be. He was beaten to death with a heavy weapon, probably a tire iron."

"The weapon hasn't been found?"

"Not that I know of. You should ask the police. The weapon is their department." He looked me over carefully. "Did you know Grimes?"

"Not really. I knew he was an art dealer in town."

"Was he an addict at one time?" Purvis said.

"I didn't know him that well. What kind of addiction do you have in mind?"

"Heroin, probably. He's got old needle marks on his arms and thighs. I asked the woman about them, but she wouldn't talk. The way she blew her top, she may be an addict herself. There's a lot of it around, even right in the hospital here."

"What woman are we talking about?"

"Dark woman—Spanish type. When I showed her the body, she did everything but climb the wall. I put her in the chapel and tried to call a priest for her but I couldn't raise one, not at this time of night. I called the police, and they want to talk to her."

I asked him where the chapel was. It was a narrow little room on the first floor, with a single small stained-glass window denoting its function. It was furnished with a lectern and eight or ten padded chairs. Paola was sitting on the floor head down, hugging her knees, her black hair almost covering her face. She was hiccuping. When I approached her, she raised a bent arm over her head as if I might be planning to murder her.

"Get away from me."

"I won't hurt you, Paola."

She tossed back her mane of hair and stared at me narrow-eyed, without recognition. She had an aura of fierce forlorn sexuality. "You're no priest."

"You can say that again."

I sat near her on the carpeted floor, which repeated the design of the stained-glass window. There were times when I almost wished I was a priest. I was growing weary of other people's pain and wondered if a black suit and a white collar might serve as armor against it. I'd never know. My grandmother in Contra Costa County had marked me for the priesthood, but I had slipped away under the fence.

Looking into Paola's opaque black eyes, I thought that the grief you shared with women was most always partly desire. At least sometimes you could take them to bed, I thought, and exchange a temporary kindness, which priests were denied. But not Paola. Both she and the woman at Sycamore Point belonged to dead men tonight. Chapel thoughts.

"What happened to Paul?" I asked her.

She looked at me with her chin on her shoulder, her lower lip protruding, her eyes defensive. "You haven't told me who you are. Are you a policeman?"

"No. I run a small business." I winced at the half-lie; the chapel was getting to me. "I heard that Paul was in the market for pictures."

"Not any more. He's dead."

"Aren't you going to carry on the business?"

She raised her shoulders and shook her head fiercely, as if she were being violently threatened. "Not me. You think I want to be killed like my father was?"

"Was Paul really your father?"

"Yes, he was."

"Who killed him?"

"I'm not saying. You're not saying much, either." She leaned toward me. "Didn't you come into the shop today?"

"Yes."

"It was something about the Biemeyers' picture,

wasn't it? What kind of business are you in? Are you a dealer?"

"I'm interested in pictures."

"I can see that. But whose side are you on?"

"The good guys."

"There are no good guys. If you don't know that, you're no use to me." She rose on her knees and swept her arm between us in a gesture of angry dismissal. "So why don't you get lost?"

"I want to help you." It wasn't entirely a lie.

"Sure you do. You want to help me. Then you want me to help you. Then you want to take the profits and run. That's the story, isn't it?"

"What profits? All you've got is a double handful of grief."

She was silent for a while. Her eyes stayed on my face. Through them I could sense the movements of her mind almost as tangibly as if she were playing chess or checkers on a board, asking herself what she had to lose to me in order to take a greater amount away.

"I admit I'm in trouble." She turned her hands palms upward on her knees, as if to offer me a share of her grief. "Only I think you're worse trouble. Who are you, anyway?"

I told her my name and what I did for a living. Her eyes changed but she didn't speak. I told her that the Biemeyers had hired me to find their stolen painting.

"I don't know anything about it. I told you that this afternoon at the shop."

"I believe you," I said with a mental reservation. "The point is that the theft of the painting and the killing of your father may be connected."

"How do you know that?"

"I don't know it, but it seems likely. Where did that painting come from, Miss Grimes?"

She winced. "Just call me Paola. I never use my father's name. And I can't tell you where he got the picture. He just used me for front; he never told me his business."

"You can't tell me, or you won't?"

"Both."

"Was the picture genuine?"

"I don't know." She was silent for an interval, during which she hardly seemed to breathe. "You say you want to help me, but all you do is ask questions. I'm supposed to supply the answers. How does it help me if I talk myself into jail?"

"Your father might have been better off in jail."

"Maybe you're right. But I don't want to end up there. Or in a hole in the ground, either." Her gaze was restless and inward, lost in the convolutions of her mind. "You think whoever painted that picture killed my father, too."

"That may be true. I have a feeling it is."

She said in a thin voice, "Is Richard Chantry still alive?"

"He may be. What makes you think he is?"

"That picture. I'm no expert like my father was, but it looked like a Chantry to me, the real McCoy."

"What did your father say about it?"

"I'm not telling you. And I don't want to talk about that picture any more. You're still asking all the questions, and I'm doing all the answering, and I'm tired. I want to go home."

"Let me take you."

"No. You don't know where I live, and I'm not telling you, either. That's my secret."

She got up from her knees, staggering a little. I supported her with my arm. Her breast touched my side. She leaned on me, breathing deeply for a moment, then pulled away. Some of her heat migrated through my body to my groin. I felt less tired than I had.

"I'll take you home."

"No, thanks. I have to wait here for the police. Anyway, all I need right now is a private cop in my life."

"You could do worse, Paola. Your father was murdered, remember, possibly by the man who painted that picture."

She took hold of my left arm above the elbow. "So you keep telling me, but do you know it?"

"No. I don't know it."

"Then stop trying to scare me. I'm scared enough already."

"I think you should be. I got to your father before he died. It happened just a couple of hundred yards from here. It was dark, and he was badly hurt, and he thought I was Chantry. In fact, he called me Chantry. And what he said implied that Chantry killed him."

Her eyes dilated. "Why would Richard Chantry kill my father? They were good friends in Arizona. My father often talked about him. He was Chantry's first teacher."

"That must have been a long time ago."

"Yes. Over thirty years."

"And people can change in thirty years."

She nodded in assent, and her head stayed down. Her hair swung forward so that it poured like black water over her face.

"What happened to your father in those years?"

"I don't know much about it. I didn't see a lot of my father until recently—until he had a use for me."

"Was he on heroin?"

She was silent for a time. Her hair was still over her face, and she didn't push it back. She looked like a woman without a face.

Finally she said, "You know the answer to that question, or you wouldn't ask it. He used to be an addict. They sent him to federal prison, and he licked it there, cold turkey." She separated her hair with her hands and looked at me between it, probably to see if I believed her. "I wouldn't have come here with him if he had been on drugs. I saw what it did to him when I was a kid in Tucson and Copper City."

"What did it do to him?"

"He used to be a good man, an important man. He even taught a course at the university once. Then he turned into something else."

"What did he turn into?"

"I don't know. He started running after boys. Or maybe he was always like that. I don't know."

"Did he kick that habit, too, Paola?"

"I guess he did." But her voice was uncertain, full of pain and doubt.

"Was the Biemeyers' painting genuine?"

"I don't know. *He* thought it was, and he was the expert."

"How do you know that?"

"He talked to me about it the day he bought it on the beach. He said it had to be a Chantry, nobody else could have painted it. He said it was the greatest find he ever made in his life."

"Did he say this to you?"

"Yes. Why would he lie to me? He had no reason." But she was watching my face as if my reaction might resolve the question of her father's honesty.

She was frightened, and I was tired. I sat down on one of the padded chairs and let my mind fray out for a couple of minutes. Paola went to the door but she didn't go out. She leaned on the doorframe, watching me as if I might steal her purse, or already had.

"I'm not your enemy," I said.

"Then don't press me so hard. I've had a rough night." She averted her face, as if she were ashamed of what she was about to say. "I liked my father. When I saw him dead, it was a terrible thing for me."

"I'm sorry, Paola. I hope tomorrow will be better."

"I hope so," she said.

"I understand your father had a photograph of the painting."

"That's right. The coroner has it."

"Henry Purvis?"

"Is that his name? Anyway, he has it."

"How do you know?"

"He showed it to me. He said he found it in my father's clothes, and he wanted to know if I recognized the woman. I told him I didn't."

"You recognized the painting?"

"Yes."

"It was the painting your father sold to the Biemeyers?"

"Yes, it was."

"How much did they pay him for it?"

"My father never told me. I think he needed the money to pay off a debt, and he didn't want me to know. I can tell you something that he did say, though. He knew the woman in the painting, and that was how he authenticated it as a Chantry."

"It is an authentic Chantry, then?"

"Yes. My father said it was."

"Did he tell you the woman's name?"

"It was Mildred. She was a model in Tucson when he was young—a beautiful woman. He said it must be a memory painting, because she's an old woman now, if she's alive at all."

"Do you remember her last name?"

"No. I think she took the names of the men she lived with."

I left Paola in the chapel and went back to the cold room. Purvis was in the anteroom, but he no longer had the photograph of the painting. He told me that he had given it to Betty Jo Siddon.

"What for?"

"She wanted to take it down to the newspaper building and have it photographed."

"Mackendrick will like that, Henry."

"Hell, it was Mackendrick who told me to let her have it. The chief of police is retiring this year, and it's made Captain Mackendrick publicity-conscious."

I started out of the hospital. A sense of unfinished business brought me to a full stop before I left the building. When Paul Grimes fell and died in my path, I had been on my way to talk to Fred's mother, Mrs. Johnson.

# XII

I went to the nurses' station at the front and asked where I could find Mrs. Johnson. The nurse in charge was a middle-aged woman with a sallow bony face and an impatient manner.

"We have several Mrs. Johnsons working in the hospital. Is her Christian name Sarah?"

"Yes. Her husband's name is Jerry or Gerard."

"Why didn't you say so in the first place? I'm afraid Mrs. Gerard Johnson is no longer employed in this hospital." She spoke with deliberate formal emphasis, like a court official pronouncing sentence on Mrs. Johnson.

"She told me that she worked here."

"Then she lied to you." The woman overheard the harshness of her words, and softened them: "Or it's possible you misunderstood her. She *is* presently employed at a convalescent home down by the highway."

"Do you know the name of it?"

"It's called the La Paloma," she said with distaste.

"Thank you. Why was she fired here?"

"I didn't say she was fired. She was allowed to leave. But I'm not authorized to discuss it." At the same time, she seemed unwilling to let me go. "Are you from the police?"

"I'm a private detective cooperating with the police."

I got out my wallet and showed her my license photostat.

She smiled into it as though it were a mirror. "She's in trouble again, is she?"

"I hope not."

"Stealing drugs again?"

"Let's just say I'm investigating Mrs. Johnson. How long ago did she leave her employment here?"

"It happened last week. The administration let her go without a black mark on her record. But they gave her no choice about leaving. It was an open-and-shut case. She had some of the pills in her pocket—and I was there when they searched her. You should have heard the language she used to the superintendent."

"What language did she use?"

"Oh, I couldn't repeat it."

Her wan face flamed red, as if I had made an indecent proposal to her. She looked at me with sudden dislike, perhaps embarrassed by her own excitement. Then she turned on her heel and walked away.

It was past midnight. I had been in the hospital so long that I was beginning to feel like a patient. I left by a route different from the one I had come in by. I didn't want to see Captain Mackendrick or Purvis or Paola or either of the dead men again.

I had noticed the La Paloma sign from the freeway and had some idea of where the convalescent home was. Driving toward it from the hospital, I passed a dark row of doctors' offices, a nurses' residence and several blocks of lower-middle-class houses, all one-storied and built before the war. Between the houses and the freeway was a narrow park studded with oak trees. In their shelter a few late lovers were parked with fog on their windshields.

The one-storied stucco complex of the La Paloma was almost as close to the freeway as a filling station. Once I had stepped inside and closed the heavy front door, the noises of late-night traffic dwindled to a far-off irregular sound like that of distant surf. I could hear the more immediate sounds of the place, snores and sighs and vague indecipherable demands.

A nurse's muted footsteps came up behind me. She was young and black and pretty.

"It's too late for visiting," she said. "We're all closed down for the night."

"I want to see a member of the staff—Mrs. Johnson?"

"I'll see if I can find her. She's getting very sought after. You're the second visitor she's had tonight."

"Who was the other one?"

She paused, then said, "Would you be Mr. Johnson?"

"No. I'm just a friend."

"Well, the other one was her son—dude with a red mustache. He stirred up quite a hassle before I got him out of here." She gave me a hard but not unfriendly look. "I hope you're not planning to stir up another hassle."

"Nothing could be further from my thoughts. I want to stir one down."

"All right, I'll get her. But keep it quiet, eh? People are sleeping."

"Sure. What was the hassle about?"

"Money. Isn't it always?"

"Not always," I said. "Sometimes it's love."

"*That* comes into it, too. He had a blonde in the car."

"Not all of us are so lucky."

She hardened her look a little in order to deflect a pass, if that was what I had offered her. "I'll get Sarah."

Mrs. Johnson came unwillingly. She had been crying, and her eyes were swollen.

"What do you want?" She made it sound as if she had very little left to give.

"I'd like to talk to you for a couple of minutes."

"I'm behind in my work already. Are you trying to get me fired?"

"No. I do happen to be a private detective, though."

Her gaze veered around the dark little anteroom and rested on the outside door. Her thick body tensed as if she were getting ready to run out onto the highway.

I stepped between her and the door. "Is there someplace we can sit down in private for a few minutes?"

"I guess so. But if I lose my job it's on your head."

She led me into a visiting room that was crowded

with mismatched furniture, and turned on a dim standing lamp. We sat down facing each other under the lamp, our knees almost touching. As though the touch of mine might contaminate hers, she pulled down her white nylon skirt.

"What do you want with me? And don't give me any more guff about being a newspaperman. I thought you were a policeman from the beginning."

"I want your son, Fred."

"So do I." She lifted her heavy shoulders and dropped them. "I'm getting worried about Fred. I haven't heard from him all day."

"He was here tonight. What was he after?"

She was silent for a moment, but not inactive. Her face worked as if she were swallowing her lie and possibly planning another.

"He needed money. That's nothing new. And it's no crime to ask your own mother for money. This isn't the first time that I've helped him out. He always pays me back as soon as he can."

I cut through her smoke screen of words. "Come off it, Mrs. Johnson. Fred's in trouble. A stolen picture is bad enough. A stolen girl compounds the felony."

"He didn't steal the girl. That's a lie, a sniveling lie. She went along with him of her own free will. In fact, it was probably her idea in the first place—she's been after Fred for some time. And if that little spade said something different, she's lying." The woman shook her fist at the door where the black nurse had disappeared.

"What about the picture, Mrs. Johnson?"

"What picture?"

"The painting that Fred stole from the Biemeyers' house."

"He didn't steal it. He simply borrowed it to make some tests on it. He took it down to the art museum, and it was stolen from there."

"Fred told me it was taken from your house."

She shook her head. "You must have misunderstood

him. It was taken from the basement of the art museum. They're responsible."

"Is that the story you and Fred have agreed on?"

"It's the truth, so naturally we agree on it. Fred is as honest as the day is long. If you can't see that, it's because your own mind is twisted. You've had too much to do with dishonest people."

"That's true enough," I said. "I think you're one of them."

"I don't have to sit here and listen to your insults."

She tried to evoke her own anger but somehow it wouldn't come. The day had been too much for her, and the night hung over her like a slowly gathering wave. She looked down into her cupped and empty hands, then put her face into them. She didn't sob or cry or say a word. But her silence in the midst of the muffled freeway noises sounded like desolation itself.

After a time she sat up and looked at me quite calmly. "It's time I got back to work."

"Nobody's watching you."

"Maybe not, but they'll blame me if things are in a mess in the morning. There are only the two of us on in this crummy place."

"I thought you worked at the hospital."

"I used to. I had a misunderstanding with one of the supervisors there."

"Do you want to tell me about it?"

"It wasn't important."

"Then tell me about it, Mrs. Johnson."

"Why should I? I've got enough on my mind without you bullying me."

"And enough on your conscience?"

"That's between me and my conscience. I don't need any help from you in straightening out my conscience."

She sat as still as stone. I admired her as I might have admired a statue without concern for its history. But I wasn't content to let her stay silent. The case, which had begun with a not very serious theft, was beginning to draw human lives into its vortex. Two men were dead, and the Biemeyers' girl had been spun off into the darkness.

"Mrs. Johnson, where is Fred going with Miss Biemeyer?"

"I don't know."

"Didn't you ask him? You wouldn't give him money without finding out what he intended to do with it."

"I did, though."

"I think you're lying."

"Think away," she said almost cheerfully.

"Not for the first time, either. You've lied to me already more than once."

Her eyes brightened with interest, and with the superiority that liars feel toward the people they lie to.

"For instance, you left the hospital because they caught you stealing drugs. You told me you left because you had a misunderstanding with a supervisor."

"Over drugs," she added quickly. "There was a discrepancy in the count. They blamed me."

"You weren't responsible?"

"Certainly not. What do you think I am?"

"A liar."

She stirred threateningly, but didn't get up. "Go ahead and call me names. I'm used to it. You can't prove anything."

"Are you on drugs now?"

"I don't take drugs."

"Not of any kind?"

"Not of any kind."

"Then who did you steal them for? Fred?"

She mimed laughter, and managed to produce a high toneless giggle. If I had heard the giggle without seeing its source, I might have taken her for a wild young girl. And I wondered if this was how she felt in relationship to her son.

"Why did Fred take the picture, Mrs. Johnson? To sell it and buy drugs?"

"He doesn't use drugs."

"To buy drugs for Miss Biemeyer?"

"That's a silly idea. She's independently wealthy."

"Is that why Fred is interested in her?"

She leaned forward with her hands on her knees, sober and dead serious. The woman who had giggled a moment ago had been swallowed up like a ghostly emanation by her body.

"You don't know Fred. You never will—you don't have the understanding. He's a good man. The way he feels about the Biemeyer girl is like a brother, an older brother."

"Where is the older brother taking his little sister?"

"You don't have to get snotty."

"I want to know where they are, or where they're going. Do you know?"

"No, I don't."

"You wouldn't give them traveling money unless you knew where they were going."

"Who says I did?"

"I say."

She clenched her fists and used them to strike both of her white nylon knees simultaneously several times. "I'll kill that little spade."

"I wouldn't, Mrs. Johnson. They'll put you in Corona if you do."

She grinned unpleasantly. "I was just kidding."

"You picked a bad subject and a bad time. A man named Paul Grimes was murdered earlier tonight."

"Murdered?"

"Beaten to death."

Mrs. Johnson pitched sideways onto the floor. She didn't move until the black girl, whom I called to help me, came and poured water on her head. Then she got up gasping and feeling her hair.

"What did you do that for? You've ruined my hairdo."

"You passed out," I said.

She swung her head from side to side, staggering a little.

The other nurse put her arm around her shoulders

and held her still. "Better sit down, hon. You were really out."

But Mrs. Johnson stayed on her feet. "What happened? Did somebody hit me?"

"I hit you with a piece of news," I said. "Paul Grimes was beaten to death tonight. I found him on the street not very far from here."

Mrs. Johnson's face went completely blank for a moment, then set in a scowling mask of ignorance. "Who's he?"

"An art dealer from Arizona. He sold that picture to the Biemeyers. Don't you know him?"

"What did you say his name was?"

"Paul Grimes."

"I never heard of him."

"Then why did you faint when I told you he'd been murdered?"

"I didn't. I have these fainting spells is all. They don't mean anything."

"You better let me take you home."

"No! I'd lose my job. I can't afford that—it's the only thing that keeps us going."

Head down and weaving slightly, she turned and moved away toward the wards.

I followed her. "Where is Fred taking the Biemeyer girl?"

She didn't answer the question or even acknowledge it.

# XIII

I followed the freeway into the center of town, which was almost deserted. A cruising police car overtook me. Its driver gave me a quick once-over as he passed, and went on.

There were lights on the second floor of the newspaper building. It faced on a grassy square fringed with tall palms. The trees stood still and silent in the calm post-midnight air.

I parked my car by the square and climbed the stairs to the lighted newsroom. A clacking typewriter led me across the large unpeopled room to a partitioned space where Betty Jo Siddon was working. She looked up with a start when I spoke her first two names.

"You shouldn't *do* that. You scared me."

"I'm sorry."

"That's all right. As a matter of fact, I'm glad you came by. I'm trying to make some kind of sense out of this murder story."

"May I read it?"

"In tomorrow's paper, if they use it. They don't always print my stuff. The news editor is a male chauvinist and he tries to keep me segregated in the women's pages." She was smiling but her dark eyes were rebellious.

"You can tell me what your theory is."

"I'm afraid I don't have a theory. I'm trying to build a story around the question of who the woman in the painting was, and who painted the picture, and of course who stole it. Actually it's a triple mystery, isn't it? Do you know who stole it?"

"I think so, but I wouldn't want to be quoted."

"I won't quote you," she said. "This is just for background."

"Okay. According to my witnesses, who frankly aren't worth much, the picture was stolen twice in quick succession. An art student by the name of Fred Johnson took it from the Biemeyers' house——"

"Fred Johnson from the museum? I wouldn't have thought he was the type."

"He may not be. He claims he took it to make some tests on it and try to authenticate it as a Chantry. But somebody stole it from his parents' house, or from the art museum——there are two versions."

Betty Jo was making penciled notes on a sheet of

typewriter paper. "Where's Fred now? Do you think I can talk to him?"

"If you can find him. He's taken off for parts unknown with the Biemeyer girl. As for your other questions, I don't know who painted the picture. It may be a Chantry and it may not. Maybe Fred Johnson knows. I did get a partial identification of the woman in the picture. Her name is Mildred."

"Is she in town here?"

"I doubt it. She was a model in Tucson a generation ago. Paul Grimes, the man who was killed, knew her. He thought the painting of her had probably been done from memory. She was much younger in it than she could be in real life."

"Does that mean it was painted recently?"

"That's one of the questions Fred was trying to answer, apparently. He was trying to date the picture to determine if Chantry could have painted it."

Betty Jo looked up brightly from her notes. "Do you think Chantry could have?"

"My opinion isn't worth anything. I haven't seen the picture or the photograph of it."

"Why didn't you say so? I'll get it."

She rose quickly and disappeared through the door marked "Photography Department." Her passage left vibrations on the air. The vibrations lingered in my body.

I was feeling lonely and late but I felt dubious about jumping the generation gap. It could open up like a chasm and swallow you, or close on you like pincers. I tried to focus my excitement on the woman in the picture that I hadn't seen yet.

Betty Jo brought it and laid it down on her desk. It was a colored photograph of a painting, measuring about four by six inches. I held it up in the fluorescent light. The pictured woman was beautiful, as Paola had said. She had classical features, delicate blond coloring. The whole painting held a sense of distance that centered in her ice-blue eyes and seemed to suggest that she was watching me, or I was watching her, from a long way off. Perhaps the suggestion came from what Paola had relayed from her father, that the woman who sat for the picture would be old or dead, her beauty only remembered.

But it seemed to have the power to focus the case for me. I wanted to reclaim the picture, meet the woman if she was alive. I wanted to find out where and when and by whom she had been painted.

"Will you be running this in tomorrow's paper?"

"I doubt it," Betty Jo said. "The photographer said the picture he took wouldn't reproduce too well."

"Even a bad print of it would be useful to me. The original has to go back to the police."

"I suppose you could ask Carlos for a copy."

"You ask him, will you? You know him. It could help me to track down Fred and the Biemeyer girl."

"And if you do you'll give me the details, right?"

"I won't forget you." The words held a double meaning for my inner ear.

Betty Jo took the picture back into the photography department. I sat down in her chair and rested my arms on her desk and my head on my arms, and slid off into sleep. I must have dreamed about violence, or the expectation of violence. When the girl's hand touched my shoulder, I lunged to my feet reaching for a gun in a shoulder holster that I wasn't wearing.

Betty Jo backed away from me with her hands half raised and fingers spread. "You frightened me."

"I'm sorry."

"Carlos is making you a picture. In the meantime, I'm afraid I have to use my typewriter. I want to have my story ready for the noon edition. Incidentally, is it all right if I mention you in it?"

"Not by name, please."

"You're modest."

"Hardly. I'm a private detective. I want to stay private."

I retreated to the City Editor's desk and put my head down on my arms again. It was some time since I had gone to sleep in the same room with a girl. Of course the room was large and reasonably well lighted, and the girl had other things than me on her mind.

This time she woke me by voice, standing well back. "Mr. Archer?"

She had a young black with her. He showed me the black-and-white copy that he had made. It was rather blurred and grimy, as if the blond woman had slipped away still further into time, out of sight of the sun. Still her features were identifiable.

I thanked the photographer and offered to pay him for the copy. He deplored the suggestion, pushing air toward me with his hands. He retreated into his workroom, and the girl sat down at her typewriter again. She typed a few words and stopped, withdrawing her hands from the keys and dropping them in her lap.

"I don't know whether I can do this piece after all. I can't name Fred Johnson or the girl. It doesn't really make for much of a story, does it?"

"It will."

"But when? I don't really know enough about the people. If the woman in the picture is alive and reachable, that would make all the difference. I could hang the whole story on her."

"You can anyway."

"It would be so much better if I could say definitely who and where she is. And that she's alive if she is alive. I might even do a follow-up interview."

"The Biemeyers might know," I said. "They may have had a personal reason for buying that picture of her."

She looked at her watch. "It's after midnight. I wouldn't dare to call them at this time of night. Anyway, the chances are that they don't know anything. Ruth Biemeyer does a lot of talking about her relationship with Richard Chantry, yet I doubt that she was ever very close to him."

I didn't argue. I didn't want to talk to my clients right now. The case had enlarged enormously since they had hired me, and I had no immediate hope of being able to explain it to them. But I did want another crack at Mrs. Chantry.

"Chantry's wife was very close to him," I said.

"You think Francine Chantry would be willing to talk to me?"

"She can hardly refuse, since there's a murder involved. Which she's taking pretty hard. She may know all about the woman in the picture. Didn't she used to model for her husband herself?"

"How do you know that?" Betty Jo said.

"She told me."

"She never told *me*."

"You're not a man."

"You noticed."

# XIV

I drove Betty Jo along the deserted waterfront to the Chantry house. It was dark and silent. The parking area was empty. The party was over.

Perhaps not entirely over. I could hear a faint sound, the sound of a woman moaning in pain or pleasure, which ended abruptly as we approached the front door. Betty Jo turned to me.

"Who was that?"

"It could have been Mrs. Chantry. But women all sound the same under certain circumstances."

She let out her breath, making a small impatient angry noise, and knocked on the door. A light went on above it.

After what seemed a long wait, the door was opened and Rico looked out at us. Lipstick was smeared on one side of his mouth. He saw me looking at it, and wiped his mouth with the back of his hand. It dragged the red smear down across his chin. His black eyes were unfriendly.

"What do you want?"

"We have a couple of questions to ask Mrs. Chantry," I said.

"She's in bed asleep."

"You better wake her up."

"I can't do that. She's had a big day. A big day and a big night." The lipstick smear on Rico's face touched his words with comic lewdness.

"Ask her if she'll see us. We're investigating a murder, as you possibly know."

"Mr. Archer and Miss Siddon," Betty Jo said.

"I know who you are."

Rico let us into the long front room and turned on the light. With his dark bald-eagle head jutting out of his long brown dressing gown, he looked like some kind of wild medieval monk. There was stale smoke in the deserted room. Through it I could almost hear the remembered buzzing hum of party conversation. Empty and half-empty glasses stood on most of the horizontal surfaces, including the keyboard of the grand piano. Except for the paintings on the walls—quiet windows into a more orderly world, which even murder didn't seem to have changed—the room was like a visible hangover.

I moved around the room inspecting the portraits and trying in an amateurish way to tell if the same hand had painted the Biemeyers' picture. I couldn't tell, and neither, she said, could Betty Jo.

But I found that the murder of Grimes, and the possible murder of Whitmore, had after all subtly changed the portraits or my perceptions of them. Their eyes seemed to regard me with suspicion and a kind of fearful resignation. Some looked at me like prisoners, some like jurors, and some like quiet animals in a cage. I wondered which, if any, reflected the mind of the man who had painted them.

"Did you know Chantry, Betty Jo?"

"Not really. He was before my time. Actually I did see him once."

"When?"

"Right here in this room. My father, who was a writer, brought me to meet him. It was a very special occasion. He hardly saw anybody, you know. All he did was work."

"How did he strike you?"

She considered the question. "He was very remote and shy, as shy as I was. He held me on his knee but he didn't really want to. He got rid of me as soon as he could, I think. And that suited me. Either he didn't like little girls at all, or he liked them too much."

"Did you really think that at the time?"

"I believe I did. Little girls are quite aware of such things, at least I was."

"How old were you?"

"I must have been four or five."

"How old are you now?"

"I'm not saying." She said it with a slightly defensive smile.

"Under thirty?"

"Barely. It was roughly twenty-five years ago, if that's what you're getting at. Chantry disappeared soon after I visited him. I often seem to have that effect on men."

"Not on me."

A little color invaded her cheeks and made her prettier. "Just don't try to hold me on your knee. You could disappear."

"Thanks for the warning."

"Don't mention it. Seriously," she added, "it gives me a funny feeling to be in this same room prying into Richard Chantry's life. It makes me wonder if certain things aren't fated. Do you think they are?"

"Of course. By the place and the time and the family

you're born into. Those are the things that fate most people."

"I'm sorry I asked. I don't really like my family. I don't like the place and time too well, either."

"So react against them."

"Is that what you do?"

"I try."

Betty Jo's eyes shifted to a point behind me. Mrs. Chantry had quietly entered the room. Her hair was brushed, her face looked newly washed. She was wearing a white robe that molded her figure from neck to knee and swept the floor.

"I do wish you'd find another place to react, Mr. Archer. And by all means another time. It's dreadfully late." She gave me a long-suffering smile, which hardened when she turned to Betty Jo. "What is this all about, dear?"

The younger woman was embarrassed. Her mouth moved, trying to find the right words.

I got out my black-and-white photograph of the stolen painting. "Do you mind taking a look at this, Mrs. Chantry? It's a photograph of the Biemeyers' picture."

"I have nothing to add to what I told you earlier. I'm sure it's a fake. I'm familiar with all of my husband's paintings, I believe, and this isn't one of them."

"Look at it anyway, will you?"

"I've already seen the painting itself, as I told you."

"Did you recognize the model who sat for it?"

Her eyes met mine in an instant of shared knowledge. She had recognized the model.

"No," she said.

"Will you take a look at this photo and try again?"

"I don't see the point."

"Try anyway, Mrs. Chantry. It may be important."

"Not to me."

"You can't be sure," I said.

"Oh, very well."

She took the photograph from my hand and studied it. Her hand was shaking, and the picture fluttered like something in a high wind from the past. She handed it back to me as if she were glad to get rid of it.

"It does bear some resemblance to a woman I knew when I was a young girl."

"When did you know her?"

"I didn't really *know* her. I met her at a party in Santa Fe before the war."

"What was her name?"

"I honestly can't say. I don't believe she had a definite surname. She lived with various men and took their names." Her eyes came up abruptly. "No, my husband wasn't one of those men."

"But he must have known her if he painted the picture."

"He didn't paint this picture. I told you that."

"Who did, Mrs. Chantry?"

"I have no idea."

Impatience had been rising in her voice. She glanced toward the door. Rico was leaning there with his hand in the pocket of his robe; and something larger than a hand, shaped like a gun. He moved toward me.

I said, "Call off your dog, Mrs. Chantry. Unless you want this written up in the paper."

She gave Betty Jo an icy look, which Betty Jo managed to return. But she said, "Go away, Rico. I can take care of this."

Rico moved reluctantly into the hallway.

I said to Mrs. Chantry, "How do you know your husband didn't paint it?"

"I would have known if he had. I know all his paintings."

"Does that mean you still keep in touch with him?"

"No, of course not."

"Then how do you know he didn't paint this some time in the last twenty-five years?"

The question stopped her for a moment. Then she said, "The woman in the painting is too young. She was older than this when I saw her in Santa Fe in 1940. She'd be a really old woman now, if she's alive at all."

"But your husband could have painted her from memory, any time up to the present. If *he's* alive."

"I see what you mean," she said in a small flat voice. "But I still don't think he painted it."

"Paul Grimes thought he did."

"Because it paid him to think so."

"Did it, though? I think this picture got him killed. He knew the model who sat for it, and she told him your husband had painted it. For some reason the knowledge was dangerous. Dangerous to Paul Grimes, obviously, and dangerous to whoever killed Grimes."

"Are you accusing my husband?"

"No. I have nothing to go on. I don't even know if your husband is alive. Do you know, Mrs. Chantry?"

She took a deep breath, her breasts rising like fists under her robe. "I haven't heard from him since the day he left. I warn you, though, Mr. Archer, his memory is all I live for. Whether Richard is dead or alive, I'll fight for his reputation. And I'm not the only one in this city who will fight you. Please get out of my house now."

She included Betty Jo in the invitation. Rico opened the front door and slammed it behind us.

Betty Jo was shaken. She crept into my car like a refugee from trouble.

I said, "Was Mrs. Chantry ever an actress?"

"An amateur one, I think. Why?"

"She reads her lines like one."

The girl shook her head. "No. I think Francine meant what she said. Chantry and his work are all she cares about. And I feel small about doing what I just did. We hurt her and made her angry."

"Are you afraid of her?"

"No, but I thought we were friends." She added as we drove away from the house, "Maybe I am a little afraid of her. But also I'm sorry that we hurt her."

"She was hurt long ago."

"Yes. I know what you mean."

I meant Rico.

I returned to my motel. Betty Jo came in with me to compare notes. We compared not only notes.

The night was sweet and short. Dawn slipped in like something cool and young and almost forgotten.

# XV

When I woke up in the morning, she was gone. A pang that resembled hunger went through me a little higher than my stomach. The phone beside the bed rang.

"This is Betty Jo."

"You sound very cheerful," I said. "Painfully cheerful."

"You had that effect on me. Also my editor wants me to do a feature on the Chantry case. He says he'll give me all the time I need. The only drawback is that they may not print it."

"Why not?"

"Mrs. Chantry talked to Mr. Brailsford first thing this morning. He owns the paper. So they're going to have an editorial conference in Mr. Brailsford's office. In the meantime, I'm supposed to go on digging. Do you have any suggestions?"

"You might try the art museum. Take along your photograph of the painting. There may be somebody in the museum who can identify the model who sat for it. And if we're very lucky the model may be able to tell us who painted it."

"That's exactly what I was planning to do."

"Good for you."

She lowered her voice. "Lew?"

"What do you want?"

"Nothing. I mean, do you mind about my thinking of it first? I mean, you're older than I am, and maybe not quite so liberated."

I said, "Cheer up. I'll probably see you at the art museum. You'll find me among the old masters."

"I did hurt your feelings, didn't I?"

"On the contrary. I never felt better. I'm going to hang up now before you hurt my feelings."

She laughed and hung up on me. I shaved and had a shower and went out for breakfast. An early wind was blowing on the water. A few small craft were out in it. But most of the boats in the harbor danced in place at their moorings, naked-masted.

I found a clean-looking restaurant and took a seat by the front window so that I could watch the boats. They gave me the empathetic feeling that I was in motion, too, scudding along under complex pressures and even more complex controls toward the open sea.

I had ham and eggs with potatoes and toast and coffee. Then I drove uptown and parked in the lot behind the art museum.

Betty Jo met me at the front entrance.

I said, "We seem to be synchronized, Betty Jo."

"Yes." But she didn't sound too happy about it.

"What's the matter?"

"You just said it. My name. I hate my name."

"Why?"

"It's a silly name. A double name always sounds like a child's name. It's immature. I don't like either of my names separately, either. Betty is such a plain name, and Jo sounds like a boy. But I suppose I have to settle for one of them. Unless you can suggest something better."

"How about Lew?"

She didn't smile. "You're making fun of me. This is serious."

She was a serious girl, and more delicate in her feelings than I'd imagined. It didn't make me sorry that I had slept with her, but it lent a certain weight to the event. I hoped she wasn't getting ready to fall in love, especially not with me. But I kissed her, lightly, philanthropically.

A young man had appeared at the entrance to the classical sculpture exhibit. He had a wavy blond head and a tapered torso. He was carrying the colored photograph of the memory painting.

"Betty Jo?"

"I've changed my name to Betty," she said. "Please just call me Betty."

"Okay, Betty." The young man's voice was precise and rather thin. "What I was going to say is, I matched up your picture with one of the Lashman pictures in the basement."

"That's marvelous, Ralph. You're a genius." She took his hand and shook it wildly. "By the way, this is Mr. Archer."

"The non-genius," I said. "Nice to meet you."

Ralph flushed. "Actually it was terribly easy to do. The Lashman painting was sitting out on one of the worktables, propped up against the wall. You'd almost think it was looking for me instead of I for it. It virtually leaped right out at me."

Betty turned to me. "Ralph has found another painting of that same blond model. One by a different painter."

"So I gathered. May I see it?"

"You certainly may," Ralph said. "The beauty of it is that Simon Lashman should be able to tell you who she is."

"Is he in town?"

"No. He lives in Tucson. We should have a record of his address. We've bought several of his paintings over the years."

"Right now, I'd rather look at the one in the basement."

Ralph unlocked a door. The three of us went downstairs and along a windowless corridor that reminded me of jails I had known. The workroom where Ralph took me was also windowless, but whitely lit by fluorescent tubes in the ceiling.

The picture on the table was a full-length nude. The woman looked much older than she had in the Biemeyer painting. There were marks of pain at the corners of her eyes and mouth. Her breasts were larger, and they drooped a little. Her entire body was less confident.

Betty looked from the sorrowful painted face to mine, almost as if she were jealous of the woman.

She said to Ralph, "How long ago was this painted?"

"Over twenty years. I checked the file. Lashman called it *Penelope,* by the way."

"She'd be really old now," Betty said to me. "She's old enough in the picture."

"I'm no spring chicken myself," I said.

She flushed and looked away as if I'd rebuffed her.

I said to Ralph, "Why would the picture be sitting out on the table like this? It isn't where it's usually kept, is it?"

"Of course not. One of the staff must have set it out."

"This morning?"

"That I doubt. There wasn't anyone down here this morning before me. I had to unlock the door."

"Who was down here yesterday?"

"Several people, at least half a dozen. We're preparing a show."

"Including this picture?"

"No. It's a show of Southern California landscapes."

"Was Fred Johnson down here yesterday?"

"As a matter of fact, he was. He put in quite a lot of time sorting through the paintings in the storage room."

"Did he tell you what he was after?"

"Not exactly. He said he was looking for something."

"He was looking for this," Betty said abruptly.

She had forgotten her jealousy of the painted woman, if that is what it had been. Excitement colored her cheekbones. Her eyes were bright.

"Fred is probably on his way to Tucson." She

clenched her fists and shook them in the air like an excited child. "Now if I could get Mr. Brailsford to pay my travel expenses—"

I was thinking the same thing about Mr. Biemeyer. But before I approached Biemeyer I decided to try to make a phone call to the painter Lashman.

Ralph got me the painter's number and address out of the file, and left me alone at the desk in his own office.

I dialed Lashman's house in Tucson direct.

A hoarse reluctant voice answered, "Simon Lashman speaking."

"This is Lew Archer calling from the Santa Teresa Art Museum. I'm investigating the theft of a picture. I understand you painted the picture of Penelope in the museum."

There was a silence. Then Lashman's voice creaked like an old door opening: "That was a long time ago. I'm painting better now. Don't tell me someone thought that picture was worth stealing."

"It hasn't been stolen, Mr. Lashman. Whoever painted the stolen picture used the same model as you used for *Penelope*."

"Mildred Mead? Is she still alive and kicking?"

"I was hoping you could tell me."

"I'm sorry, I haven't seen her in some years. She'd be an old woman by now. We're all getting older." His voice was becoming fainter. "She may be dead."

"I hope not. She was a beautiful woman."

"I used to think that Mildred was the most beautiful woman in the Southwest." His voice had become stronger, as if the thought of her beauty had stimulated him. "Who painted the picture you're talking about?"

"It's been attributed to Richard Chantry."

"Really?"

"The attribution isn't certain."

"I'm not surprised. I never heard that he used Mildred as a model." Lashman was silent for a moment. "Can you describe the picture to me?"

"It's a very simple nude in plain colors. Someone said it showed the influence of Indian painting."

"A lot of Chantry's stuff did, in his Arizona period. But none of it is particularly good. Is this one any good?"

"I don't know. It seems to be causing a lot of excitement."

"Does it belong to the Santa Teresa museum?"

"No. It was bought by a man named Biemeyer."

"The copper magnate?"

"That's correct. I'm investigating the theft for Biemeyer."

"To hell with you, then," Lashman said, and hung up.

I dialed his number again. He said, "Who is this?"

"Archer. Please hold on. There's more involved than the theft of a picture here. A man named Paul Grimes was murdered in Santa Teresa last night. Grimes was the dealer who sold the picture to Biemeyer. The sale and the murder are almost certainly connected."

Lashman was silent again. Finally he said, "Who stole the picture?"

"An art student named Fred Johnson. I think he may be on his way to Tucson with it now. And he may turn up on your doorstep."

"Why me?"

"He wants to find Mildred and see who painted her. He seems to be obsessed with the painting. In fact, he may be off his rocker entirely, and he has a young girl traveling with him." I deliberately omitted the fact that she was Biemeyer's daughter.

"Anything else?"

"That's the gist of it."

"Good," he said. "I am seventy-five years old. I'm painting my two-hundred-and-fourteenth picture. If I stopped to attend to other people's problems, I'd never get it finished. So I am going to hang up on you again, Mr. whatever-your-name-is."

"Archer," I said. "Lew Archer. L-E-W A-R-C-H-E-R. You can always get my number from Los Angeles information."

Lashman hung up again.

# XVI

The morning wind had died down. The air was clear and sparkling. Like a flashing ornament suspended from an infinitely high ceiling, the red-tailed hawk swung over the Biemeyer house.

Jack and Ruth Biemeyer both came out to meet me. They were rather conservatively dressed, like people on their way to a funeral, and they looked as if the funeral might be their own.

The woman reached me first. She had dark circles under her eyes, which she hadn't quite succeeded in covering with makeup.

"Is there any word about Doris?"

"I think she left town with Fred Johnson last night."

"Why didn't you stop her?"

"She didn't give me notice that she was leaving. I couldn't have stopped her if she had."

"Why not?" Ruth Biemeyer was leaning toward me, her handsome head poised like a tomahawk.

"Doris is old enough to be a free agent. She may not be smart enough, but she's old enough."

"Where have they gone?"

"Possibly Arizona. I have a little bit of a lead in Tucson, and I think they may be heading there. I don't know if they have the picture with them. Fred claims it was stolen from *him*."

Jack Biemeyer spoke for the first time. "That's horse manure."

I didn't argue with him. "You're probably right. If you want me to go to Tucson, it's going to cost you more, naturally."

"Naturally." Biemeyer looked past me at his wife. "I told you there would be another bite. There always is."

I felt like hitting him. Instead I turned on my heel and walked to the far end of the driveway. It wasn't far enough. A five-foot wire fence stopped me.

The hill slanted sharply downward to the edge of the barranca. On the far side stood the Chantry house, miniatured by distance like a building in a bell jar.

The greenhouse behind it had a half-painted glass roof. Through its flashing multiple panes I could make out dim movements inside the building, which was choked with greenery. There seemed to be two people facing each other and making wide sweeping motions, like duelists too far apart to hurt each other.

Ruth Biemeyer spoke in a quiet voice behind me. "Please come back. I know Jack can be difficult—God knows I know it. But we really need you."

I couldn't resist that, and I said so. But I asked her to wait a minute, and got a pair of binoculars out of my car. They gave me a clearer view of what was going on in the Chantry greenhouse. A gray-headed woman and a black-haired man, whom I identified as Mrs. Chantry and Rico, were standing among the masses of weeds and overgrown orchid plants, and using long hooked knives to cut them down.

"What is it?" Ruth Biemeyer said.

I handed her my binoculars. Standing on tiptoe, she looked over the fence.

"What are they doing?"

"They seem to be doing some gardening. Is Mrs. Chantry fond of gardening?"

"She may be. But I never saw her doing any actual work, until now."

We went back to her husband, who all this time had

been standing in a silent stony anger beside my car, like some kind of picket.

I said to him, "Do you want me to go to Tucson for you?"

"I suppose so. I have no choice."

"Sure you have."

Ruth Biemeyer interrupted, glancing from her husband to me and back again like a tennis referee. "We want you to go on with the case, Mr. Archer. If you need some money in advance, I'll be glad to give it to you out of my own savings."

"That won't be necessary," Biemeyer said.

"Good. Thank you, Jack."

"I'll take five hundred dollars from you," I said.

Biemeyer yelped and looked stricken. But he said he would write me a check, and went into the house.

I said to his wife, "What made him that way about money?"

"Getting some, I think. Jack used to be quite different when he was a young mining engineer and had nothing. But lately he's been making a lot of enemies."

"Including his own daughter." And his own wife. "What about Simon Lashman?"

"The painter? What about him?"

"I mentioned your husband's name to him this morning. Lashman reacted negatively. In fact, he told me to go to hell and hung up on me."

"I'm sorry."

"It doesn't matter to me personally. Still I may need Lashman's cooperation. Are you on good terms with him?"

"I don't know him. Naturally I know who he is."

"Does your husband know him?"

She hesitated, then spoke haltingly. "I believe he does. I don't want to talk about it."

"You might as well, though."

"No. This is really painful for me."

"Why?"

"There's so much old history involved." She shook

her head, as if it were still encumbered by the past. Then she spoke in a smaller voice, watching the doorway through which her husband had disappeared. "My husband and Mr. Lashman were rivals at one time. She was an older woman than my husband—actually she belonged to Lashman's generation—but Jack preferred her to me. He bought her away from Lashman."

"Mildred Mead?"

"You've heard of her, have you?" Her voice grew coarse with anger and contempt. "She was a notorious woman in Arizona."

"I've heard of her. She sat for that picture you bought."

She gave me a vague disoriented look. "What picture?"

"The one we're looking for. The Chantry."

"No," she said.

"Yes. Didn't you know it was a picture of Mildred Mead?"

She put her hand over her eyes and spoke blindfolded. "I suppose I may have known. If I did know, I'd blanked out on the fact. It was a terrible shock to me when Jack bought a house for her. A better house than I was living in at the time." She dropped her hand and blinked at the high harsh light. "I must have been crazy to bring that picture and hang it in the house. Jack must have known who it was. He never said a word, but he must have wondered what I was trying to do."

"You could ask him what he thought."

She shook her head. "I wouldn't dare. I wouldn't want to open that can of worms." She looked behind her as if to see if her husband was listening, but he was still out of sight in the house.

"You did open it, though. You bought the picture and brought it home."

"Yes, I did. I must be going out of my mind—do you think I am?"

"You'd know better than I would. It's your mind."

"Anybody else would be welcome to it." There was a

faint rising note of excitement in her voice: she had surprised herself with her own complexity.

"Did you ever see Mildred Mead?"

"No, I never did. When she—when she became important in my life, I was careful not to see her. I was afraid."

"Of her?"

"Of myself," she said. "I was afraid I might do something violent. She must have been twenty years older than I, at least. And Jack, who had always been such a skinflint with me, bought her a house."

"Is she still living in it?"

"I don't know. She may be."

"Where is the house?"

"In Chantry Canyon in Arizona. It's on the New Mexico border, not too far from the mine. In fact it was the original Chantry house."

"Are we talking about Chantry the painter?"

"His father, Felix," she said. "Felix Chantry was the engineer who first developed the mine. He was in charge of operations until he died. It's why it was such an insult to me when Jack bought the house from the old man's estate and gave it to that woman."

"I don't quite follow you."

"It's perfectly simple. Jack took over the mine from Felix Chantry. Actually he was related to Felix Chantry. Jack's mother was Chantry's cousin. Which was all the more reason why he should have bought the Chantry house for me." She spoke with an almost childish bitterness.

"Is that why you bought the Chantry picture?"

"Maybe it is. I never thought of it in that way. I bought it really because I was interested in the man who painted it. Don't ask me how interested, it's a moot question now."

"Do you still want the picture back?"

"I don't know," she said. "I want my daughter back. We shouldn't be standing here wasting time."

"I know that. I'm waiting for your husband to bring me my check."

Mrs. Biemeyer gave me an embarrassed look and went into the house. She didn't come out right away.

I still had my binoculars hanging around my neck, and I carried them down the driveway to the edge of the slope again. The black-haired man and the gray-haired woman were still cutting weeds in the greenhouse.

Mrs. Biemeyer came out of the house by herself. Angry tears were spilling from her eyes. The check she handed me was signed with her name, not her husband's.

"I'm going to leave him," she said to me and the house. "As soon as we get through this."

# XVII

I drove downtown and cashed the Biemeyers' check before either of them could cancel it. Leaving my car in the parking lot behind the bank, I walked a block to the newspaper building on the city square. The newsroom, which had been almost deserted in the early morning, was fully alive now. Nearly twenty people were working at typewriters.

Betty saw me and stood up behind her desk. She walked toward me smiling, with her stomach pulled in.

"I want to talk to you," I said.

"I want to talk to *you*."

"I mean seriously."

"So do I mean seriously."

"You look too happy," I said.

"I'm seriously happy."

"I'm not. I have to leave town." I told her why.

"There's something you can do for me in my absence."

She said with her wry intense smile, "I was hoping there was something I could do for you in your presence."

"If you're going to make verbal passes, isn't there someplace private where we can talk?"

"Let's try here."

She knocked on a door marked "Managing Editor," and got no answer. We went inside and I kissed her. Not only my temperature rose.

"Hey," she said. "He still likes me."

"But I have to leave town. Fred Johnson is probably in Tucson now."

She tapped me on the chest with her pointed fingers, as if she were typing out a message there. "Take care of yourself. Fred is one of those gentle boys who could turn out to be dangerous."

"He isn't a boy."

"I know that. He's the fair-haired young man at the art museum but he's very unhappy. He unburdened himself to me about his ghastly family life. His father's an unemployable drunk and his mother's in a constant state of eruption. Fred's trying to work his way out of all this, but I think in his quiet way he's pretty desperate. So be careful."

"I can handle Fred."

"I know you can." She put her hands on my upper arms. "Now what do you want me to do?"

"How well do you know Mrs. Chantry?"

"I've known Francine all my life, since I was a small child."

"Are you friends?"

"I think so. I've been useful to her. Last night was embarrassing, though."

"Keep in touch with her, will you? I'd like to have some idea of what she does today and tomorrow."

The suggestion worried her. "May I ask why?"

"You may ask but I can't answer. I don't know why."

"Do you suspect her of doing something wrong?"

"I'm suspicious of everybody."

"Except me, I hope." Her smile was serious and questioning.

"Except thee and me. Will you check on Francine Chantry for me?"

"Of course. I was intending to call her anyway."

I left my car at the Santa Teresa airport and caught a commuter plane to Los Angeles. The next plane to Tucson didn't leave for forty minutes. I had a quick sandwich and a glass of beer, and checked in with my answering service.

Simon Lashman had called me. I had time to call him back.

His voice on the line sounded still older and more reluctant than it had that morning. I told him who and where I was, and thanked him for calling.

"Don't mention it," he said dryly. "I'm not going to apologize for my show of impatience. It's more than justified. The girl's father once did me a serious disservice, and I'm not a forgiving man. Like father, like daughter."

"I'm not working for Biemeyer."

"I thought you were," he said.

"I'm working for his wife. She's very much concerned about her daughter."

"She has a right to be. The girl acts as if she's on drugs."

"You've seen her, then?"

"Yes. She was here with Fred Johnson."

"May I come and talk to you later this afternoon?"

"I thought you said you were in Los Angeles."

"I'm catching a flight to Tucson in a few minutes."

"Good. I prefer not to discuss these things on the telephone. When I was painting in Taos, I didn't even have a telephone on the place. Those were the happiest days of my life." He pulled himself up short: "I'm maundering. I detest old men who maunder. I'll say goodbye."

# XVIII

His house was on the edge of the desert, near the base of a mountain, which had loomed up on my vision long before the plane landed. The house was one-storied and sprawling, surrounded by a natural wood fence that resembled a miniature stockade. It was late in the day but still hot.

Lashman opened a gate in the fence and came out to meet me. His face was deeply seamed, and his white hair straggled down onto his shoulders. He had on faded blue denims and flat-soled buckskin slippers. His eyes were blue, faded like his clothes by too much light.

"Are you Mr. Archer?"

"Yes. It's good of you to let me come."

Informal as he seemed to be, something about the old man imposed formality on me. The hand he gave me was knobbed with arthritis and stained with paint.

"What kind of shape is Fred Johnson in?"

"He seemed very tired," Lashman said. "But excited, too. Buoyed up by excitement."

"What about?"

"He was very eager to talk to Mildred Mead. It had to do with the attribution of a painting. He told me he works for the Santa Teresa Art Museum. Is that correct?"

"Yes. What about the girl?"

"She was very quiet. I don't remember that she said a word." Lashman gave me a questioning look, which I didn't respond to. "Come inside."

He led me through an inner courtyard into his studio. One large window looked out across the desert to the horizon. There was a painting of a woman on an easel, unfinished, perhaps hardly begun. The swirls of paint looked fresh, and the woman's half-emerging features looked like Mildred Mead's face struggling up out of the limbo of the past. On a table beside it, which was scaly with old paint, was a rectangular palette containing daubs of glistening color.

Lashman came up beside me as I examined the painting. "Yes, that's Mildred. I only just started it, after we talked on the phone. I had an urge to paint her one more time. And I'm at the age where you have to put all your sudden urges to work."

"Are you painting her from the life?"

He gave me a shrewd look. "Mildred hasn't been here, if that's what you want to know. She hasn't been here in nearly twenty years. I believe I mentioned that to you on the phone," he said precisely.

"I gather you've painted her often?"

"She was my favorite model. She lived with me off and on for a long time. Then she moved to the far end of the state. I haven't seen her since." He spoke with pride and nostalgia and regret. "Another man made her what she considered a better offer. I don't blame her. She was getting old. I have to confess I didn't treat her too well."

His words set up a vibration in my mind. I'd had a woman and lost her, but not to another man. I'd lost her on my own.

I said, "Is she still living in Arizona?"

"I think so. I had a Christmas card from her last year. That's the last I've heard from Mildred." He looked out across the desert. "Frankly, I'd like to be in touch with her again, even if we're both as old as the hills."

"Where is Mildred living now?"

"In Chantry Canyon, in the Chiricahua Mountains. That's near the New Mexico border." He drew a rough map of Arizona with a piece of charcoal and told me how to get to Chantry Canyon, which was in the state's southeastern corner. "Biemeyer bought her the Chantry house about twenty years ago, and she's been in it ever since. It was the house she always wanted—the house more than the man."

"More than Jack Biemeyer, you mean?"

"And more than Felix Chantry, who built the house and developed the copper mine. She fell in love with Felix Chantry's house and his copper mine long before she fell in love with Felix. She told me it was her life-long dream to live in Chantry's house. She became his mistress and even bore him an illegitimate son. But he never let her live in the house in his lifetime. He stuck with his wife and the son he had by her."

"That would be Richard," I said.

Lashman nodded. "He grew up into a pretty good painter. I have to admit that, even if I hated his father. Richard Chantry had a real gift, but he didn't use it to the full. He lacked the endurance to stay the course. In this work, you really need endurance." Leaning into the afternoon light from the window, his face bunched, he looked like a metal monument to that quality.

"Do you think Richard Chantry is alive?"

"Young Fred Johnson asked me the same question. I'll give you the same answer I gave him. I think Richard is probably dead—as dead as his brother is—but it hardly matters. A painter who gives up his work in mid-career, as Richard apparently did—he might as well be dead. I expect to die myself the day that I stop working." The old man's circling mind kept returning with fascination and disgust to his own mortality. "And that will be good riddance to bad rubbish, as we used to say when I was a boy."

"What happened to Felix Chantry's other son by Mildred—the illegitimate brother?"

"William? He died young. William was the one I knew and cared about. He and his mother lived with me, off and on, for some years. He even used my name while he was going to art school here in Tucson. But he took his mother's name when he went into the army. He called himself William Mead, and that was the name he was using when he died."

"Was he killed in the war?"

Lashman said quietly, "William died in uniform, but he was on leave when it happened. He was beaten to death and his body left in the desert, not very far from where his mother lives now."

"Who killed him?"

"That was never established. If you want more information, I suggest you get in touch with Sheriff Brotherton in Copper City. He handled the case, or mishandled it. I never did get the full facts of the murder. When Mildred came back from identifying William's body, she didn't say a word for over a week. I knew how she felt. William wasn't my son, and I hadn't seen him for a long time, but he felt like a son to me."

The old man was silent for a moment, and then went on: "I was on my way to making a painter of William. As a matter of fact, his early work was better than his half brother Richard's, and Richard paid him the compliment of imitation. But it was William who became food for worms."

He swung around to face me, angrily, as if I had brought death back into his house. "I'll be food for worms myself before too long. But before I am, I intend to paint one more picture of Mildred. Tell her that, will you?"

"Why don't you tell her yourself?"

"Perhaps I will."

Lashman was showing signs of wanting to be rid of me before the afternoon light failed. He kept looking out the window. Before I left, I showed him my photograph of the picture that Fred had taken from the Biemeyers.

"Is that Mildred?"

"Yes, it is."

"Can you tell who painted it?"

"I couldn't be sure. Not from a small black-and-white photograph."

"Does it look like Richard Chantry's work?"

"I believe it does. It looks something like my early work, too, as a matter of fact." He glanced up sharply, half serious, half amused. "I didn't realize until now that I might have influenced Chantry. Certainly whoever did this painting had to have seen my early portraits of Mildred Mead." He looked at the painted head on the easel as if it would confirm his claim.

"You didn't paint it yourself, did you?"

"No. I happen to be a better painter than that."

"A better painter than Chantry?"

"I think so. I didn't disappear, of course. I've stayed here and kept at my work. I'm not as well known as the disappearance artist. But I've outstayed him, by God, and my work will outstay his. This picture I'm doing now will outstay his."

Lashman's voice was angry and young. His face was flushed. In his old age, I thought, he was still fighting the Chantrys for the possession of Mildred Mead.

He picked up a brush and, holding it in his hand as if it were a weapon, turned back to his unfinished portrait.

# XIX

I drove south and then east across the desert, through blowing curtains of evening. The traffic was comparatively thin and I made good time. By nine o'clock I was in Copper City, driving past Biemeyer's big hole in the ground. It looked in the fading evening light like the abandoned playground of a race of giants or their children.

I found the sheriff's station and showed my photostat

to the captain in charge. He told me that Sheriff Brotherton could be found in a substation north of the city, near his mountain home. He got out a map and showed me how to get there.

I drove north toward the mountains. They had been built by bigger giants than the ones who dug Biemeyer's hole. As I approached the mountains, they took up more and more of the night sky.

I skirted their southeastern end on a winding road that ran between the mountains on my left and the desert on my right. Other traffic had dwindled away. I had begun to wonder if I was lost when I came to a cluster of buildings with lights in them.

One was the sheriff's substation. The others were a small motel and a grocery store with a gas pump in front of it. There were a number of cars, including a couple of sheriff's cars, parked on the paved area in front of the buildings.

I added my rented car to the line of parked cars and went into the substation. The deputy on duty looked me over carefully and finally admitted that the sheriff was next door in the grocery store. I went there. The back of the store was dim with cigar smoke. Several men in wide-brimmed hats were drinking beer from cans and playing pool on a table with a patched and wrinkled top. The heat in the place was oppressive.

A sweating bald man in a once-white apron came toward me. "If it's groceries you want, I'm really closed for the night."

"I could use a can of beer. And a wedge of cheese?"

"I guess I can handle that. How much cheese?"

"Half a pound."

He brought me the beer and cheese. "That will be a dollar and a half."

I paid him. "Is Chantry Canyon anywhere near here?"

He nodded. "Second turn to the left—that's about a mile north of here. Go on up about four miles until you hit a crossroads. Turn left, another couple of miles or so, and you'll be in the canyon. Are you with the people that's taken it over?"

"What people do you mean?"

"I forget what they call themselves. They're fixing up the old house, planning to make it some kind of religious settlement." He turned toward the back of the store and raised his voice: "Sheriff? What do those people call themselves that took over Chantry Canyon?"

One of the pool players leaned his cue against the wall and came toward us, his polished boots kicking his shadow ahead of him. He was a man in his late fifties, with a gray military-style mustache. A sheriff's badge glinted on his chest. His eyes had a matching glint.

"Society of Mutual Love," he said to me. "Is that who you're looking for?"

"I wasn't. I was looking for Mildred Mead." I showed him my photostat.

"You're in the wrong state, Mister. Mildred sold out about three months ago and took off for California. She told me she couldn't stand the loneliness any more. I told her she had friends here, and she has, but she wanted to spend her last days with her folks in California."

"Where in California?"

"She didn't say." The sheriff looked uneasy.

"What was the name of her folks?"

"I don't know."

"Did she mean relatives?"

"Mildred didn't tell me. She was always close-mouthed about her family. I had to tell the same thing to the young couple that came through here earlier today."

"Young man and a girl in a blue Ford sedan?"

The sheriff nodded. "That's them. Are they with you?"

"I'm hoping to join them."

"You'll probably find them up there in the canyon. They went up about sunset. I warned them they were running the risk of getting themselves converted. I don't know what those Mutual Love people believe in, but the belief they have is certainly powerful. One of the converts told me he turned over everything he had to the organization, and they work him hard besides. Looks to me like they're coining money. I know they paid Mildred over a hundred thousand for the place. Of course that includes the acreage. So hold on to your wallet with both hands."

"I'll do that, Sheriff."

"My name is Brotherton, by the way."

"Lew Archer."

We shook hands. I thanked him and turned toward the door. He followed me outside. The night was clear and high, after the smoky interior of the store. We stood in silence for a minute. I found myself liking the man's company, in spite of his rather artificial folksiness.

"I don't want to pry," he said, "but I'm kind of fond of Mildred. Quite a few of us are. She was always generous with her money *and* her favors. Maybe too generous, I don't know. I hope she isn't in any kind of trouble in California."

"I hope not."

"You're a private detective there. Right?"

I said I was.

"Do you mind telling me what your business is with Mildred?"

"It isn't really Mildred I want to see. It's the young man and the girl who were asking for her earlier. They haven't come down the mountain again, have they?"

"I don't believe so."

"Is this the only way out?"

"They could get out the other side if they had to, towards Tombstone. But, as I told them, it's a hard road to drive at night. They on the run from something?"

"I can tell you better after I talk to them."

Brotherton's look hardened. "You're close-mouthed, Mr. Archer."

"The girl's parents hired me."

"I asked myself if she was a runaway."

"That's putting it a little strong. But I expect to take her home with me."

He let me go up the mountain by myself. I followed the storekeeper's directions, and they brought me to the head of a canyon whose open end framed the distant lights of Copper City. There were several lighted buildings in the canyon. The highest and largest was a sprawling stone house with a peaked shingled roof and a wide porch shelving out in front.

The road that led to the stone house was blocked by a wire gate. When I got out to open it, I could hear the people singing on the porch, singing a kind of song that I'd never heard before. Their refrain was something about Armageddon and the end of the world. Raising their voices on the prowlike porch, they made me think of passengers singing hymns on a sinking ship.

Fred Johnson's old blue Ford was parked in the gravel lane ahead of me. Its engine was dripping oil like something wounded. As I approached it, Fred got out and walked uncertainly into the wash of my headlights. His mustache was wet and spiky and he had a beard of blood. He didn't know me.

"Are you in some kind of trouble?"

He opened his swollen mouth. "Yeah. They've got my girl inside. They're trying to convert her."

The hymn had died in mid-phrase, as if the sinking ship had gone down abruptly. The hymn-singers were coming off the porch in our direction. From somewhere out of sight in the building, a girl's voice was raised in what sounded like fear.

Fred's head jerked. "That's her now."

I started for the gun in the trunk of my car, then remembered that I was driving a rented car. By that time, Fred and I were surrounded by half a dozen bearded men in overalls. Several long-skirted women stood to one side and watched us with cold eyes in long faces.

The oldest man was middle-aged, and he spoke to me

in a monotone. "You're disturbing our evening service."

"Sorry. I want Miss Biemeyer. I'm a licensed private detective employed by her parents. The sheriff of the county knows I'm here."

"We don't recognize his authority. This is holy ground, consecrated by our leader. The only authority we bow down to is the voice of the mountains and the sky and our own consciences."

"Tell your conscience to tell you to go and get your leader."

"You must be more respectful. He's performing an important ceremony."

The girl raised her voice again. Fred started toward it, and I went along. The overalled men came together and formed a solid phalanx blocking our way.

I stood back and shouted at the top of my voice: "Hey, leader! Get the hell out here!"

He came out onto the porch, a white-haired man in a black robe who looked as if he had been dazzled or struck by lightning. He walked toward us, smiling a wide cold smile. His followers made way for him.

"Blessings," he said to them, and to me: "Who are you? I heard you reviling and cursing me. I resent it, not so much for myself as for the Power I represent."

One of the women moaned in awe and delight. She got down on her knees in the gravel and kissed the leader's hand.

I said, "I want Miss Biemeyer. I work for Miss Biemeyer's father. He used to own this house."

"I own it now," he said, and then corrected himself: "*We* own it now. You're trespassing."

The bearded men let out an assenting growl in unison. The oldest one of them said, "We paid good money for this place. It's our refuge in time of trouble. We don't want it desecrated by cohorts of the devil."

"Then bring Miss Biemeyer out here."

"The poor child needs my help," the leader said. "She's been taking drugs. She's drowning in trouble, going down for the third time."

"I'm not leaving her here."

Fred let out a sob of frustration and grief and rage. "That's what I told them. But they beat me up."

"You gave her drugs," the leader said. "She told me you gave her drugs. It's my responsibility to purge her of the habit. Nearly all of my flock took drugs at one time. I was a sinner myself, in other ways."

"I'd say you still are," I said. "Or don't you believe that kidnapping is wrong?"

"She's here of her own free will."

"I want to hear her tell me that herself."

"Very well," he said to me, and to his followers: "Let them approach the dwelling place."

We went down the lane to the house. The bearded men crowded around Fred and me without exactly touching us. I could smell them though. They stank of curdled hopes and poisonous fears and rancid innocence and unwashed armpits.

We were kept outside on the porch. I could see through the open front door that there was reconstruction work going on inside. The central hallway was being converted into a dormitory lined with bunks two high along the walls. I wondered how large a congregation the leader hoped to gather, and how much each of them might pay him for his bunk and his overalls and his salvation.

He brought Doris out of an inner room into the hallway. His followers let me go as far as the open door, and she and I faced each other there. She looked pale and scared and sane.

She said, "Am I supposed to know you?"

"My name is Archer. We met in your apartment yesterday."

"I'm sorry, I don't remember. I think I was stoned yesterday."

"I think you were, Doris. How are you feeling now?"

"Sort of woozy," she said. "I hardly got any sleep in the car last night. And ever since we got here they've been at me." She yawned deeply.

"At you in what way?"

"Praying for me. They want me to stay with them. They won't even charge me. My father would like that, not having to pay for me." She smiled dispiritedly on one side of her mouth.

"I don't think your father feels that way about you."

"You don't know my father."

"I do, though."

She frowned at me. "Did my father send you after me?"

"No. I sort of came on my own. But your mother is paying me. She wants you back. So does he."

"I don't really think they do," the girl said. "Maybe they think they do, but they don't really."

Fred spoke up behind me. "I do, Doris."

"Maybe you do, and maybe you don't. But maybe I don't want you." She looked at him in cold unfriendly coquetry. "I wasn't what you wanted, anyway. You wanted the picture that my parents bought."

Fred looked down at the porch floor. The leader stepped between the girl and us. His face was a complex blend of exalted mystic and Yankee trader. His hands were shaking with nervousness.

"Do you believe me now?" he said to me. "Doris wants to stay with us. Her parents have neglected and rejected her. Her friend is a false friend. She knows her true friends when she sees them. She wants to live with us in the brotherhood of spiritual love."

"Is that true, Doris?"

"I guess so," she said with a dubious half-smile. "I might as well give it a try. I've been here before, you know. My father used to bring me here when I was a little girl. We used to come up and visit Mrs. Mead. They used to——" She broke off the sentence and covered her mouth with her hand.

"They used to what, Doris?"

"Nothing. I don't want to talk about my father. I want to stay here with them and get straightened out. I'm spiritually unwell." The self-diagnosis sounded like a parroting of something that she had recently been told. Unfortunately it also sounded true.

I had a strong urge to take her away from the brothers. I didn't like them or their leader. I didn't trust the girl's judgment. But she knew her own life better than I could possibly know it for her. Even I could see that it hadn't been working out.

I said, "Remember that you can always change your mind. You can change it right now."

"I don't want to change it right now. Why would I want to change it?" she asked me glumly. "This is the first time in a week that I even knew what I was doing."

"Bless you, my child," the leader said. "Don't worry, we'll take good care of you."

I wanted to break his bones. But that made very little sense. I turned and started back to my rented car. I felt very small, dwarfed by the mountains.

# XX

I locked the blue Ford and left it standing in the lane. Fred didn't look fit to drive it, and if he had been I wouldn't have trusted him not to run out on me. He climbed into my car like a poorly working automaton and sat with his head hanging on his blood-spotted chest.

He roused himself from his lethargy when I backed out onto the road: "Where are we going?"

"Down the mountain to talk to the sheriff."

"No."

He turned away from me and fumbled with the door latch on his side. I took hold of his collar and pulled him back into the middle of the seat.

"I don't want to turn you in," I said. "But that's on condition that you answer some questions. I've come a long way to ask them."

He answered after a thinking pause: "I've come a long way, too."

"What for?"

Another pause. "To ask some questions."

"This isn't a word game, Fred. You'll have to do better than that. Doris told me you took her parents' painting and you admitted it to me."

"I didn't say I stole it."

"You took it without their permission. What's the difference?"

"I explained all that to you yesterday. I took the picture to see if I could authenticate it. I took it down to the art museum to compare it with their Chantrys. I left it there overnight and somebody stole it."

"Stole it from the art museum?"

"Yes, sir. I should have locked it up, I admit that. But I left it in one of the open bins. I didn't think anyone would notice it."

"Who did notice it?"

"I have no way of knowing. I didn't tell anyone. You've got to believe me." He turned his dismayed face to me. "I'm not lying."

"Then you were lying yesterday. You said the painting was stolen from your room at home."

"I made a mistake," he said. "I got confused. I was so upset I forgot about taking it down to the museum."

"Is that your final story?"

"It's the truth. I can't change the truth."

I didn't believe him. We drove down the mountain in unfriendly silence. The repeated cry of a screech owl followed us.

"Why did you come to Arizona, Fred?"

He seemed to consider his answer, and finally said, "I wanted to trace the picture."

"The one you took from the Biemeyers' house?"

"Yes." He hung his head.

"What makes you think it's in Arizona?"

"I don't think that. I mean, I don't know whether it is or not. What I'm trying to find out is who painted it."

"Didn't Richard Chantry paint it?"

"I think so, but I don't know when. And I don't know who or where Richard Chantry is. I thought perhaps that Mildred Mead could tell me. Mr. Lashman says she was the model all right. But now she's gone, too."

"To California."

Fred straightened up in his seat. "Where in California?"

"I don't know. Maybe some of the local people can give us the information."

Sheriff Brotherton was waiting in his car, which was parked in the lighted lot outside the substation. I parked beside it, and we all climbed out. Fred was watching me intently, wanting to hear what I would tell the authorities.

"Where's the young lady?" the sheriff said.

"She decided to stay with the society overnight. Maybe longer."

"I hope she knows what she's doing. Are there any sisteren around?"

"I saw a few. This is Fred Johnson, Sheriff."

Brotherton shook the younger man's hand and looked closely into his face. "Did they attack you?"

"I took a swing at one of them. He took a swing at me." Fred seemed proud of the incident. "That was about it."

The sheriff seemed disappointed. "Don't you want to lodge a complaint?"

Fred glanced at me. I gave him no sign, one way or the other.

"No," he said to the sheriff.

"You better think it over. That nose of yours is still bleeding. While you're here, you better go into the station and get Deputy Cameron to give you first aid."

Fred moved toward the substation as if, once inside, he might never get out again.

When he was beyond hearing, I turned to the sheriff: "Did you know Mildred Mead well?"

His face was stony for a moment. His eyes glittered. "Better than you think."

"Does that mean what I think it means?"

He smiled. "She was my first woman. That was around forty years ago, when I was just a kid. It was a great favor she did me. We've been friends ever since."

"But you don't know where she is now?"

"No. I'm kind of worried about Mildred. Her health isn't the best, and she isn't getting any younger. Mildred's had a lot of hard blows in her life, too. I don't like her going off by herself like this." He gave me a long hard contemplative look. "Are you going back to California tomorrow?"

"I plan to."

"I'd appreciate it if you'd look Mildred up, see how she's doing."

"California's a big state, Sheriff."

"I know that. But I can ask around, and see if anyone here has heard from her."

"You said she went to California to stay with relatives."

"That's what she told me before she left. I didn't know she had any relatives, there or anywhere else. Except for her son William." Brotherton's voice had dropped so low that he seemed to be talking to himself.

"And William was murdered in 1943," I said.

The sheriff spat on the ground, and then withdrew into silence. I could hear the murmur of voices from the substation, and the screech owl's cry high on the mountainside. It sounded like an old woman's husky titter.

"You've been doing some research into Mildred's life," he said.

"Not really. She's the subject of a painting that I was hired to recover. But the case keeps sliding off into other cases. Mostly disaster cases."

"Give me a for-instance."

"The disappearance of Richard Chantry. He dropped out of sight in California in 1950, and left behind some paintings which have made him famous."

"I know that," the sheriff said. "I knew him when he was a boy. He was the son of Felix Chantry, who was chief engineer of the mine in Copper City. Richard came back here after he got married. He and his young wife lived in the house up the mountain, and he started painting there. That was back in the early forties."

"Before or after his half brother William was murdered?"

The sheriff walked away from me a few steps, then came back. "How did you know that William Mead was Richard Chantry's half brother?"

"It came up in conversation."

"You must have some pretty wide-ranging conversations." He stood perfectly still for a moment. "You're not suggesting that Richard Chantry murdered his half brother, William?"

"The suggestion is all yours, Sheriff. I didn't even know about William's death until today."

"Then why are you so interested?"

"Murder always interests me. Last night in Santa Teresa there was another murder—also connected with the Chantry family. Did you ever hear of a man named Paul Grimes?"

"I knew him. He was Richard Chantry's teacher. Grimes lived with him and his wife for quite some time. I never thought too much of Grimes. He lost his job at the Copper City high school and married a half-breed." The sheriff averted his head and spat on the ground again.

"Don't you want to know how he was murdered?"

"It doesn't matter to me." He seemed to have a supply of anger in him, which broke out at unexpected points. "Santa Teresa is way outside my territory."

"He was beaten to death," I said. "I understand that William Mead was also beaten to death. Two murders, in two different states, over thirty years apart, but the same *m.o.*"

"You're reaching," he said, "with very little to go on."

"Give me more, then. Was Paul Grimes living with the Chantrys when William Mead was killed?"

"He may have been. I think he was. That was back in 1943, during the war."

"Why wasn't Richard Chantry in uniform?"

"He was supposed to be working in the family's copper mine. But I don't think he ever went near it. He stayed at home with his pretty young wife and painted pretty pictures."

"What about William?"

"He was in the army. He came here on leave to visit his brother. William was in uniform when he was killed."

"Was Richard ever questioned about William's death?"

The sheriff answered after some delay, and when he did answer he spoke with difficulty: "Not to my knowledge. I wasn't in charge then, you understand. I was just a junior deputy."

"Who conducted the investigation?"

"I did, for the most part. I was the one that found the body, not too far from here." He pointed east toward the New Mexico desert. "Understand, we didn't find him right away. He'd been dead for several days, and the varmints had been at him. There wasn't much left of his face. We weren't even sure that he'd been killed by human hands until we got the medical examiner out from Tucson. By that time it was too late to do much."

"What would you have done if you'd had the chance?"

The sheriff became quite still again, as if he were listening to voices from the past that I couldn't hear. His eyes were shadowed and remote.

Finally he said, with too much angry certainty, "I wouldn't have done anything different. I don't know what you're trying to prove. I don't know why I'm talking to you at all."

"Because you're an honest man, and you're worried."

"What am I worried about?"

"Mildred Mead, for one thing. You're afraid that something has happened to her."

He took a deep breath. "I don't deny that."

"And I think you're still worried about that body you found in the desert."

He looked at me sharply but made no other response. I said, "Are you certain that it was her son William's body?"

"Absolutely certain."

"Did you know him?"

"ᴑt that well. But he was carrying his official papers. In addition to which, we brought Mildred out from Tucson. I was there when she made the identification." He went into another of his silences.

"Did Mildred take the body back to Tucson with her?"

"She wanted to. But the army decided that after we got finished with it the body should go to Mead's wife. We packed the poor remains into a sealed coffin and shipped them back to the wife in California. At first none of us knew he had a wife. He hadn't been married very long. He married her after he entered the service, a friend of his told me."

"Was this a local friend?"

"No. He was an army buddy. I disremember his name—something like Wilson or Jackson. Anyway, he was very fond of Mead and he wangled a leave to come out here and talk to me about him. But he couldn't tell me much, except that Mead had a wife and a baby boy in California. I wanted to go and see them, but the county wouldn't put up the expense money for me. Mead's army buddy got shipped out in a hurry, and I never saw him again, though later, after the war, he sent me a postcard from a vets' hospital in California. One way and another, I never did make a case." The sheriff sounded faintly apologetic.

"I don't understand why Richard Chantry wasn't questioned."

"It's simple enough. Richard was out of the state before the body was found. I made a real effort to have him brought back—you understand, I'm not saying he was guilty, in any way—but I couldn't get any support from higher authorities. The Chantrys still had a lot of political power, and the Chantry name was kept out of the William Mead case. It wasn't even publicized that Mildred Mead was his mother."

"Was old Felix Chantry still alive in 1943?"

"No. He died the year before."

"Who was running the copper mine?"

"A fellow named Biemeyer. He wasn't the official head at the time, but he was making the decisions."

"Including the one not to question Richard Chantry?"

"I wouldn't know about that."

His voice had changed. He had started to lie, or to withhold the truth. Like every sheriff in every county, he would have his political debts and his unspeakable secrets.

I wanted to ask him whom he was trying to protect, but decided not to. I was far out of my own territory, among people I didn't know or entirely understand, and there was a sense of unexpended trouble in the air.

# XXI

The sheriff was leaning toward me slightly, almost as if he could overhear my thoughts. He was as still as a perching hawk, with some of a hawk's poised threat.

"I've been open with you," he said. "But you've been holding back on me. You haven't even told me who you represent."

"Biemeyer," I said.

The sheriff smiled broadly without showing any teeth at all. "You're kidding me."

"No, I'm not. The girl is Biemeyer's daughter."

Without any obvious change, his smile turned into a grin of shock and alarm. He must have become aware that he was revealing himself. Like a hostile fist relaxing, his face smoothed itself out into blandness. Only his sharp gray eyes were hostile and watchful. He jerked a thumb toward the mountain behind him.

"The girl you left up there is Biemeyer's daughter?"

"That's right."

"Don't you know he's majority owner of the copper mine?"

"He makes no secret of it," I said.

"But why didn't you tell me?"

It was a question I couldn't answer easily. Perhaps I'd let myself imagine that Doris might possibly be better off in a world quite different from her parents' world, at least for a while. But this world belonged to Biemeyer, too.

The sheriff was saying, "The copper mine is the biggest employer at this end of the state."

"Okay, we'll put the girl to work in the copper mine."

He stiffened. "What in hell do you mean by that? Nobody said anything about putting her to work."

"It was just a joke."

"It's not funny. We've got to get her out of that funny farm before some harm comes to her. My wife and I can put her up for the night. We have a nice spare room—it used to be our own daughter's room. Let's get going, eh?"

The sheriff left Fred in the deputy's custody and drove me up the mountain in his official car. He parked it in the lane behind Fred's old blue Ford. A dented white moon watched us over the mountain's shoulder.

The big house in the canyon was dark and silent, its stillness hardly broken by a man's random snore, a girl's faint crying. The crying girl turned out to be Doris. She came to the door when I called her name. She had on a white flannelette nightgown that covered her like a tent from the neck down. Her eyes were wide and dark and her face was wet.

"Get your clothes on, honey," the sheriff said. "We're taking you out of this place."

"But I like it here."

"You wouldn't like it if you stayed. This is no place for a girl like you, Miss Biemeyer."

Her body stiffened and her chin came up. "You can't make me leave."

The leader had come up behind her, not too close. He didn't speak. He seemed to be watching the sheriff with the detachment of a spectator at somebody else's funeral.

"Don't be like that, now, will you?" the sheriff said to Doris. "I've got a daughter of my own, I know how it is. We all like a little adventure. But then it comes time to get back to normal living."

"I'm not normal," she said.

"Don't worry, you will be, honey. What you need is to find the right young man. The same thing happened to my girl. She went and lived in a commune in Seattle for a year. But then she came back and found Mr. Right, and they've got two children now and everybody's happy."

"I'm never going to have any children," she said.

But she put on her clothes and went out to the sheriff's car with him. I lingered behind with the leader. He stepped out onto the porch, moving rather uncertainly. In the light from the sky, his eyes and his white hair seemed faintly phosphorescent.

"She would have been welcome to stay with us."

"For a price?"

"We all contribute as we can. We practice tithing, each paying according to his ability. My own contribution is largely spiritual. Some of us earn our keep at humbler tasks."

"Where did you study theology?"

"In the world," he said. "Benares, Camarillo, Lompoc. I admit I don't have a degree. But I've done a great deal of counseling. I find myself able to help people. I could have helped Miss Biemeyer. I doubt that the sheriff can." He reached out and touched my arm with his long thin hand. "I believe I could help you."

"Help me do what?"

"Do nothing, perhaps." He spread his arms wide in an actorish gesture. "You seem to be a man engaged in an endless battle, an endless search. Has it ever occurred to you that the search may be for yourself? And that the way to find yourself is to be still and silent, silent and still?" He dropped his arms to his sides.

I was tired enough to be taken by his questions, and to find myself repeating them in my mind. They were questions I had asked myself, though never in just those terms. Perhaps, after all, the truth I was looking for couldn't be found in the world. You had to go up on a mountain and wait for it, or find it in yourself.

But even as I was taking a short-term lease on a piece of this thought, I was watching the lights of Copper City framed in the canyon mouth, and planning what I would do there in the morning.

"I don't have any money."

"Neither do I," he said. "But there seems to be enough for everyone. Money is the least of our worries."

"You're lucky."

He disregarded my irony. "I'm glad you see that. We're very lucky indeed."

"Where did you get the money to buy this place?"

"Some of our people have income." The idea seemed to please him, and he smiled. "We may not go in for worldly show, but this isn't exactly a poorhouse. Of course it isn't all paid for."

"I'm not surprised. I understand it cost you over a hundred thousand dollars."

His smile faded. "Are you investigating us?"

"I have no interest in you at all, now that the girl is out of here."

"We did her no harm," he said quickly.

"I'm not suggesting you did."

"But I suppose the sheriff will be bothering us now. Simply because we gave shelter to Biemeyer's daughter."

"I hope not. I'll put in a word with him, if you like."

"I would like, very much." He relaxed visibly and then audibly, letting out a long sighing breath.

"In return for which," I said, "you can do something for me."

"What is it?" He was suspicious of me again.

"Help me to get in touch with Mildred Mead."

He spread his hands, palms up. "I wouldn't know how. I don't have her address."

"Aren't you making payments to her for this house?"

"Not directly. Through the bank. I haven't seen her since she went to California. That was several months ago."

"Which bank is handling the account?"

"The Copper City branch of Southwestern Savings. They'll tell you I'm not a swindler. I'm not, you know."

I believed him, provisionally. But he had two voices. One of them belonged to a man who was reaching for a foothold in the spiritual world. The other voice, which I had just been listening to, belonged to a man who was buying a place in the actual world with other people's money.

It was an unstable combination. He could end as a con man, or a radio preacher with a million listeners, or a bartender with a cure of souls in Fresno. Perhaps he had already been some of those things.

But I trusted him up to a point. I gave him the keys to the blue Ford and asked him to keep it for Fred, just in case Fred ever came back that way.

# XXII

We drove back down the mountain to the substation and found Fred sitting inside with the deputy. I couldn't tell at first glance whether he was a prisoner or a patient. He had an adhesive bandage across the bridge of his nose and cotton stuffed up his nostrils. He looked like a permanent loser.

The sheriff, who was a small winner, went into the inner office to make a phone call. His voice was a smooth blend of confidence and respect. He was making arrangements to fly Doris home in a copper-company jet.

He lifted his head, flushed and bright-eyed, and offered me the receiver. "Mr Biemeyer wants to talk to you."

I didn't really want to talk to Biemeyer, now or ever.

But I took the receiver and said into it, "This is Archer."

"I've been expecting to hear from you," he said. "After all, I'm paying you good money."

I didn't remind him that his wife had paid me. "You're hearing from me now."

"Thanks to Sheriff Brotherton. I know how you private dicks operate. You let the men in uniform do the work and then you step in and take the credit."

For a hotheaded instant, I was close to hanging up on Biemeyer. I had to remind myself that the case was far from over. The stolen painting was still missing. There were two unsolved murders, Paul Grimes's and now William Mead's.

"There's credit enough for everybody," I said. "We have your daughter and she's in reasonably good shape. I gather she'll be flying home tomorrow in one of your planes."

"First thing in the morning. I was just finalizing the arrangement with Sheriff Brotherton."

"Could you hold that plane until late morning or so? I have some things to do in Copper City, and I don't think your daughter should travel unaccompanied."

"I don't like the delay," he said. "Mrs. Biemeyer and I are very eager to see Doris."

"May I speak to Mrs. Biemeyer?"

"I suppose you can," he said reluctantly. "She's right here."

There was some indistinct palaver at the other end, and then Ruth Biemeyer's voice came over the line. "Mr. Archer? I'm relieved to hear from you. Doris hasn't been arrested, has she?"

"No. Neither has Fred. I want to bring them both home with me tomorrow on the company plane. But I may not be able to get out of here much before noon. Is that all right with you?"

"Yes."

"Thanks very much. Good night, Mrs. Biemeyer."

I hung up and told the sheriff that the plane would

leave at noon tomorrow with me and Doris and Fred. Brotherton didn't argue. My telephone conversation had invested me with some of the Biemeyer charisma.

On the strength of this, I put in a word for the people in Chantry Canyon, as I had promised, and offered to assume responsibility for Fred. The sheriff agreed. Doris, he said, would be spending the night at his house.

Fred and I checked into a double room in the motel. I needed a drink, but the store was closed and not even beer was available. I had no razor or toothbrush. I was as tired as sin.

But I sat on my bed and felt surprisingly good. The girl was safe. The boy was in my hands.

Fred had stretched out on his bed with his back to me. His shoulders moved spasmodically, and he made a repeated noise that sounded like hiccuping. I realized he was crying.

"What's the matter, Fred?"

"You know what's the matter. My career is over and done with. It never even started. I'll lose my job at the museum. They'll probably put me in jail, and you know what will happen to me then." His voice was dulled by the cotton in his nose.

"Do you have a record?"

"No. Of course I don't." The idea seemed to shock him. "I've never been in trouble."

"Then you should be able to stay out of jail."

"Really?" He sat up and looked at me with wet red eyes.

"Unless there's something that I don't know about. I still don't understand why you took the picture from the Biemeyer house."

"I wanted to test it. I told you about that. Doris even suggested that I should take it. She was just as interested as I was."

"Interested in what, exactly?"

"In whether it was a Chantry. I thought I could put my expertise to work on it." He added in a muffled voice, "I wanted to show them that I was good for something."

He sat up on the edge of the bed and put his feet on the floor. He was young for his age, in his thirties and still a boy, and foolish for a person of his intelligence. It seemed that the sad house on Olive Street hadn't taught him much about the ways of the world.

Then I reminded myself that I mustn't buy too much of Fred's queer little story. After all, he was a self-admitted liar.

I said, "I'd like your expert opinion on that picture."

"I'm not really an expert."

"But you're entitled to an informed opinion. As a close student of Chantry, do you think he painted the Biemeyer picture?"

"Yes, sir. I do. But my statement has to be qualified."

"Go ahead and qualify it."

"Well. It certainly doesn't go back any twenty-five years. The paint is much too new, applied maybe as recently as this year. And the style has changed, of course. It naturally would. I think it's Chantry's style, his *developed* style, but I couldn't swear to it unless I saw other late examples. You can't base a theory or an opinion on a single work."

Fred seemed to be talking as an expert, or at least an informed student. He sounded honest and for once forgetful of himself. I decided to ask him a harder question.

"Why did you say in the first place that the painting had been stolen from your house?"

"I don't know. I must have been crazy." He sat looking down at his dusty shoes. "I guess I was afraid to involve the museum."

"In what way?"

"In any way. They'd fire me if they knew I'd taken the picture myself the way I did. Now they'll fire me for sure. I have no future."

"Everybody has a future, Fred."

The words didn't sound too encouraging, even to me. A lot of futures were disastrous, and Fred's was beginning to look like one of those. He hung his head under the threat of it.

"The most foolish thing you did was to bring Doris with you."

"I know. But she wanted to come along."

"Why?"

"To see Mildred Mead if I found her. She was the main source of the trouble in Doris's family, you know. I thought it might be a good idea if Doris could talk to her. You know?"

I knew. Like other lost and foolish souls, Fred had an urge to help people, to give them psychotherapy even if it wrecked them. When he was probably the one who needed it most. Watch it, I said to myself, or you'll be trying to help Fred in that way. Take a look at your own life, Archer.

But I preferred not to. My chosen study was other men, hunted men in rented rooms, aging boys clutching at manhood before night fell and they grew suddenly old. If you were the therapist, how could you need therapy? If you were the hunter, you couldn't be hunted. Or could you?

"Doris is having a hard time maintaining," Fred said. "I've been trying to help her out of it."

"By taking her on a long drive to nowhere?"

"She wanted to come. She insisted. I thought it was better than leaving her where she was, sitting in an apartment by herself and gobbling drugs."

"You have a point."

He managed to give me a quick shy smile that twitched and cowered in the shadow of his mustache. "Besides, you have to remember that this isn't nowhere for Doris. She was born in Copper City and spent at least half of her life here in Arizona. This is home for her."

"It hasn't been a very happy homecoming."

"No. She was terribly disappointed. I guess you can't go home again, as Thomas Wolfe says."

Remembering the gabled house where Fred lived with his father and mother, I wondered who would want to.

"Have you always lived in Santa Teresa?"

He was thoughtful for a moment. Then he said, "Since I was a little boy, we've lived in the same house on Olive Street. It wasn't always the wreck that it is now. Mother kept it up much better—I used to help her—and we had roomers, nurses from the hospital and such." He spoke as if having roomers was a privilege. "The best times were before my father came home from Canada." Fred looked past me at my hunched shadow on the wall.

"What was your father doing in Canada?"

Working at various jobs, mostly in British Columbia. He liked it then. I don't think he and Mother got along too well, even in those days. I've realized since that he probably stayed away from her for that reason. But it was a bit rough on me. I don't remember ever seeing my father until I was six or seven."

"How old are you now, Fred?"

"Thirty-two," he said reluctantly.

"You've had long enough to get over your father's absence."

"That isn't what I meant at all." He was flustered and angry, and disappointed in me. "I wasn't offering him as an excuse."

"I didn't say you were."

"As a matter of fact, he's been a good father to me." He thought this statement over, and amended it. "At least he was in those early days when he came back from Canada. Before he started drinking so hard. I really loved him in those days. Sometimes I think I still do, in spite of all the awful things he does."

"What awful things?"

"He rants and roars and threatens Mother and smashes things and cries. He never does a stroke of work. He sits up there with his crazy hobbies and drinks cheap wine, and it's all he's good for." His voice had coarsened, and rose and fell like an angry wife's ululation. I wondered if Fred was unconsciously imitating his mother.

"Who brings him the wine?"

"Mother does. I don't know why she does it, but she keeps on doing it. Sometimes," he added in a voice that was almost too low to hear, "sometimes I think she does it in revenge."

"Revenge for what?"

"For ruining himself and his life, and ruining *her* life. I've seen her stand and watch him staggering from wall to wall as if she took pleasure in seeing him degraded. At the same time, she's his willing slave and buys him liquor. That's another form of revenge—a subtle form. She's a woman who refuses to be a full woman."

Fred had surprised me. As he reached deeper into the life behind his present trouble, he lost his air of self-deprecating foolishness. His voice deepened. His thin and long-nosed boyish face almost supported his mustache. I began to feel faint stirrings of respect for him, and even hope.

"She's a troubled woman," I said.

"I know. They're both troubled people. It's really too bad they ever got together. Too bad for both of them. I believe my father once had the makings of a brilliant man, before he turned into a lush. Mother isn't up to him mentally, of course, and I suppose she resents it, but she isn't a negligible person. She's a registered nurse and she's kept up her profession and looked after my father, both at the same time. That took some doing."

"Most people do what they have to."

"She's done a bit more than that. She's been helping me through college. I don't know how she makes the money stretch."

"Does she have any extracurricular income?"

"Not since the last roomer left. That was some time ago."

"And I heard last night that she lost her job at the hospital."

"Not exactly. She gave it up." Fred's voice had risen, and lost its masculine timbre. "They made her a much better offer at the La Paloma nursing home."

"That doesn't sound very likely, Fred."

"It's true." His voice rose higher, his eyes were too bright, his mustache was ragged. "Are you calling my mother a liar?"

"People make mistakes."

"You're making one now, running down my mother like that. I want you to take it back."

"Take what back?"

"What you said about my mother. She doesn't peddle drugs."

"I never said she did, Fred."

"But you implied it. You implied that the hospital let her go because she was stealing drugs and peddling them."

"Is that what the hospital people said?"

"Yes. They're a bunch of sadistic liars. My mother would never do a thing like that. She's always been a good woman." Tears formed in his eyes and left snail-tracks on his cheeks. "I haven't been a good man," he said. "I've been living out a fantasy, I see that now."

"What do you mean, Fred?"

"I was hoping to pull off a coup that would make me famous in art circles. I thought if I could get to Miss Mead, she could help me find the painter Chantry. But all I've done is make an ass of myself and get the whole family into deeper trouble."

"It was a fair try, Fred."

"It wasn't. I'm a fool!"

He turned his back on me. Gradually his breathing slowed down. I felt mine slowing down with it. I realized just before I fell asleep that I was beginning to like him.

I woke up once in the middle of the night and felt the weight of the mountains squatting over me. I turned on the light at the head of my bed. There were old water-marks on the walls like the indistinct traces of bad dreams.

I didn't try to read them. I turned off the light and fell back into sleep, breathing in unison with my foolish pseudo-son.

# XXIII

When I got up in the morning, Fred was still sleeping. One arm was over his eyes as if he dreaded the new day and its light. I asked the deputy on duty in the substation to keep track of Fred. Then I drove my rented car into Copper City, guided by the plume of smoke over the smelter.

A barber sold me a shave for three dollars. For a similar amount, I got a small breakfast and directions on how to find my way to Southwestern Savings.

It was in a downtown shopping center, which looked like a piece of Southern California that had broken loose and blown across the desert. The little city that sur-rounded it seemed to have been drained of energy by the huge wound of the copper mine in its side, the end-less suspiration of the smelter. The smoke blew over the city like a great ironic flag.

The sign on the glass front door of Southwestern Sav-ings said that the building didn't open until ten. It was not quite nine by my watch. It was getting hotter.

I found a phone booth and looked for Paul Grimes in the directory. His name wasn't listed but there were two listings for Mrs. Paul Grimes, one for a residence and the other for Grimes Art & School Supplies. The latter turned out to be in the downtown area, within easy walking distance.

It was a small store on a side street, full of paper goods and picture reproductions, empty of customers. The deep dim narrow room reminded me of an ancient painted cave, but most of the modern pictures on the walls weren't quite as lifelike as the cave paintings.

The woman who emerged from a door at the back looked like Paola's sister. She was broad-shouldered and full-breasted, and she had the same dark coloring and prominent cheekbones. She was wearing an embroidered blouse, beads that jangled, a long full skirt, and open sandals.

Her eyes were black and bright in her carved brown face. She gave an impression of saved-up force that wasn't being used.

"Can I help you?"

"I hope so. I'm a friend of your daughter's." I told her my name.

"Of course. Mr. Archer. Paola mentioned you on the phone. You were the one who found Paul's body."

"Yes. I'm sorry."

"And you are a detective, is that correct?"

"I work at it."

She gave me a hard black look. "Are you working at it now?"

"It seems to be a full-time job, Mrs. Grimes."

"Am I under suspicion?"

"I don't know. Should you be?"

She shook her handsome head. "I haven't seen Paul for over a year. We've been divorced for a good many years. Once Paola was out of her childhood, there was nothing to stay together for. It was all burnt out long ago."

Mrs. Grimes spoke with a direct emotional force that impressed me. But she must have realized that she was telling me more than she needed to. She put her left hand over her mouth. I noticed that her red fingernails were bitten down to the quick, and I felt sorry that I had frightened her.

"I don't think anybody suspects you of anything."

"They shouldn't, either. I didn't do anything to Paul except try to make a man of him. Paola might tell you different—she always took his side. But I did my best for Paul whenever he let me. The truth is—the truth was, he was never meant to be married to any woman."

Her hidden life, the memories of her marriage, seemed to be very near the surface, boiling cold behind her smooth dark face.

Remembering what Paola had once told me, I asked her bluntly, "Was he homosexual?"

"Bi," she said. "I don't believe he had much to do with men while I was married to him. But he always loved the company of young men, including his high school boys when he was a teacher. It wasn't a bad thing entirely. He loved to teach.

"He taught me a lot, too," she added thoughtfully. "The most important thing, he taught me to speak correct English. That changed my life. But something went wrong with his life. Maybe it was me. He couldn't handle me." She moved her body impatiently from the waist down. "He always said it was my fault that his life went off the track. Maybe it was."

She lowered her head and clenched her fists. "I used to have a bad temper. I used to fight him hard, physically. I used to love him, too, very much. Paul didn't really love me. At least not after I became his wife and stopped being his pupil."

"Who did he love?"

She thought about the question. "Paola. He really loved Paola—not that it did her much good. And he loved some of his students."

"Does that include Richard Chantry?"

Her black gaze turned inward the past. She nodded almost imperceptibly. "Yes, he loved Richard Chantry."

"Were they lovers in the technical sense?"

"I think they were. Young Mrs. Chantry thought so. In fact, she was considering divorce."

"How do you know?"

"After Paul moved in with them, she came to me. She wanted me to break up their relationship, at least that was the way she put it to me. I think now she was trying to use me as a witness against her husband, in case it came to divorce. I told her nothing."

"Where did the conversation take place, Mrs. Grimes?"

"Right here in the shop."

She tapped the floor with her toe, and her whole body moved. She was one of those women whose sex had aged into artiness but might still flare up if given provocation. I kept my own feet still.

"What year did you have that talk with Mrs. Chantry?"

"It must have been 1943, the early summer of '43. We'd only just opened this shop. Paul had borrowed quite a lot of money from Richard to fix the place up and stock it. The money was supposed to be an advance on further art lessons. But Richard never got his money's worth. He and his wife moved to California before the summer was out." She let out a snort of laughter so explosive that it jangled her beads. "That was a desperation move if I ever saw one."

"Why do you say so?"

"I'm absolutely certain it was her idea. She pushed it through in a hurry, practically overnight—anything to get Richard out of the state and away from my husband's influence. I was glad to see the twosome broken up myself." She raised her spread hands and lifted her shoulders in a large gesture of relief, then let them slump.

"But they both ended up in Santa Teresa, after all," I said. "I wonder why. And why did your ex-husband and Paola go to Santa Teresa this year?"

She repeated the gesture with her arms and shoulders, but this time it seemed to mean that she didn't have any answers. "I didn't know they were going there. They didn't tell *me*. They just went."

"Do you think Richard Chantry had anything to do with it?"

"Anything is possible, I guess. But it's my opinion—it has been for a long time—that Richard Chantry is dead."

"Murdered?"

"It could be. It happens to homosexuals—bisexuals—whatever he is or was. I see a lot of them in this business. Some of them go in for the rough trade almost as if they wanted to be killed. Or they wander away by themselves and commit suicide. That may be what Richard Chantry did. On the other hand, he may have found a soul mate and is living happily ever after in Algiers or Tahiti."

She smiled without warmth but so broadly that I could see that one of her molars was missing. Both physically and emotionally, I thought, she was a bit dilapidated.

"Did your ex-husband go for the rough trade?"

"He may have. He spent three years in federal prison—did you know that? He was a heroin addict on top of everything else."

"So I was told. But I heard he'd kicked the habit."

She didn't answer my implied question, and I didn't put it to her more directly. Grimes hadn't died of heroin or any other drug. He had been beaten to death, like William Mead.

I said, "Did you know Richard Chantry's half brother William?"

"Yes. I knew him through his mother, Mildred Mead. She was a famous model in these parts." She narrowed her eyes as if she had remembered something puzzling. "You know, she's gone to California, too."

"Where in California?"

"Santa Teresa. She sent me a card from there."

"Did she mention Jack Biemeyer? He lives in Santa Teresa."

She knitted her black brows. "I don't think so. I don't think she mentioned anybody by name."

"Are she and Biemeyer still friends?"

"I doubt it. As you probably know, he inherited Mildred from old Felix Chantry. He stashed her in a house in the mountains and lived with her for years. But I think he broke off with her long before he retired. Mildred was quite a lot older than Jack Biemeyer. For a long time she didn't show her age, but she's feeling it now. She made that clear in the card she sent me."

"Did she give you her address?"

"She was staying in a motel in Santa Teresa. She said she was looking for a more permanent place."

"Which motel?"

Her face went vague in thought. "I'm afraid I don't remember. But it's on the front of the card. I'll see if I can find it."

# XXIV

She went to her office in the back of the store and returned brandishing a postcard. On the front was a colored picture of Siesta Village, which was one of the newer waterfront motels in Santa Teresa. A shaky hand had written on the back, beside Juanita Grimes's name and address in Copper City:

Dear Nita:
    Am staying here temporarily till I find a better place. The foggy whether does not agree with me, in fact am not feeling well. The Calif. climate is not what its cracked up to be. Don't quote me but am looking for a nursing home where I can stay tempo-

rarily and get back on my feet. Not to worry—I have friends here.

Mildred

I handed the card back to Mrs. Grimes. "It sounds as if Mildred's in some trouble."

She shook her head, perhaps not so much in denial as in resistance to the thought. "She may be. It isn't like Mildred to complain about her health. She's always been a hardy soul. She must be over seventy by now."

"When did you get this card from her?"

"A couple of months ago. I wrote her an answer and sent it to the motel, but I haven't heard from her since."

"Do you know who her friends in Santa Teresa are?"

"I'm afraid I don't. Mildred was pretty close-mouthed about her friends. She lived a very full life, to put it mildly. But old age finally caught up with her." She looked down along the slopes of her own body. "Mildred had a lot of trouble in her time. She didn't go out of her way to avoid it, either. She's always had more guts than she could use."

"Were you close to Mildred?"

"As close as any other woman in town. She wasn't—she isn't a woman's woman. She's a man's woman who never married."

"So I gather. Wasn't William an illegitimate son?"

Mrs. Grimes nodded. "She had a long love affair with Felix Chantry, the man who developed the copper mine. William was his son."

"How well did you know William, Mrs. Grimes?"

"Paul and I saw quite a lot of him. He was a budding painter, too, before the army took him. Paul thought he had more potential talent than his brother Richard. He didn't live to develop it. He was murdered by an unknown hand in the summer of '43."

"The same summer that Richard and his wife went to California."

"The same summer," she repeated solemnly. "I'll never forget that summer. Mildred drove over from

Tucson—she was living with a painter in Tucson then—and she drove over from there to view poor William's body in the morgue. Afterwards she came to my adobe, and as it turned out she spent the night. She was strong and healthy in those days, no more than forty, but the death of her son came as a terrible shock to her. She walked into my house like an old woman. We sat in the kitchen and killed a quart of bourbon between us. Mildred was a lively conversationalist most of the time, but that night she hardly said a word. She was completely used up. William was her only child, you know, and she really loved him."

"Did she have any idea who had killed him?"

"If she had, she didn't tell me. I don't think she had. It was an unsolved killing. It stayed that way."

"Do you have any thoughts on the subject, Mrs. Grimes?"

"I thought at the time it was one of those senseless killings. I still do. Poor William hitched a ride with the wrong party, and he was probably killed for the money in his pockets." She was looking intently into my face as if it were a clouded window. "I can see you don't believe that."

"It may be true. But it seems too easy. William may have hitched a ride with the wrong people, but I doubt that they were unknown to him."

"Really?" She leaned closer. The part in her hair was white and straight as a desert road. "You think William was deliberately murdered by someone he knew. What do you base that on?"

"Two things, mainly. Talking to the authorities about it, I got a feeling that they knew more than they were saying, that there may have been a deliberate or half-deliberate cover-up. I know that's vague. The other thing on my mind is even vaguer. However, I think I give it more weight. I've worked on several dozen murder cases, many of them involving multiple murders. And in nearly every case the murders were connected in some way. In fact, the deeper you go into a series of crimes, or any set of circumstances involving people who know each other, the more connectedness you find."

Her eyes were still intent on my face; I felt as if she were trying to look directly into my mind. "You believe that Paul's death the other night was connected with William Mead's death in 1943?"

"Yes. I'm working on that theory."

"Connected in what way?"

"I'm not sure."

"You think the same person killed both of them?" In spite of her age, she sounded like a young girl frightening herself with a story whose ending might frighten her more. "Who do you think it was?"

"I don't want to lead you. You seem to have known all the suspects."

"You mean you have more than one suspect?"

"Two or three."

"Who are they?"

"You tell me, Mrs. Grimes. You're an intelligent woman. You're probably acquainted with all the people involved, and you know more about them than I ever will."

Her breasts rose and fell rapidly with her breathing. In some way, I had touched and excited her. Perhaps she was feeling that something she said or did might after all make a difference to the world, or to her dead husband.

"Will I be quoted?" she said.

"Not by me."

"All right. I know something that very few people know. I got it from Mildred Mead."

"On the night when the two of you killed the bottle of bourbon?"

"No. Some time before that, not long after her son William was drafted. It must have been back in 1942. He got a girl pregnant and had to marry her, Mildred told me. But he was really in love with Richard Chantry's wife. And she was in love with William."

"Are you suggesting that Richard murdered William?"

"I'm telling you he had a motive, anyway."

"I thought you said that Richard Chantry was homosexual."

"Bisexual, like my husband. It doesn't rule anything out—I learned that the hard way."

"Do you think Richard killed your husband, too?"

"I don't know. He may have." She peered past me into the bright empty street. "Nobody seems to know where Richard is or what he's doing. As all the world knows, he's been gone for twenty-five years."

"Gone where? Do you have any ideas, Mrs. Grimes?"

"I have one. It struck me when I heard that Paul had been killed. I wondered if Richard was hiding out in Santa Teresa. And whether Paul had seen him, and been silenced." She hung her head, wagging it dolefully from side to side. "Those are terrible thoughts to have, but I've been having them."

"So have I," I said. "What does your daughter Paola think about all this? You said you talked to her on the phone."

Mrs. Grimes closed her teeth over her lower lip and looked away. "I'm afraid I don't know what she thinks. Paola and I don't communicate too well. Has she talked to you?"

"Soon after the murder. She was in shock to some extent."

"I'm afraid she still is. Would you be good enough to look her up when you go back to Santa Teresa?"

"I was planning to."

"Good. Would you take her some money from me? She says she's completely broke."

"I'll be glad to. Where is she staying?"

"The Monte Cristo Hotel."

"That sounds like swank."

"It isn't, though."

"Good." She gave me two twenties and a ten out of

the cash register. "This should at least cover her rent for a couple of days."

The morning was running out. I went back to South-western Savings, which I found open now, and approached a bright-looking woman who sat at a desk by herself. The nameplate on the desk identified her as Mrs. Conchita Alvarez.

I told her my name. "I'm looking for a friend named Mildred Mead. I understand she does her banking here."

Mrs. Alvarez gave me a hard look that was almost tangible. She must have decided I wasn't a con man, because she nodded her shiny dark head and said, "Yes. She did. But she's moved to California."

"Santa Teresa? She often talked about moving there."

"Well, now she has."

"Can you give me an address for Miss Mead? I happen to be on my way to Santa Teresa. Mr. Biemeyer is flying me over in one of the company planes."

Mrs. Alvarez stood up. "I'll see what I can find."

She went through a door and was gone for some time. She came back looking rather disappointed.

"The only address I have for Miss Mead is a motel called Siesta Village. But that address is two months old."

"Is that where you're sending her mortgage payments?"

"No. I checked into that. She rented a P.O. box." Mrs. Alvarez looked at a slip of paper in her hand. "Number 121."

"In Santa Teresa?"

"In the main post office in Santa Teresa, yes."

I drove out to the airport and turned in my rented car. The company jet was already warming up, and Doris and Fred were in it. They were sitting in separate seats, Doris in the front behind the pilot's compartment and Fred in the back. There seemed to be no communication between them, perhaps because the sheriff was standing guard at the door.

He seemed relieved to see me. "I was afraid you weren't going to make it. I thought I'd have to make the trip to California myself."

"Has there been any trouble?"

"No." He turned a cold eye on Fred, who winced away. "I've got so I don't trust anybody under forty."

"I'm afraid I qualify for your trust."

"Yeah, you're more like fifty, aren't you? And I'll be sixty on my next birthday. I never thought it would happen, but I've started to look forward to retirement. The world is changing, you know."

But not fast enough, I thought. It was still a world where money talked, or bought silence.

# XXV

The jet climbed in a long straight slant. It was a clear day. The long dry savannahs of Mexico extended themselves on my left. On my right I could see the ten-thousand-foot peak standing above Tucson. It gradually moved backward like a drifting pyramid as we flew west.

Fred kept his head turned away from me, his eyes on the scenery sliding away underneath us. The girl in the seat behind the pilot seemed equally oblivious and remote. The high sierra rose in the faded distance.

Fred looked at the mountains ahead as if they constituted the walls of a jail where he was going to be confined.

He turned to me: "What do you think they'll do to me?"

"I don't know. It depends on two things. Whether we recover the picture, and whether you decide to tell the whole story."

"I told you the whole story last night."

"I've been thinking about that, and I wonder if you did. It seems to me you left out some pertinent facts."

"That's your opinion."

"Isn't it yours, too?"

He turned his head away and looked down at the great sunlit world into which he had escaped for a day or two. It seemed to be fleeing backward into the past. The mountain walls loomed ahead, and the jet whined louder as it climbed to vault over them.

"What got you so interested in Mildred Mead?" I asked him.

"Nothing. I wasn't interested in her. I didn't even know who she was until Mr. Lashman told me yesterday."

"And you didn't know that Mildred moved to Santa Teresa a few months ago?"

He turned toward me. He badly needed a shave, and it made him look both older and more furtive. But he seemed honestly confused.

"I certainly didn't. What is she doing there?"

"Looking for a place to live, apparently. She's a sick old woman."

"I didn't know that. I don't know anything about her."

"Then what was it that got you interested in the Biemeyers' painting?"

He shook his head. "I can't tell you. Chantry's work has always fascinated me. It isn't a crime to be interested in paintings."

"Only if you steal them, Fred."

"But I didn't *plan* to steal it. I simply borrowed it overnight. I meant to return it next day."

Doris had turned in her seat. She was up on her knees, watching us over the back.

"That's true," she said. "Fred *told* me he borrowed

the picture. He wouldn't do that if he planned to steal it, would he?"

Unless, I thought, he planned to steal you, too. I said, "It doesn't seem to make sense. But nearly everything does when you understand it."

She gave me a long cold appraising look. "You really believe that, that everything makes sense?"

"I work on that principle, anyway."

She lifted her eyes in sardonic prayer and smiled. It was the first time I had seen her smile.

"Would you mind if I sat with Fred for a while?" she said.

His sensitive little smile peeked out from under his heavy mustache. He flushed with pleasure.

I said, "I don't mind, Miss Biemeyer."

I traded seats with her, and pretended to go to sleep. Their conversation was steady and low, too low to be overheard through the sound of the engine. Eventually I did to go sleep.

When I woke up, we were turning over the sea, back toward the Santa Teresa airport. We landed with a gentle bump and taxied toward the small Spanish Mission terminal.

Jack Biemeyer was waiting at the gate. His wife broke past him as we climbed out. She folded Doris in her arms.

"Oh, Mother," the girl said in embarrassment.

"I'm so glad you're all right."

The girl looked at me over her mother's shoulder like a prisoner peering over a wall.

Biemeyer began to talk to Fred. Then he began to shout. He accused Fred of rape and other crimes. He said that he would have Fred put away for the rest of his life.

Fred's eyes were watering. He was close to tears. He bit at his mustache with his lower teeth. People were coming out of the terminal to watch and listen from a distance.

I was afraid of something more serious happening.

Biemeyer might talk himself into an act of violence, or scare Fred into one.

I took Fred by the arm and marched him through the terminal into the parking lot. Before I could get him out of there, an official car drove up. Two policemen climbed out and arrested Fred.

The Biemeyer family came out of the terminal in time to see him leave. In what looked like a parody of Fred's arrest, Biemeyer took his daughter by the elbow and hustled her into the front seat of his Mercedes. He ordered his wife to get in. She refused with gestures. He drove away.

Ruth Biemeyer stood by herself in the parking lot, stiff with embarrassment and blanched by anger. She didn't appear to recognize me at first.

"Are you all right, Mrs. Biemeyer?"

"Yes, of course. But my husband seems to have driven away without me." She produced a frantic smile. "What do you think I should do?"

"It depends on what you want to do."

"But I never do what I want to do," she said. "Nobody ever does what he really wants to do."

Wondering what Ruth Biemeyer really wanted to do, I opened the right-hand door of my car for her. "I'll drive you home."

"I don't want to go home." But she got in.

It was a strange situation. The Biemeyers, for all their protestations and all their efforts, didn't really seem to want their daughter back. They didn't know how to treat her, or what to do about Fred. Well, neither did I, unless we could invent an alternative world for the people who didn't quite fit into this one.

I closed the door on Ruth Biemeyer, walked around the car, and got in behind the wheel. The air was hot and stuffy in the car, which had sat all day in the parking lot. I rolled down the window on my side.

It was a blank and desolate patch of earth, squeezed between the airport and the road and littered with empty cars. The blue sea winked and wrinkled in the distance.

Like a blind date trying to make conversation, Mrs. Biemeyer said, "This is a strange world we live in nowadays."

"It always was."

"I didn't used to think so. I don't know what will happen to Doris. She can't live at home and she can't make it on her own. I don't know what she can do."

"What did you do?"

"I married Jack. He may not have been the greatest choice in the world but at least we got through life." She spoke as if her life were already over. "I was hoping Doris would find some eligible young man."

"She has Fred."

The woman said coldly, "He isn't possible."

"At least he's a friend."

She cocked her head as if she was surprised that anyone should befriend her daughter. "How do you know that?"

"I've talked to him. I've seen them together."

"He's simply been using her."

"I don't believe that. One thing I'm pretty sure of, Fred didn't take your painting with any idea of selling it, or cashing in. No doubt he's a little hipped on it, but that's another matter. He's been trying to use it to solve the Chantry problem."

She gave me a sharp inquiring look. "Do you believe that?"

"Yes, I do. He may be emotionally unstable. Anybody with his family background would be likely to be. He's not a common thief, or an uncommon one, either."

"So what happened to the picture?"

"He left it in the museum overnight and it was stolen."

"How do you know?"

"He told me."

"And you believe him?"

"Not necessarily. I don't know what happened to the

picture. I doubt that Fred does, either. I don't believe he belongs in jail, though."

She lifted her head. "Is that where they took him?"

"Yes. You can get him out if you want to."

"Why should I?"

"Because as far as I know, he's your daughter's only friend. And I think she's just as desperate as Fred is, if not more so."

She looked around at the parking lot and the surrounding flatlands. The battlements of the university loomed on the horizon beyond the tidal slough.

She said, "What has Doris got to be so desperate about? We've given her everything. Why, when I was her age I was in secretarial school and working part-time on the side. I even enjoyed it," she said with nostalgia and some surprise. "In fact, those were the best days of my life."

"These aren't Doris's best days."

She pulled away in the seat, turning in my direction. "I don't understand you. You're a peculiar detective. I thought detectives ran down thieves and put them behind bars."

"I just did that."

"But now you want to undo it. Why?"

"I've already told you. Fred Johnson isn't a thief, no matter what he did. He's your daughter's friend, and she needs one."

The woman turned her face away and bowed her head. The blond hair fell away from her vulnerable neck.

"Jack will kill me if I interfere."

"If you mean that literally, maybe Jack is the one who belongs in jail."

She gave me a shocked look, which gradually changed into something more real and humane. "I'll tell you what I'll do. I'll take it up with my lawyer."

"What's his name?"

"Roy Lackner."

"Is he a criminal lawyer?"

"He's in general practice. He was a Public Defender for a while."

"Is he your husband's lawyer as well as yours?"

She hesitated, glancing at my face and away. "No. He isn't. I went to him to find out where I stood if I divorced Jack. And we've also discussed Doris."

"When was this?"

"Yesterday afternoon. I shouldn't be telling you all these things."

"You should, though."

"I hope so," she said. "I also hope you're discreet."

"I try to be."

We drove downtown to Lackner's office, and I told her what I knew about Fred as we went. I added in summation, "He can go either way."

That went for Doris, too, but I didn't think it was necessary to say so.

Lackner's offices were in a rehabilitated frame cottage on the upper edge of the downtown slums. He came to the front door to meet us, a blue-eyed young man with a blond beard and lank yellow hair that came down almost to his shoulders. His look was pleasant, and his grip was hard.

I would have liked to go in and talk to him, but Ruth Biemeyer made it plain that she didn't want me. Her attitude was proprietorial and firm, and I wondered in passing if there was some attachment between the young man and the older woman.

I gave her the name of my motel. Then I went down to the waterfront to give Paola her mother's fifty dollars.

# XXVI

The Monte Cristo was a three-story stucco hotel that had once been a large private residence. Now it advertised "Special Rates for Weekenders." Some of the weekenders were drinking canned beer in the lobby and matching coins to see who was going to pay for it. The desk clerk was a little doll-faced man with an anxious look that intensified when he saw me. I think he was trying to decide whether I was a cop.

I didn't tell him whether I was or not. Sometimes I didn't even tell myself. I asked him if Paola Grimes was in. He gave me a puzzled look.

"She's a dark girl with long black hair. Good figure."

"Oh. Yeah. Room 312." He turned and examined her key slot. "She isn't in."

I didn't bother asking him when to expect Paola. He wouldn't be likely to know. I kept her fifty dollars in my wallet and made a mental note of her room number. Before I left the hotel, I looked into the bar. It was a kind of post-historic ruin. All the girls waiting there were blond. Outside, along the beach front, there were a number of women with long black hair but none of them was Paola.

I drove uptown to the newspaper building and left my car at a fifteen-minute curb in front of it. Betty was at her typewriter in the newsroom. Her hands were quiet on the keys. She had faint blue circles under her eyes, no lipstick on her mouth. She looked dispirited, and she failed to brighten appreciably when she saw me.

"What's the matter, Betty?"

"I haven't been making good progress on the Mildred

148

Mead thing. I can't seem to find out enough about her."

"Why don't you interview her?"

She screwed up her face as if I'd threatened to slap her. "That isn't funny."

"It wasn't meant to be. Mildred Mead has a box in the Santa Teresa post office, number 121 in the main branch. If you can't get to her through that, she's probably in one of the local nursing homes."

"Is she sick?"

"Sick and old."

Betty's eyes, her whole face, changed and softened. "What on earth is she doing here in Santa Teresa?"

"Ask her. And when she tells you, you tell me."

"But I don't know which nursing home she's in."

"Call all of them."

"Why don't *you?*"

"I want to talk to Captain Mackendrick. Besides, you can do a better job on a phone check. You know the people in this town and they know you. If you locate her, don't say anything to scare her off. I wouldn't mention that you work for a newspaper."

"What *shall* I say?"

"As little as possible. I'll check back with you."

I drove across the center of town to the police station. It was a stucco oblong that lay like a dingy sarcophagus in the middle of an asphalt parking lot. I talked my way past an armed and uniformed woman guard into Mackendrick's office, which was small and bleak. It contained a wall of files, a desk and three chairs, one of which was occupied by Mackendrick. Across the single window there were bars.

Mackendrick was studying a typed sheet that lay flat on the desk in front of him. He was slow in looking up. I wondered if this was meant to imply that he was more important than I was, but not important enough. He finally raised his impervious eyes to mine.

"Mr. Archer? I thought you'd left town for good."

"I went to Arizona to pick up the Biemeyer girl. Her father flew us back in one of his company's jets."

Mackendrick was impressed, and slightly startled, as I had meant him to be. He massaged the side of his crumpled face with his hand, as if to reassure himself of its solidity.

"Of course," he said, "you're working for the Biemeyers. Right?"

"Right."

"Does he have some special interest in the Grimes killing?"

"He bought a picture from Grimes. There's some question whether it's a phony or a genuine new Chantry."

"If Grimes had anything to do with it, it probably is a phony. Is that the picture that was stolen?"

"It wasn't exactly stolen," I said, "at least not the first time around. Fred Johnson took it to make some tests on it at the art museum. Somebody stole it from there."

"Is that Johnson's story?"

"Yes, and I believe it." But even to me the story had sounded weak in my retelling.

"I don't. Neither does Biemeyer. I've just been talking to him on the phone." Mackendrick smiled in cold pleasure. He had taken a point from me in the endless game of power that complicated his life. "If you want to go on working for Biemeyer, you better check with him about some of those little details."

"He isn't my only source. I've talked to Fred Johnson at some length, and I don't believe he's a criminal type."

"Nearly everybody is," Mackendrick said. "All they need is the opportunity. And Fred Johnson had that. He may even have been in cahoots with Paul Grimes. That would be quite a trick, to sell a phony Chantry, then steal it back before it could be detected."

"I thought of that possibility. But I doubt that it happened. Fred Johnson isn't capable of planning and carrying out an action like that. And Paul Grimes is dead."

Mackendrick leaned forward with his elbows on his desk, his left palm and his right fist forming a ball joint under his chin. "There may be others involved. There almost certainly are. We may be dealing with an art-theft ring of queers and addicts. It's a crazy world." He disengaged his hands and waved his fingers in front of his face, miming the wildness of the world. "Did you know Grimes was a queer?"

"Yes. His wife was telling me that this morning."

The captain's eyes widened in astonishment. "He has a wife?"

"He had. She told me they've been separated for years. She runs an art shop in Copper City under her married name."

Mackendrick penciled a note on a yellow pad. "Is Fred Johnson queer?"

"I doubt it. He has a girl."

"You just got finished telling me that Grimes had a wife."

"It's true, Fred could be bisexual. But I've spent a fair amount of time with him now, and haven't seen any evidence of it. Even if he is, it doesn't make him a thief."

"He stole a picture."

"He took it with the knowledge and permission of the owner's daughter. Fred is a budding art expert. He wanted to test the picture for age and authenticity."

"So he says now."

"I believe him. I honestly don't think he belongs in jail."

Mackendrick's palm and fist came together again like parts of a machine. "Is Fred Johnson paying you to say this?"

"Biemeyer is paying me to recover his picture. Fred Johnson says he hasn't got it. I think it's time we looked elsewhere. In fact, that's what I've been doing, more or less accidentally."

Mackendrick waited. I told him what I had learned about Paul Grimes's early life in Arizona, and about his relationship with Richard Chantry. I also told him about the death of Mildred Mead's illegitimate son, William, and the quick departure of Richard Chantry from Arizona in the summer of 1943.

Mackendrick picked up his pencil and began to draw connected squares across the yellow paper, a series of squares like a random chessboard representing the precincts of the city or his mind.

"This is new information to me," he admitted finally. "Are you sure that it's good information?"

"I got most of it from the sheriff who handled the William Mead killing. You can check with him if you want to."

"I'll do that. I was in the army when Chantry came here and bought that house on the ocean. But I got out and joined the force in 1945 and I was one of the few people who got to know him personally." Mackendrick spoke as if his own experience and the history of the city had become almost synonymous to him. "I patrolled the beach front there for several years, until I made sergeant. That was how I became acquainted with Mr. Chantry. He was very security-conscious. He did a lot of complaining about people loitering around his house. You know how the beach and the ocean always attract out-of-towners."

"Was he nervous?"

"I guess you'd say that. He was a loner, anyway. I never knew him to give a party, or even invite friends into his house. As far as I knew, he had no friends. He kept himself locked up in the house with his wife and a man called Rico, who cooked for them. And he worked. As far as I know, all he did was work. Sometimes he'd be up painting all night and I'd see the lights still burning in his house when I cruised by on the early-morning shift." Mackendrick lifted his eyes, which had been emptied of the present and now became filled and perplexed by it again. "Are you sure that Mr. Chantry was a homo? I never knew one of them who liked hard work."

I didn't mention Leonardo for fear of confusing the issue. "I'm fairly certain. You could ask around."

Mackendrick shook his head abruptly. "Not in this town I couldn't. He's Santa Teresa's claim to fame—gone for twenty-five years, and still our leading citizen. And *you* be careful what you say about him."

"Is that a threat?"

"It's a warning. I'm doing you a favor giving it. Mrs. Chantry could sue you, and don't think she wouldn't. She's got the local paper so bulldozed that they let her read it ahead of time whenever they mention her husband. Especially when they mention his disappearance, it has to be handled with kid gloves."

"What do you think happened to him, Captain? I've told you what I know."

"And I appreciate it. If he was a homo, as you say he was, then there's your answer right there. He stayed with his wife for seven years and couldn't stick it any longer. It's one thing I've often noticed about homos. Their lives run in cycles; they can't stay the course. And they have a tougher course to run than most of us."

Mackendrick had succeeded in surprising me. There was a vein of tolerance in his granite after all.

I said, "Is that the official theory, Captain? That Chantry simply took off of his own accord. No murder? No suicide? No blackmailing pressure?"

Mackendrick took in a deep whistling breath through his nose, and blew it out through his lips. "I wouldn't attempt to tell you how many times I've been asked that question. It's just about my favorite question by now," he said with irony. "And I always give the same answer. We never came up with any evidence at all that Chantry had been killed, or forced to leave. As far as we were able to establish the facts, Chantry left here because he wanted to start a new life. And what you tell me about his sexual background only confirms it."

"I assume his farewell letter was checked out in every way."

"Every way possible. Handwriting, fingerprints,

source of stationery—everything. The writing and the prints and the stationery were all Chantry's. There was no evidence that the letter was written under duress, either. And no new evidence has come up in the twenty-five years since then. I've had a special interest in the case from the beginning, because I knew Chantry, and you can take my word for all this. For some reason, he got sick and tired of his life here in Santa Teresa, and he dropped out."

"He may have dropped in again, Captain. Fred Johnson seems to think that the stolen picture is a Chantry, and a fairly recent one."

Mackendrick made an impatient flinging gesture with his left hand. "I'd want a better opinion than Fred Johnson's. And I don't buy his story that the picture was stolen from the museum. I think he's got it stashed someplace. If it is a genuine Chantry, it's worth real money. And in case you don't know it, Fred Johnson's family is on the rocks financially. His father's a hopeless drunk who hasn't worked for years; his mother lost her job at the hospital under suspicion of stealing drugs. And no matter whether he lost it or sold it or gave it away, Fred is criminally responsible for the loss of that picture."

"Not until he's proved responsible."

"Don't give me that, Archer. Are you a lawyer?"

"No."

"Then stop trying to act the part of one. Fred is where he belongs. You're not. And I have an appointment with the deputy coroner."

I thanked Mackendrick for his patience, without irony. He had told me a number of things I needed to know.

Leaving the police station, I passed my friend Purvis coming in. The young deputy coroner had the bright glazed look of a dedicated public servant on his way to get his picture in the paper. He didn't even break stride as he went by.

I waited beside his official station wagon. Squad cars

came and went. A flock of starlings flew over in a twittering cloud, and the first early shadow of evening followed them across the sky. I was worried about what might happen to Fred in jail, and regretful that I hadn't been able to spring him.

Purvis came out of the station eventually, walking more slowly, with a certain weight of confidence.

I said, "What's the word?"

"Remember the cadaver I showed you the night before last in the morgue?"

"I'm not likely to forget him. Jacob Whitmore, the painter."

Purvis nodded. "He wasn't drowned in the ocean after all. We completed a very careful autopsy this afternoon. Whitmore was drowned in fresh water."

"Does that mean he was murdered?"

"Probably. Mackendrick seems to think so. Drowned in somebody's bathtub and chucked into the ocean afterwards."

# XXVII

I drove out to Sycamore Point and knocked on the door of Jacob Whitmore's cottage. It was opened by the girl he had left behind. The low sun touched her face with a rosy glow and made her narrow her eyes. She didn't appear to recognize me.

I had to remind her who I was. "I was here the night before last. I bought some of Jake's pictures from you."

She shaded her eyes and studied my face. Hers was pale and unfocused. Her blond hair was uncombed, and it was lifted by the sundown wind pouring down the draw.

She said, "Are the pictures okay?"

"They're okay."

"I have some more if you want them."

"We'll talk about it."

She let me into her front room. Nothing in it had changed essentially, but it had lapsed into more extreme disorder. A chair was lying on its back. There were bottles on the floor, fragments of enchilada on the table.

She sat at the table. I picked up the fallen chair and sat facing her. "Have you heard from the coroner this afternoon?"

She shook her head. "I haven't heard from anybody; not that I remember, anyway. Excuse the condition of the room, will you, please? I drank too much wine last night and I must have had a tantrum. It seemed—it seems so unfair that Jake had to drown." She was silent for a time, and then said, "They asked my permission to do an autopsy yesterday."

"They did it today. Jake drowned in fresh water."

She shook her bleached head again. "No, he didn't. He drowned in the ocean."

"His body was found in the ocean, but the water that killed him was fresh water. You can take the coroner's word for it."

She looked at me dimly through her half-closed eyes. "I don't understand. Does that mean he drowned in a creek and his body was washed down into the sea?"

"That isn't likely. The creeks are low in the summer. It probably means that he was drowned in a bathtub or a swimming pool, and whoever did it dumped his body here in the ocean."

"I don't believe it." She looked around the room as if the murderer might be lurking behind the furniture. "Who would do that to Jake?"

"You tell me, Mrs. Whitmore."

She shook her head. "We weren't married. My name is Jessie Gable." The sound of her name brought tears to her eyes. She blinked and the tears ran down her cheeks. "You're telling me that Jake was murdered, aren't you?"

"Yes."

"I don't understand. He never hurt a living soul. Except me. But I forgave him."

"Murder victims don't usually deserve it."

"But he had nothing worth stealing."

"Maybe he had. Didn't Paul Grimes buy some of his pictures?"

She nodded. "That's true, he did. But it wasn't really the pictures that he wanted. I was here in the room when Grimes was talking to Jake. He was trying to get some information out of him, and he bought Jake's pictures just to get him talking."

"Talking about what?"

"The other picture. The picture that Jake had sold him at the beach art show, the day before."

"And did Jake tell him what he wanted to know?"

"I don't know. They went outside to talk about it. They didn't want me to hear what they were saying."

I got out my photograph of the Biemeyers' stolen painting and showed it to her in the light from the window. "Is this the picture that Jake sold to Grimes the day before?"

She took the picture and nodded. "It certainly looks like it. It's a really good picture and Jake got a lot of money for it. He didn't tell me how much, but it must have been several hundred, anyway."

"And Grimes probably sold it for several thousand."

"Really?"

"I'm not fooling, Jessie. The people who bought the picture from Grimes had it stolen from them. I was hired to recover it."

She sat up straight and crossed her legs. "You don't think *I* stole it, do you?"

"No. I doubt you ever stole anything."

"I didn't," she said firmly. "I never did. Except Jake from his wife."

"That isn't a felony."

"I don't know," she said. "I'm being punished like it was. And so was Jake punished."

"Everybody dies, Jessie."

"I hope that I die soon."

I waited. "Before you do," I said, "I want you to do Jake a favor."

"How can I? He's already dead."

"You can help me find the person or persons who killed him." I took the photograph from her limp hands. "I think he was killed over this."

"But why?"

"Because he knew or figured out who painted it. I'm winging, you understand. I don't know for certain that that's true. But I think it is. This picture was the connecting link between the two men who were killed, Jake and Paul Grimes."

I remembered as I said it that a third man had been killed: William Mead, whose body was found in the Arizona desert in 1943, and whose mother was the subject of the picture. These facts coming together in my mind gave me a kind of subterranean jolt, like an earthquake fault beginning to make its first tentative move. I was breathing quickly and my head was pounding.

I leaned across the littered table. "Jessie, do you have any idea where Jake got this picture?"

"He bought it."

"How much did he pay for it?"

"Fifty dollars at least—probably more. He wouldn't tell me how much more. He took the fifty dollars I had in my safety fund—that's money I kept in case we couldn't pay the rent. I told him he was crazy to put out cash for the picture, that he should take it on consignment. But he said he had a chance to make a profit. And I guess he did."

"Did you ever see the person he bought it from?"

"No, but it was a woman. He let that slip."

"How old a woman?"

Jessie spread her hands like someone feeling for rain. "Jake didn't tell me, not really. He said that it was an older woman but that doesn't mean it was. She could be seventeen and he'd still tell me she was an older woman. He knew that I was jealous of the chicks. And I had reason to be."

Tears rose in her eyes. I didn't know whether they stood for anger or grief. Her feelings seemed to be fluctuating between those two emotions. So did mine. I was weary of questioning the widows of murdered men. But I still had questions to ask.

"Did the woman bring the picture here to the house?"

"No. I never saw her. I told you that. She took it down to the waterfront on a Saturday. These last years, Jake had a sideline buying and selling pictures at the Saturday art show. He bought the picture there."

"How long ago was that?"

She was slow in answering, perhaps looking back over a flickering passage of days that seemed all the same: sun and sea, wine and pot and grief and poverty.

"It must have been a couple of months ago. It's at least that long since he took my safety fund. And when he sold the picture to Paul Grimes he didn't replace my fund. He kept the money himself. He didn't want me to know how much it was. But we've been living on it ever since." She scanned the room. "If you can call this living."

I got a twenty out of my wallet and dropped it on the table. She scowled at it and then at me.

"What's that for?"

"Information."

"I couldn't give you much. Jake was secretive about this deal. He seemed to think he was on to something big."

"I think he was, too, or trying to get on to it. Do you want to try and dig up some more information for me?"

"What kind of information?"

"Where this picture came from." I showed her the portrait of Mildred Mead again. "Who Jake bought it from. Anything else that you can find out about it."

"Can I keep that photo?"

"No. It's the only one I have. You'll have to describe it."

"Who to?"

"The dealers at the Saturday art show. You know them, don't you?"

"Most of them."

"Okay. If you come up with anything usable, I'll give you another twenty. If you can give me the name or address of the woman who sold Jake this picture, I'll give you a hundred."

"I could use a hundred." But she looked at me as if she didn't expect to see it in this life. "Jake and I had bad luck. He's had nothing but bad luck since he joined up with me." Her voice was harsh. "I wish I could of died instead of him."

"Don't wish it," I said. "We all die soon enough."

"It can't come too soon for me."

"Just wait awhile. Your life will start again. You're a young woman, Jessie."

"I feel as old as the hills."

Outside, the sun had just gone down. The sunset spread across the sea like a conflagration so intense that it fed on water.

# XXVIII

The red sky was darkening when I got downtown. The stores were full of light and almost empty of customers. I parked near the newspaper building and climbed the stairs to the newsroom. There was nobody there at all.

A woman in the hall behind me spoke in a husky tentative voice: "Can I help you, sir?"

"I hope so. I'm looking for Betty."

She was a small gray-haired woman wearing strong glasses that magnified her eyes. She looked at me with sharp friendly curiosity.

"You must be Mr. Archer."

I said I was.

The woman introduced herself as Mrs. Fay Brighton, the librarian of the paper. "Betty Jo asked me to relay a message to you. She said she'd be back here by half past seven at the latest." She looked at the small gold watch on her wrist, holding it close to her eyes. "It's almost that now. You shouldn't have long to wait."

Mrs. Brighton went back behind the counter of the room that housed her files. I waited for half an hour, listening to the evening sounds of the emptying city. Then I tapped on her door.

"Betty may have given up on me and gone home. Do you know where she lives?"

"As a matter of fact, I don't. Not since her divorce. But I'll be glad to look it up for you."

She opened a directory and transcribed Betty's number and address onto a slip of paper: "Seabrae Apartments, number 8, phone 967-9152." Then she brought out a phone from under the counter. Her eyes clung to my face as I dialed and listened. Betty's phone rang twelve times before I hung up.

"Did she give you any idea where she was going?"

"No, but she made a number of calls. She used this phone for some of them, so that I couldn't help hearing. Betty was calling various nursing homes in town, trying to locate a relative of hers. Or so she said."

"Did she mention the name?"

"Mildred Mead, I think it was. In fact, I'm sure of it. I think she found her, too. She took off in a hurry, and she had that light in her eyes—you know?—a young news hen on a breaking story." She let out a sighing breath. "I used to be one myself."

"Did she tell you where she was going?"

"Not Betty Jo." The woman smiled with shrewd pleasure. "When she's on a story, she wouldn't give her best friend the time of day. She started late in the game, you know, and the virus really got to her. But you probably know all that if you're a friend of hers."

The unspoken question hung in the air between us.

"Yes," I said. "I am a friend of hers. How long ago did she leave here?"

"It must have been two hours ago, or more." She looked at her watch. "I think she took off about five-thirty."

"By car?"

"I wouldn't know that. And she didn't give me any hint at all as to where she was heading."

"Where does she eat dinner?"

"Various places. Sometimes I see her in the Tea Kettle. That's a fairly good cafeteria just down the street." Mrs. Brighton pointed with her thumb in the direction of the sea.

"If she comes back here," I said, "will you give her a message for me?"

"I'd be glad to. But I'm not staying. I haven't eaten all day, and I really only waited for you to give you Betty's message. If you want to write one to her, I'll put it on her desk."

She slid a small pad of blank paper across the counter to me. I wrote: "Sorry I missed you. I'll check back in the course of the evening. Later you can get me at the motel."

I signed the message "Lew." Then, after a moment's indecision, I wrote the word "Love" above my name. I folded the note and gave it to Mrs. Brighton. She took it into the newsroom.

When she came back, she gave me a slightly flushed and conscious look that made me wonder if she had read my message. I had a sudden cold urge to recall it and cross out the word I had added. So far as I could remember, I hadn't written the word, or spoken it to a woman, in some years. But now it was in my mind, like a twinge of pain or hope.

I walked down the block to the Tea Kettle's red neon sign and went in under it. It was nearly eight o'clock, which was late for cafeteria patrons, and the place looked rather desolate. There was no line at the serving counter, and only a few scattered elderly patrons at the tables.

I remembered that I hadn't eaten since morning. I picked up a plate, had it filled with roast beef and vegetables, and carried it to a table from which I could watch the whole place. I seemed to have entered another city, a convalescent city where the wars of love were over and I was merely one of the aging survivors.

I didn't like the feeling. When Mrs. Brighton came in, she did nothing to relieve it. But when she brought her tray into the dining room, I stood up and asked her to share my table.

"Thank you. I hate eating alone. I spend so much time alone as it is, since my husband died." She gave me an anxious half-smile as if in apology for mentioning her loss. "Do you live alone?"

"I'm afraid I do. My wife and I were divorced some years ago."

"That's too bad."

"I thought so. But she didn't."

Mrs. Brighton became absorbed in her macaroni and cheese. Then she added milk and sugar to her tea. She stirred it and raised it to her lips.

"Have you known Betty long?"

"I met her at a party the night before last. She was covering it for the paper."

"She was supposed to be. But if you're talking about the Chantry party she never did submit any usable copy. She got wound up in a murder case, and she hasn't thought about anything else in two days. She's a terribly ambitious young woman, you know."

Mrs. Brighton gave me one of her large-eyed impervious looks. I wondered if she was offering me a warning or simply making conversation with a stranger.

"Are you involved in that murder case?" she said.

"Yes. I'm a private detective."

"May I ask who has employed you?"

"You may ask. But I better not answer."

"Come on." She gave me a roguish smile that wrinkled up her face yet somehow improved it. "I'm not a reporter any more. You're not talking for print."

"Jack Biemeyer."

Her penciled eyebrows rose. "Mr. Bigshot's involved with a murder?"

"Not directly. He bought a picture which was later stolen. He hired me to get it back."

"And did you?"

"No. I'm working on it, though. This is the third day."

"And no progress?"

"Some progress. The case keeps growing. There's been a second murder—Jacob Whitmore."

Mrs. Brighton leaned toward me suddenly. Her elbow spilled the rest of her tea. "Jake was drowned three days ago, accidentally drowned in the ocean."

"He was drowned in fresh water," I said, "and put into the ocean afterwards."

"But that's terrible. I knew Jake. I've known him since he was in high school. He was one of our delivery boys. He was the most harmless soul I ever knew."

"It's often the harmless ones that get killed."

As I said that, I thought of Betty. Her face was in my mind, and her firm harmless body. My chest felt hot and tight, and I took a deep breath and let it out, without intending to, in a barely audible sigh.

"What's the matter?" Mrs. Brighton said.

"I hate to see people die."

"Then you picked a strange profession."

"I know I did. But every now and then I have a chance to prevent a killing."

And every now and then I precipitated one. I tried to

keep that thought and the thought of Betty from coming together, but the two thoughts nudged each other like conspirators.

"Eat your vegetables," Mrs. Brighton said. "A man needs all the vitamins he can get." She added in the same matter-of-fact tone: "You're worried about Betty Jo Siddon, aren't you?"

"Yes, I am."

"So am I. Particularly since you told me Jake Whitmore was murdered. Somebody I've known half my life—that's striking close to home. And if something happened to Betty—" Her voice broke off and started again in a lower register: "I'm fond of that girl, and if anything happened to her—well, there's nothing I wouldn't do."

"What do you think happened?"

She looked around the room as if for a portent or a prophet. There was no one there but a few old people eating.

"Betty's hooked on the Chantry case," she said. "She hasn't been talking about it much lately but I know the signs. I had it myself at one time, over twenty years ago. I was going to track Chantry down and bring him back alive and become the foremost lady journalist of my time. I even wangled my way to Tahiti on a tip. Gauguin was one of Chantry's big influences, you know. But he wasn't in Tahiti. Neither was Gauguin."

"But you think Chantry's alive?"

"I did then. Now I don't know. It's funny how you change your views of things as you get older. You're old enough to know what I mean. When I was a young woman, I imagined that Chantry had done what I would have liked to do. He thumbed his nose at this poky little town and walked away from it. He was under thirty, you know, when he dropped out of sight. He had all the time in the world ahead of him—time for a second life. Now that my own time is running short, I don't know. I think it's possible that he was murdered all those years ago."

"Who had reason to kill him?"

"I don't know. His wife, perhaps. Wives often do have reason. Don't quote me, but I wouldn't put it past her."

"Do you know her?"

"I know her quite well, at least I did. She's very publicity-conscious. When I stopped being a reporter, she lost all interest in me."

"Did you know Chantry himself?"

"I never did. He was a recluse, you know. He lived in this town for seven or eight years, and you could count on the fingers of one hand the number of people who knew him to speak to."

"Can you name any of them?"

"I can think of one," she said. "Jake Whitmore knew Chantry. He used to deliver their paper. I think it was knowing Chantry that made a painter of him."

"I wonder if it was knowing Chantry that killed him."

Mrs. Brighton took off her glasses and wiped them with a lace-edged handkerchief. She put them on again and studied me through them.

"I'm not sure I follow you. Could you tell me just what you mean by that, in words of one syllable? I've had a long hard day."

"I have a feeling that Chantry may be here in town. It's something more than a feeling. Jack Biemeyer's stolen painting was probably a Chantry. It passed through two pairs of hands on its way to Biemeyer—Jake Whitmore's and Paul Grimes's. Both Whitmore and Grimes are dead. I guess you know that."

She bowed her gray head under the weight of the knowledge. "You think Betty's in real trouble, don't you?"

"She may be."

"Can I help? Do you want me to start phoning the nursing homes?"

"Yes. But please be careful. Don't mention any names. You have an aged aunt who needs custodial care. Get them to describe the facilities. Listen for sounds of guilt or any sign of trouble."

"I'm good at that," she said dryly. "I hear a lot of those kinds of sounds in the office. But I'm not sure that that's the best approach."

"What do you suggest?"

"I don't have anything specific in mind. It depends on what theory we're working on. Is it your idea that Betty located the nursing home where Mildred Mead is staying, was inveigled into going there, and got snatched? Isn't that a little melodramatic?"

"Melodramatic things are happening all the time."

She sighed. "I suppose you're right. I hear a lot of *them* in the office, too. But isn't it just as likely that Betty simply took off on the track of something, and she'll be turning up again any time?"

"It may be just as likely," I said. "But don't forget that Jake Whitmore turned up drowned. Paul Grimes turned up beaten to death."

Her face absorbed the knowledge and grew heavy with it, like an old sponge absorbing water. "You're right, of course. We have to do what we can. But shouldn't we be going to the police?"

"As soon as we have something definite to take to them. Mackendrick is hard to convince."

"Is he not. Okay. I'll be in the office if you want me."

She gave me the number, and I wrote it down. I asked her further to make me a list of the nursing homes and their numbers as she called them.

# XXIX

I drove up the dark hill to Biemeyer's house feeling angry and powerless. The house was blazing with lights but entirely silent.

Biemeyer answered the door with a drink held securely in his hand. He gave the impression that the drink was holding him up. Everything else about him, shoulders and knees and face, seemed to be sagging.

"What in the hell do you want?" His voice was husky and frayed, as if he had been doing a lot of shouting.

"I'd like to have a serious talk with you, Mr. Biemeyer."

"I can translate that. You want more money."

"Forget about the money for a change. I don't care about your money."

His face lengthened. He had hoisted his money up the mast, but I had failed to salute it. Slowly his face came together again, wrinkling around his dark hostile eyes.

"Does that mean you won't be sending me a bill?"

I was tempted to turn my back on him and leave, perhaps taking a swing at him first. But Biemeyer and his household possessed knowledge that I had to have. And working for them gave me standing with the police that I couldn't get in any other way.

"Please take it easy," I said. "The money you've advanced will probably cover it. If it doesn't, I'll send you a bill. After all, I did recover your daughter."

"But not the picture."

"I'm working on the picture, getting closer to it. Is there some place we could have a private talk?"

"No," he said. "There is not. All I'm asking you to do is to respect the sanctity of my home. If you won't do that, to hell with you."

Now even the glass in his hand was no longer steady. He waved it in a declamatory gesture and sloshed some liquor on the polished floor. Mrs. Biemeyer appeared behind him, as if the spilling of liquor was an understood signal in the family. Much farther back, half hidden by the edge of a partition, Doris stood still and silent.

"I think you should talk to him, Jack," Ruth Biemeyer said. "We've been through quite a lot in the last couple of days. And thanks in good part to Mr. Archer, we've survived it."

Her face was calm and smooth, and she was dressed for evening. Her voice was resigned. I guessed that she had made a bargain with whatever fates she recognized: bring Doris home and I'll put up with Jack. Well, Doris was there, standing like a Chirico figure in the receding distances of the house.

Biemeyer failed to put up an argument. He didn't even acknowledge his wife's remarks. He simply turned on his heel and led me through the house to his study. Doris gave me a small propitiatory smile as we went by. Her eyes were bright and scared.

Biemeyer sat down at his desk in front of the picture of his copper mine. He set down his drink and swiveled his chair toward me. "All right. What do you want from me now?"

"I'm looking for a pair of women. I think they may be together. One of them is Betty—Betty Jo Siddon."

Biemeyer leaned forward. "The society reporter? Don't tell me she's turned up missing."

"Just tonight. But she may be in danger. You may be able to help me find her."

"I don't see how. I haven't seen her in weeks. We don't go to many parties."

"She didn't get lost at a party, Mr. Biemeyer. I'm not sure how it happened, but I think she went to a nursing home in town here and got waylaid. That's the theory I have to work on, anyway."

"Where do I come in? I've never been in a nursing home in my life." He gave me a macho look and reached for his drink.

"Miss Siddon was looking for Mildred Mead."

His hand jerked and closed on his drink, spilling part of it on his trousers. "I never heard of her," he said without conviction.

"She was the subject of the painting I've been looking for. You must have recognized her."

"How?" he said. "I never met the woman in my life. What did you say her name was?"

"Mildred Mead. You bought her a house in Chantry Canyon quite a few years ago. That was a generous gift to a woman you say you never met. Incidentally, your daughter, Doris, ended up in that house last night. It's been taken over by a commune. Mildred sold them the house a few months ago and moved here. Don't tell me this is news to you."

"I'm not telling you anything."

Biemeyer's face had turned fiery red. He got to his feet. I expected him to take a swing at me. Instead he rushed out of the room.

I thought that was the end of our conversation. But he came back with a fresh drink and sat down opposite me again. His face had turned pale in blotches.

"Have you been researching me?"

"No."

"I don't believe you. How did you find out about Mildred Mead?"

"Her name came up in Arizona, together with yours."

He sighed. "They hate me there. There were times when I had to close down the smelter and put half of Copper City out of work. I know how it feels—I'm a Copper City boy myself. Back before the war, my family didn't have two nickels to rub against each other. I worked my way through high school and played football to stay in college. But I suppose you know all that already?"

I gave him a knowing look, which didn't come hard. I knew now.

"Have you talked to Mildred?" he said.

"No. I haven't seen her."

"She's an old woman now. But she was something to see in the old days. A beautiful thing." He opened and closed his free hand and gulped part of his drink. "When I finally got hold of her, it made everything worthwhile—all the work and the goddam football games getting my bones beaten. But she's old now. She finally got old."

"Is she here in town?"

"You know she is, or you wouldn't ask me the question. Or she was." He reached out with his free hand and grasped my shoulder. "Just don't tell Ruth. She's insanely jealous. You know how women are."

Just beyond the open door of the study the light stirred. Ruth Biemeyer moved into the doorway, trampling on the heels of her own shadow.

She said, "It isn't true that I'm insanely jealous. I may have been jealous at times. But it gives you no right to speak like that."

Biemeyer stood facing her, not quite as tall as she was on her heels. His face was set in creases of bitter loathing that gave it the character it had lacked.

"You were eaten up with jealousy," he said. "You have been all your life. You wouldn't give me normal sex, but when I got it from another woman you couldn't stand it. You did your dirty damnedest to break it up. And when you couldn't, you ran her out of town."

"I was ashamed for you," she said with acid sweetness. "Chasing after that poor old woman, when she was so sick and tired she could hardly walk."

"Mildred isn't so old. She's got more sex in her little finger than you ever had in your body."

"What would you know about sex? You were looking for a mother, not a wife."

"Wife?" He swept the room with an exaggerated glance. "I don't see any wife, I see a woman who cut me off when I was in my prime."

"Because you chose that old hag."

"Don't call her that!"

Their quarrel had had from the start a self-conscious dramatic aspect. They looked sideways at me as they spoke, as if I were their judge or referee. I thought of their daughter, Doris, and wondered if she had been used in this way as the audience and fulcrum of their quarrels.

I remembered Doris's memory of the scene when she had hidden in the clothes hamper in the bathroom, and I began to get angry again. This time I kept my anger hidden. Doris's parents were telling me some of the things I had to know. But both of them were looking at me now, perhaps wondering if they had lost their audience.

I said to Ruth Biemeyer, "Why did you buy that picture of Mildred Mead and hang it on the wall?"

"I didn't know it was Mildred Mead. It's an idealized portrait, and she's a wrinkled old crone by now. Why should I connect her with the picture?"

"You did, though," Biemeyer said. "And she still was better-looking than you ever were on your best day. That was the thing you couldn't stand."

"*You* were the thing I couldn't stand."

"At least you're admitting it now. You used to pretend that all the trouble originated with me. I was the King Kong of Copper City and you were the delicate maiden. You're not so bloody delicate, *or* maidenly."

"No," she said. "I've grown scar tissue. I've needed it."

I was getting sick of them. I had gone through quarrels like theirs myself, when my own marriage was breaking up. Eventually the quarrels reached a point where nothing hopeful, and nothing entirely true, was being said.

I could smell the sour animal anger of their bodies,

and hear them breathing quickly, out of phase. I stepped between them, facing Biemeyer.

"Where is Mildred? I want to talk to her," I said.

"I don't know. Honestly."

"He's lying," the woman said. "He brought her to town and set her up in an apartment on the beach. I have friends in this town, I know what's going on. They saw him beating a path to her door, visiting her every day." She turned on her husband. "What kind of a creep are you, anyway, sneaking away from your lawful home to make love to a crazy old woman?"

"I wasn't making love to her."

"Then what were you doing?"

"Talking. We'd have a few drinks and some conversation. That's all it amounted to."

"Just an innocent friendship, eh?"

"That's right."

"And that's all it ever was," she said sardonically.

"I don't claim that."

"What do you claim?"

He pulled himself together and said, "I loved her."

She looked at him in a lost way. It made me wonder if he had ever told her that before. She burst into tears and sat down in his chair, bending her streaming face close to her knees.

Biemeyer seemed upset, almost disoriented. I took him by the arm and led him to the far end of the room.

"Where is Mildred now?"

"I haven't seen her for weeks. I don't know where she went. We got into an argument about money. I was looking after her, of course, but she wanted more. She wanted me to set her up in a house with a staff of servants and a nurse to look after her. Mildred always did have big ideas."

"And you didn't want to pay for them?"

"That's right. I was willing to pay my share. But she wasn't penniless. And she was getting old—she's in her seventies. I told her a woman has to adjust when she gets into her seventies. She can't expect to go on living like a queen."

"Where did she go?"

"I can't tell you. She moved out several weeks ago without telling me anything. She said she was going someplace to move in with relatives."

"In town here?"

"I don't know."

"You didn't try to find her?"

"Why should I?" Biemeyer said. "Why the hell should I? There wasn't anything going on between us any more. With the money from the house in Chantry Canyon, she had enough to live on for the rest of her life. I didn't owe her anything. Frankly, she was turning into a nuisance."

So was Biemeyer, but I stayed with him. "I need to get in touch with her, and you may be able to help me. Do you have any contacts at the Southwestern Savings branch in Copper City?"

"I know the resident manager. Delbert Knapp."

"Can you find out from him where Mildred Mead has been cashing her mortgage checks?"

"I guess I can try."

"You can do better than try, Mr. Biemeyer. I hate to press you, but this could be a matter of life or death."

"Whose death? Mildred's?"

"Possibly. But I'm more immediately concerned with Betty Siddon. I'm trying to trace her through Mildred. Will you get in touch with Delbert Knapp?"

"I may not be able to do it tonight. He wouldn't have the information at home with him, anyway."

"What about Mildred's local contacts? Can you help me with those?"

"I'll think about it. But you understand I don't want my name in the paper. I don't want my name mentioned at all in connection with Mildred. In fact, the more I think about it, the less I like the whole idea of getting involved."

"A woman's life may be at stake."

"People die every day," he said.

I stood up and spoke down to him. "I got your daughter back. Now I want some help from you. And if I don't get it, and something happens to Miss Siddon, I'll fix you."

"That sounds like a threat."

"It is. There's enough crap in your life to make you fixable."

"But I'm your client."

"Your wife is."

My voice sounded calm in my ears, a little distant. But my eyes felt as if they had shrunk, and I was shaking.

"You must be crazy," he said. "I could buy and sell you."

"I'm not for sale. Anyway, that's just talk. You may have money, but you're too tight to use it. The other day you were bellyaching about five hundred measly bucks to get your daughter back. Half the time you're the king of the world, and the other half you talk like poor white trash."

He stood up. "I'm going to report you to Sacramento for threatening to blackmail me. You're going to regret this for the rest of your life."

I was already regretting it. But I was too angry to try to conciliate him. I walked out of the study and headed for the front door.

Mrs. Biemeyer caught me before I reached it. "You shouldn't have said what you did."

"I know that. I'm sorry. May I use your phone, Mrs. Biemeyer?"

"Don't call the police, will you? I don't want them here."

"No. I'm just calling a friend."

She led me into the huge bricked kitchen, seated me at a table by the window, and brought me a telephone on a long cord. The window overlooked the distant harbor. Closer, near the foot of the hill, the Chantry house had lights on in it. While I was dialing the number Fay

Brighton had given me, I took a second, longer look and saw that some of the lights were in the greenhouse.

I got a busy signal, and dialed again.

This time Mrs. Brighton answered on the first ring: "Hello?"

"This is Archer speaking. Have you had any luck?"

"Yes, sir, but all of it was bad. The trouble is that a whole lot of the people sound suspicious. It may be something in *my* voice that does it to them. I'm sort of scared sitting here by myself, you know. And I don't seem to be accomplishing anything."

"How far down the list are you?"

"Maybe halfway. But I feel that I'm not accomplishing anything. Is it all right with you if I quit for the night?"

I didn't answer her right away. Before I did, she let out an apologetic snuffling sob and hung up.

# XXX

I switched off the kitchen lights and took another look at the Chantry place. There were definitely movements in the greenhouse. But I couldn't make out their significance.

I went out to the car for my binoculars, and ran into Ruth Biemeyer for the second time.

"Have you seen Doris?" she said. "I'm getting a little concerned about her."

She was more than a little concerned. Her voice was thin. Her eyes were dark and craterous in the brilliant outside lights. I said, "Has Doris left the house?"

"I'm afraid she has, unless she's hiding somewhere. She may have run away with Fred Johnson."

"How could she? Fred's in jail."

"He was," she said. "But my lawyer got him out today. I'm afraid I made a mistake. Please don't tell Jack about it, will you? He'd never let me forget it."

She was a woman in trouble, sinking still deeper into trouble. She had lost her poise and started to lose her hope.

"I'll tell your husband what I have to—no more. Where is Fred? I want to talk to him."

"We dropped him off at his parents' home. I'm afraid it wasn't a good idea, was it?"

"It isn't a good idea," I said, "for you and me to be standing here with all the outside lights on. There's something funny going on at the Chantry place."

"I know there is. It's been going on a good part of the day. Today they were cutting down weeds in there. Tonight they've been digging a hole."

"What kind of a hole?"

"Go and look for yourself. They're still at it."

I went down the driveway to the edge of the slope, where the wire fence stopped me. The lights went out behind me. I leaned on the fence and focused my binoculars on the greenhouse. A dark man and a woman with shining gray hair—Rico and Mrs. Chantry—were working inside the building. They seemed to be filling in a hole with shovels, using a pile of dirt that stood between them.

Rico slid down into the half-filled hole and jumped up and down, packing the loose dirt. He appeared to be sinking upright into the earth, like a damned soul sinking into hell by his own volition. Mrs. Chantry stood and watched him.

I caught her face in my binoculars. She looked rosy and rough and dangerous. There was dirt on her face, and her hair curved like glistening gray hawk wings over her temples.

She reached a hand down to Rico and helped him out

of the hole. They teetered together on its edge and then returned to their task of filling it in. The earth fell soundlessly from their spades.

A black thought bit at the edge of my mind and gradually eclipsed it. The people in the greenhouse had dug a grave and now they were filling it in. It didn't seem quite possible. But if it was, then it was possible that Betty Siddon's body was under the dirt.

I went back to the car for my gun and had it in my hand when Ruth Biemeyer said behind me, "What are you planning to do with that?"

"I want to know what's happening down there."

"For God's sake, don't take a gun with you. So many innocent people get shot. And I still haven't found my daughter."

I didn't argue. But I slipped the gun, a medium-caliber automatic, into my jacket pocket. I went back to the fence and climbed over it and started down the slope to the barranca. It had been planted and overgrown with succulent plants that felt rubbery under my feet.

Farther down, the succulents gave way to sage and other native bushes. Nestled among the bushes, like a giant golden egg, was a girl's blond head. Doris was crouched there, watching what was going on in the greenhouse.

"Doris?" I said. "Don't be scared."

But she jumped like a fawn and went crashing down the slope. I caught her and told her to be quiet. She was trembling and breathing hard. Her body kept making unwilled or half-willed movements, trying to jerk away from me. I held her with both arms around her shoulders.

"Don't be afraid, Doris. I won't hurt you."

"You're hurting me now. Let me go."

"I will if you promise to stay where you are and keep quiet."

The girl quieted down a bit, but I could still hear her breathing.

The couple in the greenhouse had stopped filling in the hole and were standing together in listening attitudes. Their eyes ranged up the dark hillside. I got down among the sagebrush and pulled Doris down with me. After a long tense minute, the people in the greenhouse resumed their work. It looked like gravediggers' work.

"Did you see what they were burying, Doris?"

"No, I didn't. It was already covered when I got here."

"What brought you here?"

"I saw the light in the greenhouse; then I came down the hill and saw the big pile of dirt. Do you think they're burying a body?"

There was awe in her voice. There was also familiarity, as if her nightmares were coming true at last.

"I don't know," I said.

We moved across the slope to the corner of the wire fence and along it to her parents' driveway. Ruth Biemeyer was waiting at the top.

"What do you think we ought to do?" she said.

"I'll phone Captain Mackendrick."

She left me in the kitchen. I kept my eye on the greenhouse through the window. All I could see was barred light crossed by occasional shadows.

Mackendrick wasn't in his office, and the police operator couldn't locate him right away. I had time to remember that he had known Chantry when he was a young cop, and to wonder if he was going to see him again shortly.

I got Mackendrick at home. His phone was answered by a woman with a semi-official voice who sounded both impatient and resigned. After a certain amount of explanation, I persuaded her to let me talk to her husband. I told him what was happening in the greenhouse.

"Digging in your own greenhouse isn't a crime," he said. "I can't do anything about it officially. Hell, they could sue the city."

"Not if they buried a body."

"Did you see them bury a body?"

"No."

"Then what do you expect me to do?"

"Think about it," I said. "People don't dig grave-sized holes and fill them up just for the fun of it."

"You'd be surprised at what they do. Maybe they're looking for something."

"Such as?"

"A leaky water main. I've seen people dig up a whole yard looking for a water pipe with a hole in it."

"People like Mrs. Chantry?"

He was slow in answering. "I don't think we better continue this conversation. If you decide to take any action, I don't want to know about it."

"There's something else you don't want to know about," I said. "But I want to tell you."

Mackendrick sighed, or grunted. "Make it fast, eh? I've got a lot on my agenda, and it's late."

"You know a young woman named Betty Siddon."

"That I do. She's been in my hair."

"You haven't seen her tonight, have you?"

"No."

"She seems to be missing."

"What does that mean?"

"She's dropped out of sight. I haven't been able to contact her."

"For how long?"

"For several hours."

Mackendrick shouted at me, in a voice that was half angry and half jocose, "For God's sake, that doesn't mean anything. If she'd been gone for a week or two, you might say she was missing."

"Let's wait twenty years," I said. "Then we'll all be dead."

My voice sounded strange in my own ears, high and angry.

Mackendrick lowered his voice, as if to set me an example. "What's the trouble, Archer, are you stuck on the girl or something?"

"I'm worried about her."

"Okay, I'll tell my people to be on the lookout for her. Good night."

I sat with the dead receiver in my hand, feeling an angry pain that I had felt before. I lived at the intersection of two worlds. One was the actual world where danger was seldom far from people's lives, where reality threatened them with its cutting edge. The other was the world where Mackendrick had to operate in a maze of tradition and a grid of rules—a world where nothing officially happened until it was reported through channels.

From where I sat in the dark kitchen, I could see the gravediggers putting the final touches to the hole they had filled in. They seemed to be gathering up armfuls of cuttings and scattering them over the raw dirt. Finally Rico picked up a brown sack, swung it over his shoulder, and carried it out to a car standing in the courtyard. He opened the trunk of the car and slung the brown sack in.

Mrs. Chantry turned out the lights in the greenhouse and followed Rico into the main house.

I went out to my car and drove it down the hill, parking just around the corner from Mrs. Chantry's street. Though the movements of the night and its people were far beyond the range of my understanding, I was beginning to pick up some of the smaller rhythms. In less than fifteen minutes, there was a glow of headlights from the direction of the Chantry house. The Chantry car, with Rico driving alone in the front seat, passed me and turned toward the freeway.

I followed at a distance, but close enough to see him enter the northbound lane. There was fairly heavy traffic at this mid-evening hour, crawling like an endless luminescent worm into the tunneled darkness. We passed the university's lighted towers, the crowded buildings of the student annex where I had first met Doris, the narrow entrance to the dark beach where Jake Whitmore's body had been found.

Rico stayed on the freeway, and so did I. The traffic

was dwindling down to its intercity components, trucks and night-driving tourists and the like. I let the distance between us lengthen out, and almost lost him. He made an unexpected right turn off the freeway, then a quick left through an underpass. I left the highway and waited out of sight for a minute, then followed him down to the sea with my car lights out.

The object of his journey was a wooden pier that extended out over the water for a couple of hundred yards. Three or four miles beyond the end of the pier, a half-dozen oil platforms blazed with lights like leafless Christmas trees. And off to the north, like a menacing West Coast Statue of Liberty, a giant gas flame flared.

Against the several lights I could see Rico approaching the foot of the pier, hunchbacked by the sack he had slung across his shoulder. I left my car and followed him on foot, walking softly and narrowing my distance. By the time Rico had reached the seaward end, I was close behind him.

"Drop it, Rico," I said. "Get your hands up."

He made a move to heave the sack overside. It struck the top rail and fell clanking on the deck of the pier. Rico turned on me swinging. I moved inside his flailing arms and hit him several times in the belly, then once on the jaw. He went down and stayed for a while. I searched his clothes. No gun.

I untied the twine that closed the mouth of his sack, and spilled some of its contents on the planking. There were human bones caked with dirt, a damaged human skull, rusted engine parts from an old car.

Rico sighed and rolled over. Then he was on me, heavy and strong but dull in his reactions. His head swung loose and undefended. I didn't hit him again. I backed away and got out my gun and told him to calm down.

Instead he turned and ran staggering to the outer end of the pier. He started to climb over the railing, or try to. His feet kept slipping. The tide was low and the water was a long way down.

For some reason, it became important to me that Rico shouldn't make it into the black water. I pocketed my gun and got my arms around his waist. Dragged him back onto the deck and held him down.

As I marched Rico back to my car and got him safely inside of it, I understood one source of my satisfaction. Twenty-odd years ago, near an oil-stained pier like this, I had fought in the water with a man named Puddler and drowned him.

Rico, whatever his sins, had served as an equalizer for one of mine.

# XXXI

Captain Mackendrick was glad to see Rico, too. The three of us convened in Mackendrick's office with a male police stenotypist ready to record what was said. Rico didn't say anything at all until we brought in the sack of bones and iron. Mackendrick held it up in front of Rico's face and shook it. It made a strange dull clatter.

Mackendrick brought out the damaged skull and placed it on his desk. It looked empty-eyed at Rico. Rico returned the stare for a long moment. He tried to wet his lips with his dry tongue. Then he tried to scratch his head, but his fingers got tangled in the bandages he was now wearing.

"You used to be a pretty good young fellow," Mackendrick said. "I remember when you used to play volleyball on the beach, you liked good clean sport. You liked good clean work—mowing the lawn, washing the car. You thought Mr. Chantry was the greatest boss a young fellow ever had. You said so to me, remember?"

Tears had begun to roll from Rico's eyes and find twin downward channels on either side of his nose.

He said, "I'm sorry."

"What are you sorry for, Rico? Did you kill him?"

He shook his head, and the tears flew out from his face. "I don't even know who he is."

"Then why did you dig up his poor bones and try to get rid of them?"

"I don't know."

"You mean you do things without knowing why?"

"Sometimes. When people tell me."

"Who told you to get rid of these bones, weight them with iron, and chunk them in the sea? Who told you to do that?" Mackendrick said.

"I don't remember."

"Was it your own idea?"

The man recoiled from the suggestion. "No."

"Whose idea was it?"

Rico stared into the empty eyes of the skull. His face became even more sober, as if he had looked into a mirror and recognized his own mortal condition. He raised his hands and touched his cheeks with his fingertips, feeling the skull behind them.

"Is this Mr. Richard Chantry's skull?" Mackendrick said.

"I don't know. Honest to God, I don't know."

"What do you know?"

He looked at the floor. "Nothing much. I always was a dumbhead."

"That's true, but not that dumb. You used to look out for yourself in the old days, Rico. You went for the girls, but you didn't let them lead you around by the nose. You didn't go out and commit a crime because a woman jiggled her hips at you. You used to have more sense than to do that."

The stenotypist's fingertips danced a rapid minuet on the keys of his machine. Rico was watching them as if they were miming a dance of death, telling his past or perhaps foretelling his future. His mouth opened and closed several times in an effort to find words. Then he began to whisper to himself, too low to be heard.

Mackendrick leaned forward, speaking quietly: "What did you say, Rico? Speak up, man, it may be important."

Rico nodded. "It is important. I had nothing to do with it."

"Nothing to do with the murder, you mean?"

"That's right. It was all her doing. My conscience is clear on that. She told me to bury him, which I did. Then twenty-five years later she told me to dig him up. That's all I did."

Rico was looking into the empty eyes of the skull. They seemed to be draining all the life from his own eyes.

"All you did." Mackendrick echoed him softly and sardonically. "All you did was bury a murdered man and later dig him up and try to dispose of his bones in the sea. Why would you do that if you didn't kill him?"

"Because she told me to."

"Who told you to?"

"Mrs. Chantry."

"She told you to bury her husband's body?"

Mackendrick had risen and stood over Rico, who moved his head from side to side, trying to evade the weight of Mackendrick's shadow.

"It isn't her husband's body."

"Who is it, then?"

"It was just a guy that came to the door one day about twenty-five years ago. He wanted to see Mr. Chantry. I told him that Mr. Chantry was working in his studio and anyway he didn't see people without an appointment. But the guy said Mr. Chantry would see *him* if I gave him his name."

"What *was* his name?" Mackendrick said.

"I'm sorry. I don't remember."

"What did he look like?"

"He just looked ordinary. Kind of pale and flabby, not in good shape. The most outstanding thing about him, he didn't talk too good. I mean, he talked like he had a stroke or something. He sounded like an old bum, only he wasn't that old."

"How old was he?"

"Early thirties, maybe. Older than I was, anyway."

"How was he dressed?"

"Not too good. He had on a kind of brown suit that didn't fit too well. I remember thinking at the time, it looked like he got it at the Salvation Army."

"Did you take him in to see Mr. Chantry?"

"*She* did. They were in the studio talking for quite a while, all three of them."

"What were they talking about?" I said.

"I didn't listen in. They closed the door, and that's a solid oak door about three inches thick. After a while, she brought him out and sent him on his way."

Mackendrick made a contemptuous dry spitting sound. "You just got through telling us that you buried him. Are you withdrawing that statement?"

"No, sir. That was later in the week, when he came back with the woman and the little boy."

"What woman? What little boy?"

"She was a woman around thirty, I'd say. Pretty good figure, otherwise nothing much to look at—kind of a blah brunette. Her little boy was around seven or eight. He was very quiet. He didn't ask questions the way kids usually do. In fact, I didn't hear him say a word the whole time he was there. And no wonder. He must have been right there when it happened."

"What did happen?"

Rico answered slowly, "I don't know for sure. I didn't *see* it happen. But after it was over, there was this body in the greenhouse scrunched up in a big old sack. She said he had a stroke and fell and hit his head and died on her. She said she didn't want any trouble, so I should bury him. She said if I would be nice to her and bury him, then she would be nice to me."

"So you've been in her bed for the last twenty-five years," Mackendrick said with distaste. "And this poor bastard has been in the ground feeding her orchids. Isn't that right?"

Rico lowered his head and looked at the scarred floor between his feet. "I guess it is. But I didn't kill him."

"You covered up for whoever did. Who did?"

"I don't know. I didn't see it happen."

"In the course of twenty-five years in her bed, did you ever think of asking her who killed him?"

"No, sir. It wasn't my business."

"It is now. You're all in this together, I guess you know that—you and Mr. Chantry and Mrs. Chantry and the brunette with the little boy." Mackendrick picked up the skull again and held it, like a memento mori, close to Rico's face. "Are you sure this isn't Mr. Chantry?"

"No, sir. I mean yes, sir, I'm sure it isn't."

"What makes you sure? You buried him in a sack."

"She said it was the other man—the man in the brown suit."

"But all you have is her word for it?"

"Yes, sir."

"Mrs. Chantry's word for it?"

"Yes, sir."

Mackendrick gave the skull a long sad look, which he transferred to me. "Do you have any questions you want to ask him?"

"Thanks, I do, Captain." I turned back to Rico. "Assuming this skull isn't Richard Chantry's, what do you think happened to Richard Chantry?"

"I always thought he just walked away."

"Why?"

"I don't know why."

"Did you ever see him again, or hear from him?"

"No, sir. He left this letter behind—you've probably seen it in the art museum."

"I've seen it. When did he write it?"

"I don't know."

"Between the time he killed this man and the time he walked away?"

"I don't know when he wrote it. I never saw him or talked to him after that day."

"Did Mrs. Chantry tell you where he went?"

"No, sir. I don't believe she knew."

"Did he take anything with him?"

"Not that I know of. *She* looked after his things after he left."

"Was Mrs. Chantry unhappy about his leaving?"

"I don't know. She didn't talk to me about it."

"Not even in bed?"

Rico flushed. "No, sir."

"What about the dark-haired woman and the little boy? Did you ever see them again?"

"No, sir. I didn't go out looking for them, either. They were none of my business."

"What is your business, Rico?"

"Looking after the house and the people. I do the best I can."

"There's only one person left in the house, isn't that right?"

"I guess so. Mrs. Chantry."

I turned to Mackendrick. "Do you think she'll answer questions?"

"I'm not ready to ask them," Mackendrick said in a strained voice. "I have to check with the higher-ups on this."

I wanted to go on checking with the lower-downs, but I needed Mackendrick's cooperation. I waited until Rico had been taken out and placed in a holding cell. When Mackendrick and I were alone in his office with the skull and bones, I told him briefly what had happened, or what I thought had happened, to Betty Siddon.

Mackendrick fidgeted at his desk. His face flushed and became obtuse, as if his circuits were getting overloaded.

Finally he broke in: "I can't do anything about the

Siddon woman tonight. I wouldn't even if I had the men. Women are always taking off on their own little business. She's a good-looking piece; she's probably sacked out in her boyfriend's apartment."

I came close to taking a swing at Mackendrick. I sat and contained my rage, which boiled cold in my head like liquid gas. I told myself to watch it. If I let myself go out of control, as I had been threatening to do all evening, I could find myself locked out of the case, or possibly locked into a holding cell, like Rico.

I concentrated on the skull on the desk, reminding myself that men were supposed to calm down as they got older. When I had myself in hand, I said, "I sort of am her boyfriend."

"I thought so. I still don't have the men to go around knocking on doors. You don't have to worry about her, take my word for it. She's a smart girl and this is her town. If she doesn't turn up overnight, we'll reassess the situation in the morning."

He was beginning to talk like a chief of police. I caught myself hoping that he would never make it. But I seemed to have been elected to help him on his way.

"May I make a couple of suggestions, Captain? And a couple of requests?"

He cast an impatient glance at the electric clock on the wall: it registered close to midnight. "You've earned the right to that."

"We should try to pinpoint the date of this man's death. It should coincide with the date of Chantry's disappearance. That date should be checked for other disappearances, here and in the whole Southern California area, particularly the hospitals and asylums. This man sounds like a possible mental patient." I reached out and touched the poor broken skull.

"We do all that as a matter of routine," Mackendrick said.

"Sure. But this isn't a routine situation. I think you should start burning up the wires."

"Because you're worried about your girl?"

"I'm worried about her and several other people. This isn't just past history that we're dealing with. There are crimes in the present, too, including the crime of murder. And I have a feeling that they're all connected."

"How?"

"Probably through the disappearance of Chantry. That seems to be the central event in the series." I briefly rehearsed the others, beginning with the apparent murder of William Mead in Arizona thirty-two years before, and concluding with the deaths of the art dealers Paul Grimes and Jacob Whitmore.

"What makes you so certain that they're connected?"

"Because the people are connected. Grimes was Chantry's teacher and very good friend. Grimes bought the picture of Mildred Mead from Whitmore. William Mead was Chantry's half brother, and incidentally the son of Mildred Mead. Mildred seems to be one of the two central women in the case. The other one is Mrs. Chantry, of course. If we could get hold of those women and get them talking—"

"Mrs. Chantry is out," Mackendrick said, "at least for the present. I can't bring her in for questioning on Rico's say-so." He looked at me as if he were about to say more, but fell silent.

"What about Mildred Mead?"

Mackendrick reddened in anger or embarrassment. "Who is this Mildred Mead? I never heard of her before."

I showed him my photograph of her picture and told him the story that went with it. "She probably knows more about the background of this case than anybody else. With the possible exception of Mrs. Chantry."

"Where can we find Mildred Mead? Does she live here in town?"

"She did until recently. She probably still does, in one of the nursing homes. She's the woman that Betty Siddon was looking for."

Mackendrick sat and looked at me. His face passed

moon-like through a number of phases, from anger and disgust to acceptance touched with heavy humor.

"Okay," he said, "you win. We'll make the rounds of the nursing homes and see if we can find those two women."

"May I come?"

"No. I'm going to supervise this search myself."

# XXXII

I told myself that it was time I talked to Fred again. It was Mrs. Chantry I really wanted to talk to. But Mackendrick had placed her off-limits and I didn't want to cross him just as he was beginning to cooperate.

I drove across town and parked on Olive Street. The shadows under the trees were as thick and dark as old blood. The tall gray gabled house looked cheerful by comparison, with lights on all three stories. There was an interplay of voices behind the front door.

My knocking silenced the voices. Mrs. Johnson came to the door in her white uniform. Her eyes were bright with emotions I couldn't read. Her face was gray and slack. She looked like a woman who had been pushed to her limit and might break down under further pressure.

"What is it?" she said.

"I thought I'd come by and see how Fred is doing. I just found out that he'd been released."

"Thanks to Mr. Lackner." Her voice had risen, as if I weren't the only one she was talking to. "Do you know Mr. Lackner? He's in the front room with Fred."

The long-haired young lawyer gave me a grip that seemed to have become more powerful in the course of the day. He smiled and called me by name and said that it was nice to see me again. I smiled and congratulated him on his quick work.

Even Fred was smiling for a change, but rather dubiously, as if he had no established right to feel good. The room itself had a tentative air, like a stage set for a play that had closed down soon after opening, a long time ago. The old chesterfield and matching chairs sagged almost to the floor. The curtains at the windows were slightly tattered. There were threadbare places in the carpet where the wooden floor almost showed through.

Like a ghost who haunted the ruined house, Mr. Johnson appeared at the doorway. His face—including his eyes—was red and moist. His breath was like an inconstant wind that had lost its way in a winery. He looked at me without recognition but with dislike, as if I had done him a bad turn in his unremembered past.

"Do I know you?"

"Of course you do," Mrs. Johnson said. "Certainly you know him. This is Mr. Archer."

"I thought so. You're the man who put my boy in jail."

Fred jumped up white and shaking. "That isn't so, Dad. Please don't say things like that."

"I'll say them when they're true. Are you calling me a liar?"

Lackner stepped between the father and son. "This is no time for family quarrels," he said. "We're all happy here—all together and all happy, isn't that right?"

"I'm not happy," Johnson said. "I'm miserable, and you want to know why? Because this sneaking bastard here"—he pointed a wavering forefinger at me—"is lousing up the atmosphere in my front room. And I want it clearly understood that if he stays one minute longer I'll bloody well kill him." He lurched toward me. "Do you understand that, you bastard? You bastard that brought my son home and put him in jail."

"I brought him home," I said. "I didn't put him in jail. That was somebody else's idea."

"But you masterminded it. I know that. You know that."

I turned to Mrs. Johnson. "I think I better leave."

"No. Please." She pressed her doughy face with her fingers. "He isn't himself tonight. He's been drinking heavily all day. He's terribly sensitive; he can't stand all these pressures. Can you, dear?"

"Stop sniveling," he said. "You've been sneaking and sniveling all your life, and that's all right when there's no one around but us chickens. Just don't let down your guard when this man is in the house. He means us no good, you know that. And if he doesn't get out of here while I count to ten, I'll throw him out bodily."

I almost laughed in his face. He was a stout unsteady man whose speech was fed by synthetic energy. Perhaps there had been a time, many years ago, when he was capable of carrying out his threats. But he was fat and flaccid, prematurely aged by alcohol. His face and frame were so draped with adipose tissue that I couldn't imagine what he had looked like as a young man.

Johnson began to count. Lackner and I looked at each other and left the room together. Johnson came stumbling after us, still counting, and slammed the front door behind us.

"Gosh," Lackner said. "What makes a man act that way?"

"Too much to drink. He's a far-gone alcoholic."

"I can see that for myself. But why does he drink like that?"

"Pain," I said. "The pain of being himself. He's been cooped up in that run-down house for God knows how many years. Probably since Fred was a boy. Trying to drink himself to death and not succeeding."

"I still don't understand it."

"Neither do I, really. Every drunk has his own reason. But all of them tend to end up the same, with a soft brain and a diseased liver."

As if we were both looking for someone to blame, Lackner and I glanced up at the sky. Above the dark olive trees that marched in single file along this side of the street, the sky was clouded and the stars were hidden.

"The fact is," Lackner said, "I don't know what to make of the boy, either."

"Do you mean Fred?"

"Yes. I realize I shouldn't call him a boy. He must be almost as old as I am."

"I believe he's thirty-two."

"Really? Then he's a year older than I am. He seems terribly immature for his age."

"His mental growth has been stunted, too, living in this house."

"What's so much the matter with this house? Actually, if it were fixed up, it could be quite elegant. It probably was at one time."

"The people in it are the matter," I said. "There are certain families whose members should all live in different towns—different states, if possible—and write each other letters once a year. You might suggest that to Fred, provided you can keep him out of jail."

"I think I can do that. Mrs. Biemeyer isn't feeling vindictive. In fact, she's a pretty nice woman when you talk to her outside of the family circle."

"It's another one of those families that should write letters once a year," I said. "And forget to mail them. It's really no accident that Fred and Doris got together. Neither of their homes is broken, exactly, but they're both badly bent. So are Fred and Doris."

Lackner wagged his coiffed and bearded head. In the dim clouded moonlight, I felt for a moment that some ancient story was being repeated, that we had all been here before. I couldn't remember exactly what the story was or how it ended. But I felt that the ending somehow depended on me.

I said to Lackner, "Did Fred ever explain to you why he took that picture in the first place?"

"Not in any satisfactory way, no. Has he talked to you about it?"

"He wanted to demonstrate his expertise," I said. "Prove to the Biemeyers that he was good for something. Those were his conscious reasons, anyway."

"What were his unconscious reasons?"

"I don't really know. It would take a panel of psychiatrists to answer that, and they won't tell. But, like a lot of other people in this town, Fred seems to have a fixation on Richard Chantry."

"Do you think the painting was really Chantry's work?"

"Fred thinks so, and he's the expert."

"He doesn't claim to be," Lackner said. "He's just a student."

"Fred's entitled to an opinion, though. And I think it's his opinion that Chantry painted the picture recently, maybe sometime this year."

"How could he know?"

"By the condition of the paint. He says."

"Do you believe that, Mr. Archer?"

"I didn't until tonight. I was pretty well taking it for granted that Richard Chantry was long dead."

"But now you don't."

"Now I don't. I think Chantry is alive and kicking."

"Where?"

"Possibly here in town," I said. "I don't go in much for hunches. But I've got a funny feeling tonight, as if Chantry was breathing on the back of my neck and looking over my shoulder."

I was on the verge of telling Lackner about the human remains that Mrs. Chantry and Rico had dug up in her greenhouse. It wasn't public knowledge yet, and it would have been a violation of my basic rule. Never tell anyone more than he needs to know, because he'll tell somebody else.

At this point, Gerard Johnson came out onto the porch and staggered down the uneven steps. He looked like a dead man walking blind, but his eyes or his nose or his alcoholic's radar picked me up and dragged him through the weeds in my direction.

"Are you still here, you bastard?"

"I'm still here, Mr. Johnson."

"Don't 'mister' me. I know how you feel. You treat me with disrespect. You think I'm a stinking old drunk. But I'm here to tell you with my last breath that I'm a better man—right here as I stand, I'm a better man than you ever were and I'm ready to prove it."

I didn't ask him how. I didn't have to. He thrust his right hand into the sagging pocket of his pants and brought it out holding a nickel-plated revolver, the kind cops like to call a "Saturday-night special." I heard the click of the hammer, and dived for Johnson's legs. He went down.

I climbed rapidly up his recumbent body and took the gun away from him. It was empty. My hands were shaking.

Gerald Johnson struggled to his feet and began to shout. He shouted at me and at his wife and son as they came out on the porch. The words he used were mostly scatological. He raised his voice and shouted at his house. He shouted at the houses across the road and down the street.

More lights came on in those houses, but no one appeared at the windows or opened the doors. Perhaps if someone had appeared, Johnson might have felt less lonely.

It was his son, Fred, who took pity on him. Fred came down off the porch and put his arms around Johnson from behind, encircling his laboring chest.

"Please act like a human being, Dad."

Johnson struggled and surged and swore, and gradually left off shouting. Fred's face was wet with tears. The sky tore like a net and the moon swam out.

Suddenly the night had changed its weather. It was higher and brighter and stranger. Holding Johnson around the shoulders, Fred walked him up the steps and into the house. It was a sad and touching thing to see the lost son fathering his father. There was no real hope for Johnson, but there was still hope for Fred. Lackner agreed. I turned the gun over to him before he drove away in his Toyota.

Fred had left the front door open, and after a moment Mrs. Johnson came out and down the steps. Her body moved aimlessly, like a stray animal. The light from the sky silvered her uniform.

"I want to apologize."

"For what?"

"Everything."

She flung out her arm in an awkward sideways gesture, as much a brushing away as an embracing. It seemed to take in the gabled house and everyone and everything in it, her family and the neighbors, and the street, the thick dark olive trees and their darker shadows, the moon that drenched her in its cold light and deeply scored her face.

"Don't apologize to me," I said. "I chose this job, or it chose me. There's a lot of human pain involved in it, but I'm not looking for another job."

"I know what you mean. I'm a nurse. I may be an unemployed nurse by tomorrow. I just had to come home on account of Fred getting out, and I walked off my shift. It's about time I walked back on."

"Can I offer you a lift?"

She gave me a quick suspicious look, as if I might have designs on her heavy middle-aged body. But she said, "You're very kind, sir. Fred left our car someplace in Arizona. I don't know if it's even worth bringing back."

I opened the door for her. She reacted as if this hadn't happened to her for some time.

When we were both in the car, I said, "There's a question I'd like to ask you. You don't have to answer it. But if you do, I don't plan to pass your answer on to anybody."

She stirred in her seat and turned toward me. "Has somebody been bad-mouthing me?"

"About those drugs that were missing at the hospital, do you want to discuss it some more?"

She said, "I admit I took a few sample pills. But I didn't take them for myself, or for any wrong purpose. I wanted to try them out on Gerard, and see if I could get him to cut down on his drinking. I guess they could get me on a technical charge of prescribing medicine without being a doctor. But nearly every nurse I ever knew does that." She gave me an anxious look. "Are they thinking about bringing charges?"

"Not to my knowledge."

"Then how did the subject come up?"

"One of the nurses at the hospital mentioned it. She was explaining why you'd been fired."

"That was the excuse they used. But I'll tell you why I was fired. There were people in that institution that didn't like me." We were passing the hospital, and she pointed an accusing finger at the great lighted building. "I may not be the easiest person to get along with. But I am a good nurse, and they had no right to fire me. You had no right to bring it up with them, either."

"I think I had, Mrs. Johnson."

"What gives you the right?"

"I'm investigating a couple of murders, as well as the missing picture. You know that."

"You think I know where the picture is? I don't. Fred doesn't either. We're not thieves. We may have problems in the family, but we're not that kind of people."

"I never said you were. People can change, though, if they get involved with drugs. It gives other people a handle to use on them."

"Nobody's got that kind of a handle on me. I took a few pills, I admit it. I gave them to Gerard. And now I'm paying for it. I'll be spending the rest of my working days in understaffed nursing homes. That is, if I'm lucky enough to hold any job at all."

She fell into a glum silence that lasted most of the way to the La Paloma. Before she left the car, I told her about the women I was looking for, Mildred Mead and Betty Siddon.

She listened gravely. "I'll do what I can. I won't have much time for phoning on *this* night shift. But I'll pass the word along to some nurses I know in the other nursing homes." She added haltingly, as if it cost her a moral effort to acknowledge any debt: "Fred told me how you treated him in Arizona. I appreciate that. After all, I'm his mother," she said in something like surprise.

She stepped out onto the asphalt and moved heavily toward the half-lighted building. Beyond the wall that enclosed the parking lot, cars went by in unceasing flight and pursuit on mourning tires. Mrs. Johnson turned as she reached the doorway and lifted her hand to me.

A moment after she entered, Mrs. Johnson backed out of the doorway. She was closely followed by two cops. One was in uniform. The other was Captain Mackendrick. I heard her complaining as I approached that they had no right to jump on her in the dark, she was an innocent woman on her way to work.

Mackendrick scanned her angry frightened face. "You're Mrs. Johnson, aren't you? Fred Johnson's mother?"

"That is correct," she said coldly. "It doesn't give you any license to scare me out of my wits."

"I didn't mean to do that, ma'am. I'm sorry."

"You ought to be sorry." Mrs. Johnson was pressing her advantage. "You have no right to harry me and harass me. We've got a good lawyer working on our behalf, and you'll be hearing from him if you don't look out."

Mackendrick gazed helplessly at the sky and then at me. "Look, did I do anything wrong? I bumped into a woman accidentally in the dark. I apologized. Do I have to get down on my knees?"

"Mrs. Johnson is a little nervous tonight."

She nodded approvingly in my direction. "You bet I am. What are you doing here, anyway, Captain?"

"We're making a search for a woman."

"Miss Siddon?"

"That's correct, ma'am." Mackendrick gave her a sharp inquiring look. "Who told you about Miss Siddon?"

"Mr. Archer here. He asked me to phone some of my friends in the other nursing homes. I said I would if I got the time, and I will. May I go now?"

"Please do," Mackendrick said. "Nobody's interfering with your movements in any way, shape, or form. But it may not be a good idea to call the other nursing homes. We'd rather surprise 'em."

Mrs. Johnson went into the building for a second time, and didn't reappear.

"She's a tough old babe," Mackendrick said.

"She's had a tough couple of days. Could you and I have a word in private, Captain?"

He jerked his head at the man in uniform, who climbed into the police car. We walked to the far corner of the lot, as far as possible from the building and the highway. A native oak that had somehow kept itself alive in this waste of pavement extended its faint moon-shadow to us.

I said, "What brought you here?"

"We got a tip. Someone phoned in and said we should look here for Miss Siddon. That's why I came over myself. We went through the place with a fine-toothed comb and found no trace of her or anybody like her."

"Who provided the tip?"

"It was anonymous—evidently some woman trying to stir up trouble. Mrs. Johnson's the kind who makes enemies. She got herself fired from the hospital, you know."

"So she was telling me. You don't need my opinion, Captain, but I'll give it to you anyway. I think I gave you a bum steer on this search of the nursing homes. I'm not suggesting you call it off entirely. But I think it's time to concentrate your own energies on something else."

Mackendrick was slow to answer. "You mean Mrs. Chantry, don't you?"

"She seems to be at the center of this case."

"We don't know that."

"I think we do."

"What you think isn't good enough, Archer. I can't move against that woman without enough evidence to sink her."

# XXXIII

I parked at the head of Mrs. Chantry's street and walked down to her house. Fog was crawling up the barranca behind it. On the hill above, the Biemeyers' place was full of cold light. But Mrs. Chantry's house was dark and still.

I knocked on the front door. I must have half expected to find her dead, or gone, because her immediate response took me by surprise.

As if she'd been waiting there all night, she said through the door, "Who is that? Rico?"

I didn't answer her. We stood on opposite sides of the door in a long waiting silence. It was unevenly filled by the noise of the waves that mounted the beach like giant blundering footsteps and then slid back again.

"Who is that?" she said on a rising note.

"Archer."

"Go away."

"Should I go and get Captain Mackendrick?"

There was another silence, measured by the thumping, slumping footsteps of the sea. Then she unlocked the door and opened it.

There were no lights in the hallway or, so far as I

could see, in the house. Against the interior darkness, her hair and her face were the same silvery color. She had on a high-necked dark dress, which suggested that she was a widow and made me wonder if she was.

"Come in if you must," she said in a small cold voice.

I followed her into the main room where her party had been held. She switched on a floor lamp above an armchair and stood beside it waiting. We faced each other in dead silence. Her party had left no echoes in the room.

Finally she said, "I know your type. You're one of those self-elected experts who can't keep his sharp little nose out of other people's business. You just can't bear to see them live their lives without your horning in, can you?"

She flushed, perhaps partly in anger. But what she was saying seemed to have other pressures behind it, too.

I said, "You call this a life that you're living? Covering up a murder for a man you haven't seen in twenty-five years. Sleeping with a boy-man like Rico to keep him quiet."

As if the lighting in the room had changed drastically, the color left her face and her eyes darkened.

"Nobody talks to me like that."

"You might as well get used to it. When the D.A.'s men make their case in Superior Court, they won't be mincing their words."

"The case will never get to court. There is no case." But her eyes were strained and questioning, trying to see over the sharp edge of the present.

"Come off it, Mrs. Chantry. Twenty-five years ago, a man was killed in this house. I don't know who he was but you probably do. Rico buried him in the greenhouse. Tonight, with some help from you, he dug up his bones and put them in a weighted sack. Unfortunately for both of you, I caught him before he threw them in the sea. Do you want to know where they are now?"

She turned her face away. She didn't want to know.

Suddenly, as if her legs had collapsed, she sat down in the armchair. She covered her face with her hands and appeared to be trying to cry.

I stood and listened to her painful noises. Handsome as she was, and deep in trouble, I couldn't feel much sympathy for her. She had built her life on a dead man's bones, and death had taken partial possession of her.

As if our minds had been tracking each other, she said, "Where are the bones now?"

"Captain Mackendrick has them. He has your friend Rico, too. And Rico's been talking."

She sat and absorbed the knowledge. It seemed to make her physically smaller. But the hard intelligence in her eyes didn't fade.

"I think I can handle Mackendrick. He's ambitious. I'm not so sure about you. But you do work for money, don't you?"

"I have all the money I need."

She leaned forward, her ringed fists on her knees. "I'm thinking about quite a lot of money. More than you can ever accumulate in a lifetime. Enough to retire on."

"I like my work."

She made a bitter face, and succeeded in looking quite ugly. She struck her knees with her fists. "Don't play with me. I'm serious."

"So am I. I don't want your money. But you could try bribing me with information."

"Bribe you to do what, exactly?"

"Give you an even break if you've got one coming."

"All you want to do is play God, right?"

"Not exactly. I would like to understand why a woman like you, with everything going for her, would try to cover up a lousy murder."

"It wasn't a murder. It was an accident."

"Who committed the accident?"

"You don't believe me, do you?"

"You haven't given me anything to believe, or not to believe. All I know is that you and Rico dug up a dead man's bones; then you sent Rico to sink them in the sea. That was a foolish thing to do, Mrs. Chantry. You should have left them underground in the greenhouse."

"I don't think so. My mistake was getting Rico to handle it. I should have disposed of the body myself."

"Whose body was it, Mrs. Chantry?"

She shook her head as if the past were swarming like bees around her. "He was a stranger to me. He came to the house asking to see my husband. Richard shouldn't have seen him, and normally wouldn't have. But evidently the man's name meant something to him. He told Rico to send the man into his studio. And when I saw the man again, he was dead."

"What was the dead man's name?"

"I don't remember."

"Were you there when the dead man talked to Rico?"

"Yes, at least part of the time."

"And later when Rico buried the body?"

"I knew what was being done. I didn't participate in the burial."

"Rico said you ordered it."

"I suppose I did, in a sense. I was relaying my husband's wish."

"Where was your husband at the time of the burial?"

"He was in his studio, writing his farewell letter. It's a strange thing," she added after a moment. "He'd often spoken of taking off in that way. Dropping everything, starting a new, unencumbered life. And then the occasion came up, and he did just that."

"Do you know where he went?"

"No. I haven't heard from him since. Neither has anyone else, to my knowledge."

"Do you think he's dead?"

"I hope he isn't. He was—he is a great man, after all."

She let herself cry a little. She seemed to be trying to regain lost emotional ground, rebuilding the Chantry myth with the materials that came to hand, partly old and partly new.

"Why did he kill the man in the brown suit?"

"I don't know that he did. It may have been an accident."

"Did your husband claim it was an accident?"

"I don't know. We didn't talk about it. He wrote his letter and went."

"You have no idea how or why the man was killed?"

"None whatever."

"Your husband gave you no explanation at all?"

"No. Richard left in such a hurry there was no time for explanations."

"That isn't the way I heard it, Mrs. Chantry. According to Rico, you and your husband and the man in the brown suit did some talking in the studio. What were you talking about?"

"I don't remember that," she said.

"Rico does."

"He's a liar."

"Most men are, when they get into real trouble. So are most women."

She was losing her self-assurance, and anger seemed to be taking its place again. "Could you possibly spare me your generalizations? I've been through quite a lot in the last twenty-four hours and I don't have the strength to listen to a cheap private detective mouthing moral maxims."

Her voice was high, and she looked tormented.

I said, "You've been through quite a lot in the last twenty-five years. It'll go on and get worse unless you do something to end it."

She sat in silence for a while, her gaze turned inward on the unburied past. "End it how?" she said finally.

"Tell me what actually happened, and why."

"I have been."

"Not really, Mrs. Chantry. You've left out some of the most important things. Who the man in the brown suit was, and why he came here. The fact that he came

here twice, and when he came here the second time—
the time that he was killed—he had a woman and a
small boy with him. The fact that you told Rico the
man had a stroke and died more or less by accident."

She sat and absorbed this, too, like someone un-
dergoing a rapid aging process. She didn't try to evade
it or push it away. In a sense, it appeared to be what she
had been waiting for.

"So Rico did a lot of talking," she said.

"All he had time for. You picked a lousy co-
conspirator."

"I didn't pick him. He simply happened to be here."
She looked me over carefully, as if perhaps I might be
used to take Rico's place in her life. "I had no choice."

"People always have some kind of choice."

She hung her pretty head and brushed it with her
hand in a desolate twisting gesture. "That's easy to say.
Not so easy to act on."

"You have a choice to make now," I said. "You can
cooperate with me—"

"I thought I had been."

"Some. But you're holding back. You can help me to
sort out this case. And if you do, I'll make it as easy for
you as I can."

"Don't do me any favors." But she was studying my
face for the exact meaning of what I had said.

"You wouldn't be well advised," I said, "to go on
trying to cover up for your husband. You could end up
with your own share of a murder rap."

"It wasn't a murder. It was an accident. The man was
in poor shape. My husband may have struck or pushed
him. He had no intention of killing him."

"How do you know?"

"He told me. He wasn't lying."

"Did he tell you who the man was?"

"Yes."

"What was his name?"

She shook her head in a quick distracted movement.
"I don't remember. He was simply a man my husband

had known in the army. The man had been wounded in the Pacific, and spent some years in a veterans' hospital. When they finally released him, he came here to see my husband. Apparently he'd heard of Richard's success as a painter and came here to bask in reflected glory."

"Who were the woman and the little boy?"

"They were the man's wife and son. The second time he came, he brought them to meet my husband."

"Were they aware that your husband killed the man?"

"I don't know. I'm not even certain that that's what happened."

"But you assumed it."

"Yes. I had to. I kept waiting to hear from the woman. I hardly slept for weeks. But I never did hear from her. Sometimes I wonder if I imagined the whole thing."

"The bones Rico dug up aren't imaginary."

"I know that. I meant the woman and the little boy."

"What happened to them?"

"They simply went away—I don't know where. And I went on with my life as best I could."

There was self-pity in her voice, but she was watching me in cold surmise. The contours of her body appeared to be aware of me, more in resignation than anything else.

Below the house, the sea thumped and fumbled and slid like a dead man trying clumsily to climb back into life. I shivered. She touched my knee with her tapered fingers.

"Are you cold?"

"I suppose I am."

"I suppose I could turn on the heat."

The smile that went with the offer lent it a double meaning, but it was forced.

"I won't be staying, Mrs. Chantry."

"I'll be all alone here."

She uttered a mock sigh, which ended on a note of

genuine desolation. She seemed to be realizing how completely alone she was.

"You'll be having visitors before long."

Her hands came together and clenched. "You mean the police, don't you?"

"You can probably expect Mackendrick in the morning, if not before."

"I thought you were going to help me," she said in a small voice.

"I will if you let me. You haven't told me enough. And some of the things you've told me aren't true."

She gave me an angry look, but it was calculated and controlled. "I haven't been lying."

"Maybe not consciously. When you live a phony life for twenty-five years, it's possible to get a bit out of touch."

"Are you telling me I'm out of my mind?"

"More likely you're simply lying, to yourself as well as me."

"What did I say that wasn't true?"

"You said the dead man was an old army friend of your husband's. I happen to know that Chantry was never in the army. That one discrepancy casts doubt on your whole story."

She flushed and bit her lower lip and looked at me like a thief. "I was just talking loosely. I meant that the dead man had been in the army at the time they met. But of course Richard wasn't."

"Do you want to make some other corrections in your account?"

"If you'll tell me where I went wrong."

A spurt of anger went through me. "It isn't so funny, Mrs. Chantry. Several people have been killed. Others are in danger."

"Not from me. I've never injured anyone in my life."

"You've stood by and let it happen."

"Not by choice." She tried to project a look of candor, which failed to come off. "I don't know what happened between Richard and the dead man. I have no idea what their relationship actually was."

"I've been told your husband was bisexual."

"Really? This is the first I've heard of it."

"Are you telling me he wasn't?"

"The question never came up. Why is it so important to you?"

"It may be an essential part of the case."

"I doubt it. Richard wasn't a very sexual man at all. He was more excited by his work than he ever was by me."

She made a doleful mouth and looked at me to measure its effect. For some reason, it made me angrier. I had had enough of the woman and her lies, enough of her truth as well. While I sat trading words with her, a woman I cared about was lost in the dangerous night.

"Do you know where Betty Siddon is?"

She shook her silver head. "I'm afraid I don't. Has something happened to Betty Jo?"

"She went looking for Mildred Mead and got lost herself. Do you know where I can find Mildred Mead?"

"No. I don't. She phoned me a few months ago, when she'd just come to town. But I didn't want to see her. I didn't want to stir up all the old memories."

"Then you should never have dug up those bones," I said.

She swore at me violently, damning me to hell. But the wish rebounded, almost as if she'd meant it for herself in the first place. A gray look of self-loathing dropped like a veil across her face. She covered it with her hands.

"Why did you dig them up?" I said.

She was silent for a while. Then she said behind her hands, "I simply panicked."

"Why?"

"I was afraid the place would be searched, and I would be blamed for the man's death."

She was watching me between her fingers, like a woman behind bars.

"Did somebody threaten you with exposure?"

She didn't answer. I took this to mean yes. "Who was it, Mrs. Chantry?"

"I'm not sure. She didn't come here. She phoned me last night and threatened to go to the police with what she knew. I think it was the woman who came here with the little boy the day the man was killed."

"What did she want from you?"

"Money." She dropped her hands: her mouth was twisted and her eyes were hard.

"How much?"

"She didn't specify. A large amount, I gather."

"When does she want it?"

"Tomorrow. She said she'd call me again tomorrow, and meanwhile I should raise all the money I could."

"Do you plan to do that?"

"I had planned to. But there's no point in it now, is there? Unless you and I can come to some arrangement."

She thrust her hands into her hair and held her head between them, chin high, like a work of art that she was offering for lease or outright sale.

I said, "I'll do what I can. But you can't keep Mackendrick out of this. If you can help him to close the case, he'll be grateful. I think you should get in touch with him right away."

"No. I need time to think. Will you give me until morning?"

"I will on one condition. Don't do anything rash."

"Like run away, you mean?"

"Like kill yourself."

She shook her head in a short angry movement. "I'm going to stay here and fight. I hope you'll be on my side."

I didn't commit myself. As I got up to leave, the eyes of Chantry's portraits seemed to be watching me from the shadowed walls.

Mrs. Chantry followed me to the door. "Please don't judge me harshly. I know I appear to be a wicked person. But I've really had very little choice about the things I've done, or left undone. My life wasn't easy even before my husband took off. And since then it's been a kind of shabby hell."

"With Rico."

"Yes. With Rico. I said I had no real choice."

She was standing close to me, her eyes hooded and calculating, as if she might be getting ready to make another unfortunate choice.

I said, "A young soldier named William Mead was murdered in Arizona over thirty years ago. He was the illegitimate son of Felix Chantry by Mildred Mead— your husband's half brother."

She reacted as though I had struck her and she was about to cry out. Her eyebrows rose and her lower lip dropped. For a moment, her face was open. But she didn't make a sound.

"Your husband left Arizona immediately afterwards, and there was some suspicion that he had killed William Mead. Did he?"

"Certainly not. What reason would he have?"

"I was hoping you could tell me. Weren't you quite close to William at one time?"

"No. Of course not."

But there was no conviction in her denial.

# XXXIV

I left her and drove south along the waterfront. The traffic was still fairly heavy. It wasn't really late, but I was tired. The long indeterminate conversation with Mrs. Chantry had drained my energy.

I checked in at my motel, hoping that Betty might have left a message for me.

She hadn't. But there was one from Paola Grimes, who wanted me to call her at the Monte Cristo Hotel. I got the front desk of the hotel after some difficulty.

Paola answered her room phone on the first ring: "Hello?"

"This is Archer."

"It's about time." Her voice was flat and angry. "My mother told me she gave you some money for me. Fifty dollars. I need it. I can't get out of this flea-trap without it, and my van won't start, either."

"I'll bring you your fifty now. I tried to deliver it earlier."

"You could have left it at the desk."

"Not that desk. I'll see you, Paola."

I found her waiting for me in the Monte Cristo lobby. She had evidently brushed her hair and washed her face and put on fresh lipstick. But she looked sad and out of place among the night-blooming girls and their followers.

I handed her the fifty dollars. She counted and rolled the bills, and thrust them into her brassière.

I said, "Will that cover your hotel bill?"

"Up until now I guess it will. I don't know about to-morrow. The police want me to stick around but they won't release any of my father's money. He was carrying quite a lot of money."

"You'll get it back, or your mother will."

"Or my great-grandchildren will," she said bitterly. "I don't trust cops and I don't like this town. I don't like the people here. They killed my father and I'm afraid they'll kill me."

Her fear was contagious. I followed the movements of her eyes and began to see the place as she was seeing it, an anteroom where lost souls waited for a one-night stand that was never going to end.

"Who killed your father?"

She shook her head, and her black hair fell like night

around her face. "I don't want to talk about it. Not here."

"We could talk in your room."

"No, thanks." She gave me a sharp dark paranoid look, like a frightened animal peering out from the cover of her hair. "The room may be bugged. That's one reason I can't stay in it."

"Who would bug it?"

"Maybe the cops. Maybe the killers. What difference does it make? They're all in this together."

"Come out and sit in my car."

"No, thanks."

"Then let's take a walk, Paola."

Surprisingly she agreed. We went out and joined the people on the sidewalk. Across the road, a line of palms tossed their plumes above the empty booths of the weekly art show. Beyond them the phosphorescent white waves broke and rose and receded as if they had been set the eternal task of marking time and measuring space.

Gradually, as we moved along the sidewalk, Paola became less tense. Our movements seemed to relate to the natural rhythms of the sea. The sky opened out above us, poorly lit by the low sinking moon on the horizon.

Paola touched my arm. "You asked me who killed my father."

"Yes."

"You want to know what I think?"

"Tell me what you think."

"Well, I've been going over in my mind everything my father said. You know, he believed that Richard Chantry was alive and staying here in town under a different name. And he thought that Chantry actually painted that picture of Mildred Mead. I thought so, too, when I saw it. I don't claim to be an expert, like my father, but it looked like a Chantry to me."

"Are you sure your father's opinion was honest,

Paola? The picture was worth a lot more to him if it was a Chantry."

"I know that, and so did he. That's why he did his best to authenticate it. He spent the last days of his life trying to locate Chantry and trace the picture to him. He even looked up Mildred Mead, who is living here in town. She was Chantry's favorite model, though of course she didn't actually sit for that particular portrait. She's an old woman now."

"Have you seen her?"

She nodded. "My father took me to see her a couple of days before he was killed. Mildred was a friend of my mother's in Arizona, and I've known her ever since I was a child. My father probably thought that having me there would get her talking. But Mildred didn't say much the day we visited her."

"Exactly where was this?"

"She has a little place in a court. She was just moving in. I think it's called Magnolia Court. There's a big magnolia tree in the middle of it."

"In town here?"

"Yes. It's in the downtown section. She said she took it because she couldn't do much walking any more. She didn't talk much, either."

"Why not?"

"I think she was scared. My father kept pressing her about Richard Chantry. Was he alive or dead? Did he paint that picture? But she didn't want to talk about him. She said she hadn't seen him in over thirty years and he was probably dead, and she hoped he was. She sounded very bitter."

"I'm not surprised. Chantry may have killed her son William."

"And he may have killed my father, too. My father could have traced the picture to him and got himself killed for his trouble."

Her voice was low and frightened. She looked around suspiciously at the palms and the low moon, as if they were parts of a shabby stage set hiding the actual jungle life of the world. Her hands grasped at each other and pulled in opposing directions.

"I've got to get out of this town. The police say I have to stick around, they need me for a witness. But they're not even protecting me."

"Protecting you from what?" I said, though I knew the answer.

"Chantry. Who else? He killed my father—I know that in my bones. But I don't know who he is or where he is. I don't even know what he looks like any more. He could be any man I meet on the street."

Her voice was rising. Other people on the sidewalk had begun to notice us. We were approaching a restaurant-bar that was spilling jazz through its open front door. I steered her in and sat her at a table. The room was narrow and deep, resembling a tunnel, and the band at its far end was like a train coming.

"I don't like that music," she said.

"No matter. You need a drink."

She shook her dark head. "I can't drink. Alcohol drives me crazy. It was the same with my father. He told me that was why he went on drugs." She covered her ears with her hands and closed her eyes. "I've got to get out of here."

I took her hand and drew her to her feet. Pulling and jerking against my movements, she followed me out. She stared at the people on the street in profound distrust, ready to yell if anyone looked twice at her. She was on the narrow edge of hysteria or something worse.

I gripped her arm and walked her quickly in the direction of the hotel.

She hung back. "I don't want to go back there. I don't like it there. They kept me up all night, knocking and fooling around and whispering. They think that any woman is their meat."

"Then check out of the place."

"I wouldn't know where to go. I guess I could go back to the gallery. I have a little room in the back there. But I'm afraid to."

"Because your father isn't there?"

"No." She hugged herself and shuddered. "Because he might come back."

That sent a chill through me. I didn't quite believe that the woman was losing her mind, but she was trying hard to. If she went on like this, she might succeed before morning.

For various reasons, I felt responsible for her. I made a kind of superstitious bargain with the controlling forces of the world, if any. If I tried to look after Paola, then maybe Betty would be looked after.

I took Paola into the Monte Cristo and paid her bill and helped her pack her suitcase and carried it out to my car.

She trotted along beside me. "Where are we going?"

"I'll get you a room in my motel. It's across from the yacht harbor, and it's quieter. There's an all-night restaurant on the corner if you get hungry."

"I'm hungry now," she said. "I haven't been eating."

I took her to the restaurant for a sandwich, then got her checked into the motel. Biemeyer could pay for her room. She was a witness.

I left the motel without going into my own room. But when I was out in the parking lot getting into my car, I had a sudden wild idea that Betty might be waiting for me in that room. I went and looked. The room was empty, the bed unslept-in.

There was only one thing I could do: follow my case until it took me to her. Not too late. Please.

# XXXV

The magnolia tree hung like a tethered cloud over the court to which it had given its name. There was light in only one of the small cottages, shining dimly through drawn blinds. I tapped on the screen door.

I heard a movement behind it, and then a breathing silence. A woman's voice finally said, "Who is that?"

"My name is Archer. I'm a private detective working for Jack Biemeyer."

"Then you can go plumb to hell," she said quietly. "But before you do you can go back and tell Jack Biemeyer to do the same."

"I'll be glad to, Miss Mead. I don't like that s.o.b. either."

She opened the inner door, a small and dainty figure against the light. "What did you say your name was?"

"Lew Archer."

"Did Jack Biemeyer send you here?"

"Not exactly. He had a picture stolen—a painting of you. I thought you might be able to help me trace it."

"How did Jack know I was here? I haven't told a living soul."

"Paola Grimes sent me."

"I see. I should have known better than to let her into my house." Her body had stiffened as if she were getting ready to slam the door in my face. "She's a bad-luck member of a bad-luck family."

"I talked to her mother, Juanita, this morning in Copper City. She sent her best wishes to you."

"Did she? That's nice."

I had said the right thing. She moved to unlatch the

outer door. Until then, she hadn't shown her age. She was lame, and her hips moved awkwardly. I was reminded of certain kinds of pelagic birds that move at ease in the air or on the ocean, but have a hard time walking.

Her white head was like a bird's. It was sparse and elegant, with hollow cheeks, a thin straight nose, eyes that still had distance and wildness. She caught me looking at her, and smiled. One of her front teeth was missing. It gave her a gamine touch.

"Do you like my looks? I can't say they've improved with age."

"That's true."

She went on smiling. "Who would want them to? My looks got me into more trouble. I don't mean to complain. A woman can't have everything in her life. I traveled a lot—first class a good deal of the time. I knew some talented and famous men."

"I met one of them in Tucson yesterday."

"Lashman?"

"Yes."

"How is he?"

"Getting old. But he's still painting. As a matter of fact, when I left him he was working on another portrait of you."

She was silent for a moment. Her head was poised and her eyes were empty. "The way I am now, or the way I was?"

"The way you were."

"Of course, it would have to be. He hasn't seen me since I got really old." She talked about herself as if she were an object of art that unfortunately hadn't been made to last—a Japanese flower arrangement or a song by a composer who didn't know musical notation. "But that's enough about me. Tell me about Juanita."

She sat in an armchair under a standing lamp, and I sat facing her. I gave her a brief report on Juanita Grimes, then on Juanita's ex-husband, Paul, and his death.

She seemed shocked by the knowledge. "I can't believe Paul Grimes is dead. He was here just the other day, with his daughter."

"So she told me. I understand he wanted you to authenticate a painting of you."

"That was the general idea. Unfortunately I couldn't place it. All he had was a small photograph of it, and I've been painted so many times I lost track long ago. As a matter of fact, I've got very bored with pictures, especially pictures of my own face. I haven't hung any pictures since I moved in, though I've got a ton of them in the back room." She waved her fingers at the bare walls. "It's no fun being reminded of what you've lost."

"I know that. But would you mind taking another look at a photograph of a picture?"

"A picture of me?"

"I think so. It's the same picture that Paul Grimes was interested in."

I got out my photograph of the painting and handed it to her. She held it up to the light and studied it. Then she let out a little wordless grunt of recognition.

"Have you seen it before, Miss Mead?"

"This is the third time I've seen it. The second time tonight. But I still can't say for sure who painted it, or when. It looks like a Chantry, all right, but I don't remember him painting it."

"It's been suggested that it was a memory picture, one you never sat for—maybe done quite recently."

"That's what the young woman was saying this evening."

"What young woman?"

"The girl from the local paper. I told her I don't give interviews. But she was very persistent and I finally let her come. I must admit she was nice enough. I wasn't much help to her, though."

"Was her name Betty Siddon?"

"That's it. Betty Siddon. Do you know her?"

"I've been trying to get in touch with her. Did she tell you where she was going from here?"

"She said something about a beach—Sycamore Beach?"

"Sycamore Point?"

"I guess that was it. Anyway, the man who sold the picture to Paul Grimes drowned in the ocean there the other day. What was his name?"

"Jake Whitmore. He didn't drown in the ocean, though. He was drowned in fresh water, probably in somebody's bathtub."

Without intending to, I had succeeded in shocking her. The life and color drained from her face. Its bones still made it handsome, though her eyes had gone as dead as any statue's.

Her pale mauve mouth said, "This Whitmore was murdered, too?"

"The police and the coroner think so."

"Jesus." She was breathing like a runner.

"Can I get you some water, Miss Mead?"

"Got something better than that." She pointed at a cabinet against the wall. "There's a fifth of Jack Daniel's in there. And glasses. Pour yourself one, too. I take mine straight. Double."

I got out the whisky and poured her a double shot and myself a single. She took hers in a single gulp. She asked for another double. I poured it, and she drank it. I watched the color rise in her face.

"Drink yours down," she said. "I hate to drink alone."

I wondered if she was an alcoholic, and decided she probably was.

"Why are you looking at me like that?" she said. "Do I look funny? Do my eyes look funny?"

"No. They look fine."

"Then quit staring at me like that."

"I'm sorry. I have to leave, anyway."

"You're interested in that Siddon girl, aren't you?"

"Yes, I am. You're a mind reader."

"I know men," she said. "Isn't she a little young for you?"

"Maybe. How long ago was she here?"

"I didn't look at the time. It was early in the evening."

"How did she find you?"

"She called the—" The old woman's mouth clamped shut. After a short period of strained silence, she said, "I have no idea."

"You were going to say she called somewhere."

"Was I? Then you know more than I do. I must have been thinking about something else. Don't let me keep you—you say you have to go. Just leave that bottle where I can reach it, will you?"

She touched the table beside her chair with one of her wrinkled white hands.

I said, "I'm not leaving yet."

"I wish you would. I'm very tired. Anyway, I've told you all I know."

"I seriously doubt that, Miss Mead. When I was in Arizona, I stumbled into some very interesting facts. Back in the early forties, your natural son William was killed by someone and left in the desert."

Her face grew paler and longer. "Juanita Grimes always did talk a lot."

"She wasn't my main source. Your son's murder was and is public knowledge. I talked to the man who discovered his body and investigated his death. Sheriff Brotherton."

"So?"

"Aren't you interested in who killed your son?"

"It doesn't matter now," she said. "What difference can it possibly make? He's dead. He's been dead for over thirty-two years."

"But I think the man who killed him is still alive."

"How can you know that?"

"I feel it in my bones. Not that there isn't plenty of evidence. There have been other deaths. Paul Grimes, Jacob Whitmore. And the man whose remains were dug up tonight in Richard Chantry's greenhouse."

She tried to speak, and succeeded on her second attempt. "What man?"

"He hasn't been identified yet, but he will be. He came to Chantry's house about twenty-five years ago with a woman and a little boy. There was an argument, and a fight between him and Chantry. According to the account I heard, the man fell down and hit his head and died. The Chantrys buried him."

"Did Mrs. Chantry tell you this?" she said.

"Some of it."

Her eyes widened while the rest of her face had tightened and thinned. She looked like a kestrel or some other small bird of prey.

"What else did Mrs. Chantry tell you?"

"That was the gist of it. What else was there to tell?"

"I'm asking you," she said.

"But I think you're the one who knows the answer. Why did Jack Biemeyer buy you the house in Chantry Canyon?"

"Because I asked him to."

"Jack Biemeyer isn't that generous."

"He was to me, in those days." A little color came into her face and gathered on her cheekbones. "I admit he hasn't improved with age. But then neither have I."

"I suggest that Biemeyer bought you that house on behalf of the Chantry family. Or possibly they gave it to you, by way of him, for nothing."

"What reason would they have to do that?"

"To keep you quiet about your son William's murder."

"William's death was public knowledge. What was there to be quiet about?"

"Who killed him. I think it was Richard Chantry. He left Arizona for California right after the murder and never went back. The case against him was quashed, or never developed. If you had any suspicions, you kept them to yourself."

She shook her head. "You don't know me. I loved my son. When they showed me William's body, I almost died myself. And don't forget he was a Chantry, too.

Felix Chantry was his natural father. And there was no bad blood between William and Richard."

"Then why did Richard leave Arizona immediately after William's death?"

"I don't know. Perhaps he was afraid of being murdered, too."

"Did he say that?"

"I never discussed it with him. As a matter of fact, I haven't seen Richard since then."

"Since William's death?"

"That's right. I haven't seen Richard once in thirty-two years. Nobody's seen him in the last twenty-five years. And I didn't find out why until tonight, from you." She moved restlessly, and looked at the bottle beside her. "If you're planning to stay around for a while, you might as well pour me another. And yourself, too."

"No, thanks. I have a few more questions, and that should do it. I understand that when your son William was killed he left behind a wife and a small son."

Her eyes changed as if she were looking inward and downward into the past. "I believe he did."

"You mean you don't know?"

"I've been told about them. I've never seen them."

"Why not?"

"It wasn't through any wish of mine. They simply dropped out of sight. I did hear a rumor that the woman, William's widow, married another man and changed the boy's name to his."

"Do you know the name?"

"I'm afraid I don't. They never contacted me."

"Do you think they contacted Richard Chantry?"

She looked away. "I wouldn't know about that."

"The woman and the little boy who came to Chantry's house twenty-five years ago—could they have been William's widow and son?"

"I don't know. It seems to me you're really reaching."

"I have to. It's all a long way back in the past. Do

you have any idea who the man was—the man who got himself killed and buried in the greenhouse?"

"I haven't the slightest."

"Could it have been your son William?"

"You must be crazy. William was killed in Arizona in 1943—seven years before that."

"Did you see his body?"

"Yes."

"I understand it was pretty chewed up. Were you able to make a positive identification?"

"Yes. I was. My son William died thirty-two years ago."

"What happened to his body after you identified it?"

"I don't know exactly."

"That's surprising."

"Is it? He had a wife in California, you know. She wanted his body shipped back here for final burial. And I had no objections. Once a man is dead, he's dead. It doesn't matter where he's finally planted."

Her voice was rough and careless, and I got the impression that she was deliberately violating her own feelings.

As if she realized this, she added, "I want my own body cremated—it won't be long now—and the ashes scattered on the desert near Tucson."

"Near Lashman's?"

She looked at me with irritation, and renewed interest. "You know too damn much."

"You tell me too damn little, Mildred. Where *was* your son William buried?"

"Someplace in California, I was told."

"Did you ever visit his grave?"

"No. I don't know where it is."

"Do you know where his widow lives now?"

"No. I never was much interested in family. I left my own family in Denver when I was fourteen years old, and never went back. I never looked back, either."

But her eyes were in long focus now, looking back

over the continent of her life. She may have been feeling what I felt, the subterranean jolt as the case moved once again, with enough force to throw a dead man out of his grave.

# XXXVI

It was nearly three by my car clock when I got out to Sycamore Point. At the foot of the beach, the sea was coughing in its sleep. My own tides were at a low ebb and I was tempted to go to sleep sitting up in the front seat.

But there was a light in Jacob Whitmore's cottage. I let myself hope for a minute that Betty was there. But Jessie Gable turned out to be alone.

I noticed the difference in Jessie as soon as she let me into the lighted room. Her movements were more assured, her eyes more definite. There was wine on her breath, but she didn't seem to be drunk.

She offered me a chair and said, "You owe me a hundred dollars. I found out the name of the woman who sold Jake the picture."

"Who was it?"

She reached across the table and laid her hand on my arm. "Wait a minute, now. Don't be in such a hurry. How do I know you *have* a hundred dollars?"

I counted out the money onto the table. She reached for the stack of bills. I picked them up again from under her hands.

"Hey," she said, "that's my money."

"You haven't told me the woman's name yet."

She tossed her blond hair. It fell like a soiled silk shawl over her shoulders. "Don't you trust me?"

"I did until you started not trusting me."

"You sound like Jake. He was always turning things around and upside down."

"Who sold Jake the picture?"

"I'll tell you when you give me the money."

I dealt fifty onto the table. "There's half. I'll give you the other half when you tell me who she is."

"It's worth more than that. This is an important case. I was told I should get a big reward."

I sat and studied her face. Two days before, when I had first come here, she hadn't seemed to care about money.

"Who's going to pay the reward?" I said.

"The newspaper."

"Did Betty Siddon tell you that?"

"More or less. She said I'd be well paid for my information."

"Did you tell Betty who the woman was?"

She disengaged her eyes from mine and looked away into a shadowed corner of the room. "She said it was important. And I didn't know if you were coming back or not. You know how it is. I really need the money."

I knew how it was. She was selling Jake Whitmore's bones, as survivors often do. And I was buying them. I dealt the rest of the hundred onto the tabletop.

Jessie reached for the bills, but her hand fell on the table short of them. She looked at me as if I might interfere, or possibly hit her.

I was sick of the game. "Go ahead and take it."

She picked up the tens and twenties, and put them inside her shirt against her breast. She looked at me guiltily, close to tears.

I said, "Let's not waste any more time, Jessie. Who was the woman?"

She said in a low hesitant voice, "Her name is Mrs. Johnson."

"Fred's mother?"

"I don't know whose mother she is."

"What's her first name?"

"I don't know. All I got from Stanley Meyer was her last name."

"Who is Stanley Meyer?"

"He's a hospital orderly who paints in his spare time. He sells his stuff at the beach art show. His booth is right next to Jake's. He was there when Jake bought the picture from her."

"You're talking about the portrait of a woman that Jake later sold to Paul Grimes."

She nodded. "That's the one you're interested in, isn't it?"

"Yes. Did your informer Stanley Meyer describe the woman to you?"

"Sort of. He said she was a middle-aged woman, maybe in her fifties. A big woman, broad in the beam. Dark hair with some gray in it."

"Did he say how she was dressed?"

"No."

"How did he happen to know her name?"

"He knew her from the hospital. This Mrs. Johnson worked there as a nurse, until they fired her."

"Why did they fire her?"

"Meyer said he didn't know. He said that the last he heard she was working at the La Paloma nursing home."

"What else did he tell you about Mrs. Johnson?"

"That's about all I remember."

"Did you tell all this to Betty Siddon?"

"Yes."

"How long ago?"

"I don't really know. Jake didn't believe in clocks. He thought that we should tell time by the sun, like the Chumash Indians."

"Was it before or after sundown that Betty Siddon was here?"

"After sundown. I remember now—it was right after you were here."

"Did you tell her you'd seen me?"

"No."

"Did she say where she was going when she left?"

"She didn't say it in so many words. But she asked me about the La Paloma nursing home. She wanted to make sure she had it straight that that was where Mrs. Johnson was working now."

I drove back down the highway, which was empty except for a few long-distance trucks. I felt as though I had climbed the ridge between the late dead middle of the night and chilly early morning. I could go on now, for another day if I had to.

I parked in the La Paloma lot and rang the bell at the service entrance. Someone inside groaned and muttered in reply. I rang again and heard rapid quiet footsteps. The door was opened six inches on a chain, and the young black nurse peered out at me.

"I was here the other night," I said.

"I remember you. If it's Mrs. Johnson you're after, she isn't here. It's the second time tonight she left me to handle the whole place by myself. I'm just about beat now and I've got hours to go yet. Talking to you isn't getting my work done, either."

"I know how you feel. I've been working all night, too."

She gave me an incredulous look. "What at?"

"I'm a detective. May I come in and talk to you for a minute, Miss?"

"Mrs.—Mrs. Holman." She sighed and unlatched the chain. "I guess so. But make it fast, please."

We leaned against the wall in the dark hallway. The breathings and groans of the patients and the intermittent sounds from the highway made a late-night undersong. Her face merged with the darkness so that her eyes appeared to be the night's own glowing eyes.

"What do you want to know?" she said.

"Why Mrs. Johnson went home."

"Well, she got a call from Fred. Fred is her son. He said the old man was on the rampage again. He's a terrible drunk—she's the only one who can handle him when he's that way. So she took a taxi home. I don't hold it against her, because you gotta do what you gotta do." She took a big breath and let it out: I could feel the warm exhalation in the darkness. "I don't mean to bear down hard on Mrs. Johnson. There are drinkers in my family, too."

"Did you ever visit the Johnson house?"

"No," she said abruptly. "If that's all you want to know, you're wasting my time."

"It isn't, though. This is very important, Mrs. Holman—a matter of life and death."

"Whose life?" she said. "Whose death?"

"A woman named Betty Siddon. She works for the local paper."

I heard the woman draw in her breath.

"Do you recognize the name?"

"Yeah. I do. She called here from the newspaper office right after I came on duty. She wanted to know if we had a patient here named Mildred Mead. I said we did have but not any more; Miss Mead got independent and moved out to Magnolia Court. The only reason she came here in the first place was on account of her connection with Mrs. Johnson."

"What connection?"

"Her—Miss Mead and Mrs. Johnson were relatives."

"What kind of relatives?"

"I never got that straight."

"Did you mention Miss Siddon's call to Mrs. Johnson?"

"No. I didn't want to get her stirred up. She didn't like it at all, you know, when old Miss Mead moved out of here. She took it personally, you might say. They had quite an argument when Miss Mead left. As a matter of fact, they almost came to blows. They're both a couple of blowtops, if you want my opinion."

I got the impression that the woman was talking too freely, sending up a smoke screen of words between me and the thing I wanted to know.

I said, "Has Miss Siddon been here tonight?"

"No." Her answer was firm. But her eyes seemed to

flicker a little, as if a counter-thought had moved behind them.

"If she has been, you better tell me. She may be in serious danger."

"I'm sorry about that. I haven't seen her."

"Is that the honest truth, Mrs. Holman?"

She flared up. "Why don't you stop bugging me? I'm sorry there's trouble in the air, and that your friend's in trouble. But I'm not responsible. And I've got work to do, if you haven't."

I left her reluctantly, feeling that she knew more than she was willing to tell. The atmosphere of the nursing home, compounded of age and sickness and blurred pain, followed me across town to the Johnson house.

# XXXVII

The high old house was completely dark. It seemed to hang over me like a dismal past piled generation on generation against the stars. I knocked on the front door, knocked repeatedly and got no answer.

I felt like shouting at the house as Gerard Johnson had done, and I wondered if I was going crazy, too. I leaned on the wall and looked out at the quiet street. I had parked my car around the corner, and the road was empty. Above the dense masses of the olive trees, a pallor was slowly spreading up the sky.

The dawn chill made my bones ache. I threw off my lethargy and pounded on the door and skinned my knuckles and stood in the gray dark sucking them.

Gerard Johnson spoke through the door: "What is it?"

"Archer. Open the door."

"I can't. She went away and locked me in." His voice was a hoarse whine.

"Where did she go?"

"Probably the La Paloma—that's the nursing home. She's supposed to be on night duty."

"I just came from there. Mrs. Johnson walked off the job again."

"She shouldn't do that. She'll lose that job, too. We'll have to go on welfare. I don't know what will happen to us."

"Where's Fred?"

"I don't know."

There were other questions I wanted to ask him, about his wife and the missing picture, but I despaired of getting useful answers. I gave Johnson a curt good night through the door and drove to the police station.

Mackendrick was in his office, looking not much different from the way he had looked seven or eight hours before. There were tender-looking blue patches under his eyes, but the eyes themselves were stern and steady, and he was freshly shaven.

"You look as if you didn't get much sleep," he said.

"I didn't get any. I've been trying to catch up with Betty Siddon."

Mackendrick drew in a long breath that made the chair creak under him. He let it out with a sigh.

"Why is it so important? We can't keep twenty-four-hour tabs on every reporter in town."

"I know that. This is a special case. I think the Johnson house ought to be searched."

"Do you have any reason to think Miss Siddon's in there?"

"Nothing definite, no. But there's a possibility, more than a possibility, that the missing picture is ʌidden in that house. It passed through Mrs. Johnson's hands once before, and then through her son Fred's."

I reminded Mackendrick of the facts of the case: Fred Johnson's theft or borrowing of the picture from the Biemeyer house; its subsequent theft from the art museum or, according to Fred's original story, from the Johnson house. I added what Jessie Gable had told me, that Whitmore had bought the picture from Mrs. Johnson in the first place.

"All this is very interesting," Mackendrick said in a flat voice. "But I haven't got time to look for Miss Siddon right now. And I haven't got time to look for a lost or stolen or mislaid picture which probably isn't worth very much anyway."

"The girl is. And the picture is the key to the whole bloody case."

Mackendrick leaned heavily forward across his desk. "She's your girl, right?"

"I don't know yet."

"But you're interested in her?"

"Very interested," I said.

"And the picture is the one you were hired to reclaim?"

"I guess so."

"And that makes it the key to the case, right?"

"I didn't say that, Captain. My personal connection with the girl and the picture aren't the reasons they're important."

"You may not think so. I want you to go into my washroom and take a good look at your face in the mirror. Incidentally, while you're in there, you can use my electric razor. It's in the cabinet behind the mirror. The light switch is to the left inside the door."

I went into the little room and looked at my face. It was drawn and pale. I grimaced to bring it to life but my eyes didn't change. They were at the same time dull and glaring.

I shaved and washed. It made some improvement in my looks. But it didn't touch the anxiety and fatigue that I was carrying inside my head and body.

When I came back into Mackendrick's office, he gave me a hard stare.

"Are you feeling any better?"

"Some."

"How long is it since you've eaten?"

I looked at my watch. It was ten to seven. "About nine or ten hours."

"No sleep?"

"No."

"Okay, let's get some breakfast. Joe's opens at seven."

Joe's was a workingman's restaurant whose booths and bar were already filling up with customers. There was a low-key half-kidding kind of hopefulness in the smoky atmosphere, as if the day might turn out to be not so bad after all.

Mackendrick and I sat across from each other in one of the booths. We discussed the case over coffee while we waited for our breakfasts to arrive. I was becoming painfully aware that I hadn't told Mackendrick about my interview with Mrs. Chantry. I was going to have to tell him before he found out for himself, if he hadn't already. I was going to have to tell him very soon. But I put it off until I had fortified myself with some solid food.

Both Mackendrick and I had ham and eggs and fried potatoes and toast. On top of that, he ordered a piece of apple pie with vanilla ice cream on the side.

When he had eaten it and ordered a fresh cup of coffee, I said, "I went to see Mrs. Chantry last night."

His face hardened, cracking at the corners of the mouth and eyes. "I asked you not to."

"It seemed necessary. We work under different rules, Captain."

"You can say that again."

I had meant that he had to work under special political constraints. He was the iron fist of the city, embodying all its crushing force, but he had to listen to what the city told him to do with it. He seemed to be listening now to the city's multitudinous voices, some of which were speaking in the big smoky room where we sat.

Gradually his face smoothed out and lost its cracked-cement look. His eyes remained impassive.

"What did you find out from Mrs. Chantry?"

I told him in some detail, with special emphasis on the man in the brown suit whose bones Mrs. Chantry and Rico had dug up. By this time, Mackendrick's face was flushed with interest.

"Did she tell you where the man came from?"

"Apparently he'd been in a veterans' hospital."

Mackendrick hit the table once with his hand. The dishes jumped and rattled. Everyone at our end of the restaurant was probably aware of this, but nobody turned to look.

"I wish to hell," he said, "that you'd told me about this earlier. If the man was ever in a veterans' hospital, we should be able to trace him through his bones."

Mackendrick laid three dollar bills on the table and got up and walked out.

I put down my own money and went outside. It was past eight, and the city was coming to life. I walked down the main street, hoping that I would come to life along with it, and ended up at the newspaper building.

She hadn't been seen or heard from.

I walked back to the parking lot and reclaimed my car and drove it down to the waterfront. I was guided by a half-admitted half-unconscious fantasy: if I went back to the room where Betty and I had started, she would be there.

She wasn't. I threw myself down on the bed and tried to turn my mind off. But it was invaded by dreams of the angry dead.

I woke up clear-minded in strong daylight. It was nearly twelve by my watch. I looked out the window at the harbor, sliced into long bright sizzling strips by the partly closed Venetian blinds. A few sailors were taking their boats out in the light noon wind. And my mind released the memory I needed.

When I was in Arizona, Sheriff Brotherton had told me about a soldier whose name was "something like Wilson or Jackson," and who had been a friend of

Mildred Mead's murdered son, William. The sheriff had had a postcard from the soldier after the war, sent from a veterans' hospital in California.

I picked up the room phone and placed a call to Sheriff Brotherton's office in Copper City. After a period of waiting, Brotherton himself came on the line.

"I'm glad you caught me, Archer. I was just going out to lunch. How's everything with the little Biemeyer girl? I take it she's home safe with her family."

"She's home. I don't know how safe she is."

"Isn't she safe with her own family?" Brotherton seemed to resent the implication that his rescue of Doris had not been permanent, like an ascent into heaven.

"She's a troubled girl, and she isn't too happy with her father. Speaking of whom, and forgive me if I've asked you this before, did Biemeyer have anything to do with shutting off the investigation of William Mead's death?"

"You have asked me that before. I said I didn't know."

"What are the probabilities?"

"It wouldn't make sense for Biemeyer to do that. He was very close to William Mead's mother at that time. I'm not telling you anything that isn't generally known."

"Did Mildred Mead want the investigation pressed?"

"I don't know whether she did or not. She did her talking to the higher echelons." Brotherton's voice was stiff, on the point of freezing up completely.

"Did Mildred want Richard Chantry brought back from California for questioning?"

"I don't remember that she did. What are you looking for, Archer?"

"I may not know till I see it. But one of the things you told me about the Mead case may be important. You mentioned that an army friend of Mead's came out to Arizona and talked to you about his death."

"That's correct. As a matter of fact, I've been thinking about him. I heard from him after the war, you know. He sent me a postcard from a veterans' hospital in L.A. He wanted to know if there were any further developments in the Mead case. I wrote him back that there weren't."

"Do you remember how he signed his postcard?"

The sheriff hesitated, and then said, "Jackson, I think. Jerry Jackson. His writing wasn't too clear."

"Could the name have been Jerry Johnson?"

The sheriff was silent for a while. I could hear faint voices talking somewhere on the line, like half-forgotten memories coming home to roost.

"It could have been," he said. "The postcard may still be in my files. I hoped that someday I could write and give that poor buddy of Mead's a positive answer. But I never did."

"You may be able to do it yet."

"I keep hoping, anyway."

"Do you have a suspect, Sheriff?"

"Do you?"

"No. But it wasn't my case."

I had touched a nerve. "It wasn't mine either," he said with some bitterness. "It was taken out of my hands."

"Who did that?"

"The powers that be. I'm not naming any names."

"Was Richard Chantry a suspect in his half brother's death?"

"That's no secret. I told you how they hustled Richard out of the state. He never came back, to my knowledge."

"Was there trouble between the two brothers?"

"I don't know if you could call it trouble. Healthy rivalry, anyway. Competition. They both wanted to be painters. They both wanted to marry the same girl. I guess you could say that Richard won on both counts. He even ended up with the family money."

"But his luck only lasted seven years."

"So I heard."

"Do you have any idea what happened to him?"

"No, I don't. It's away outside my territory. And incidentally I have to talk to some people and you're making me late. Goodbye."

The sheriff hung up abruptly. I went down the hall and tapped on the door of Paola's room. I heard her moving quietly inside.

She said through the door, "Who is it?"

I told her. She opened the door. She looked as though she'd been having bad dreams like mine, and hadn't fully awakened.

"What do you want?"

"A little more information."

"I've already told you everything."

"I doubt that."

She made an effort to close the door. I held it open. Each of us could feel the other's weight and the presence of an opposing will.

"Aren't you interested in who killed your father, Paola?"

Her dark eyes searched my face, not very hopefully. "Do you know for certain?"

"I'm working on it. But I need your help. May I come in?"

"I'll come out."

We sat in a pair of basket chairs beside a window at the end of the hall. Paola moved her chair away from the window.

"What are you afraid of, Paola?"

"That's a stupid question. My father was killed the other night. And I'm still here in this same lousy town."

"Who are you afraid of?"

"Richard Chantry. Who else? He seems to be a hero around here. That's because people don't know what an s.o.b. he was."

Did you know him?"

"Not really. He was before my time. But my father knew him very well; so did my mother. There were some queer stories floating around about him in Copper City. About him and his half brother, William Mead."

"What stories?"

Two deep clefts formed between her black eyebrows. "The way I heard it, Richard Chantry stole his brother's work. They were both serious painters, but William Mead was the one with the real talent. Richard imitated him, and after William was drafted Richard grabbed his drawings and some of his paintings, and passed them off as his own. He grabbed William's girl, too."

"Is that the present Mrs. Chantry?"

"I guess so."

Gradually she had leaned toward the window, like a heliotropic plant that loved the light. Her eyes remained sullen and fearful. She pulled back her head as if she had spotted snipers in the street.

She followed me into my room and stood just inside the door while I called Mackendrick. I told him the two main facts that I had learned that morning: Richard Chantry had stolen and misrepresented as his own some of his half brother William's work; and after William's death an army buddy of his who called himself Jerry Johnson had turned up in Arizona.

Mackendrick stopped me. "Johnson's a common name. But I wouldn't be surprised if that's our Gerard Johnson on Olive Street."

"Neither would I. If Gerard was injured in the war and spent time in a hospital, it could explain some of his peculiarities."

"Some of them, anyway. All we can do is ask him. First I want to put out an additional query to the vets' hospitals."

"An additional query?"

"That's right. Your friend Purvis has been examining those bones you brought in last night. He found traces of what looked like shrapnel wounds, and apparently they were given expert treatment. So Purvis has been getting in touch with the hospitals on his own hook."

"What are you doing about Betty Siddon?"

"Hasn't she turned up yet?"

Mackendrick sounded bored. I slammed the receiver down. Then I sat regretting my show of anger and wondering what to do next.

# XXXVIII

I drove uptown to the newspaper office. Betty had not been heard from. Her friend Fay Brighton was red-eyed. She told me she had had one call that had made her suspicious, but the woman who called had left neither name nor number.

"Was it a threatening call?"

"I wouldn't say that exactly. The woman sounded worried. She wanted to know if Betty was all right. I asked her why she wanted to know, and she hung up on me."

"When did the call come in?"

"This morning about ten o'clock. I shouldn't have let the woman rattle me. If I'd handled her with more tact, she might have told me more."

"Did you get the impression she knew something?"

She thought about the question. "Yes, I did. She sounded scared—guilty, maybe."

"What kind of a woman was she?"

"I've been trying to figure that out. She talked intelligently, like a professional woman. But her voice was a little different." She hesitated, in a listening attitude. "She may have been a black woman, an educated black."

It took me a minute to remember the name of the black nurse at the La Paloma. Mrs. Holman. I borrowed Mrs. Brighton's phone directory and looked for the name Holman, but there was no listing under it.

I needed a black connection. The only one I could think of in the city was the proprietor of the liquor store where I had bought two half-pints of whisky for Jerry Johnson. I went there, and found him on duty behind the counter.

"Some Tennessee whisky?" he said.

"I can always use some."

"Two half-pints?" He smiled indulgently over my eccentricity.

"I'll try a whole pint this time."

While he was putting the bottle in a bag, I asked him if he knew a nurse named Mrs. Holman. He gave me an interested look that was careful not to stay on my face too long.

"I may have heard of her. I wouldn't say I know her. I know her husband."

"She's been looking after a friend of mine," I said. "At the La Paloma nursing home. I was thinking of giving her a little present."

"If you mean this"—he held the bottle up—"I can deliver it."

"I'd rather do that in person."

"Whatever you say. Mrs. Holman lives near the corner of Nopal and Martinez. Third house up from the corner—there's a big old pepper tree in front of it. That's five blocks south of here and one block over toward the ocean."

I thanked him and paid him for the whisky and drove south. The pepper tree was the only spot of green in a block of one-story frame houses. Under its lacy shadow, several small black children were playing in the wheelless body of a 1946 Chevrolet sedan.

Mrs. Holman was watching them from the porch. She started when she saw me and made an involuntary movement toward the door. Then she stood with her back to it and tried to smile at me, but her eyes were somber.

"Good morning," I said.

"Good morning."

"Are these your children?"

"One of them is." She didn't tell me which one. "What can I do for you, sir?"

"I'm still looking for Miss Siddon. I'm worried about her. I thought maybe you were, too."

"I don't know where you got that idea," she said blankly.

"Didn't you call the newspaper office this morning?"

She looked past me at the children. They were silent and still, as if the feathery shadow of the pepper tree had become oppressive.

"What if I did?" she said.

"If you can do that, you can talk to me. I'm not trying to pin anything on you. I'm trying to find Betty Siddon. I think she may be in danger, and you seem to think so, too."

"I didn't say that."

"You don't have to. Did you see Miss Siddon last night at the La Paloma?"

She nodded slowly. "I saw her."

"When was that?"

"It was still the early part of the evening. She came to visit Mrs. Johnson, and the two of them went into a huddle in one of the empty rooms. I don't know what they were talking about, but it ended up with both of them walking out of there together. They drove off in Miss Siddon's car without a word to me."

"So Mrs. Johnson went home twice last night?"

"I guess she did."

"The police were at the La Paloma when Mrs. Johnson came back there. Isn't that right?"

"I guess they were."

"You know very well they were. And they must have told you what they were looking for."

"Maybe they did. I don't remember." Her voice was low. She was still, and very ill at ease.

"You must remember, Mrs. Holman. The cops were

looking for Mildred Mead and Betty Siddon. They must have asked you about them."

"Maybe they did. I'm tired. I've got a lot on my mind and I had a rough night."

"You could have a rougher day."

She flared up. "Don't you dare threaten me."

The children in the Chevrolet were still and frightened. One of them, a little girl whom I guessed to be Mrs. Holman's, began to weep quietly into her hands.

I said to the little girl's mother, "Don't you dare lie to me. I've got nothing against you. I don't want to put you in the slammer. But that's where you'll end up if you don't tell the truth."

She looked past me at the weeping child. "Okay," she said, "okay. Mrs. Johnson asked me not to tell the police about either of them being there—Miss Mead *or* Miss Siddon. I knew then there was trouble coming up. I might have known it would end up on my doorstep."

She brushed past me and climbed into the Chevrolet. I left her there with her daughter in her lap, and the other children silent around her.

# XXXIX

I went back to Olive Street. In the full white blast of noon, the Johnson house looked grim and strange, like a long old face appalled by the present.

I parked across the street and tried to imagine what had happened inside the house, and what was happening now. If Betty was there, she might not be easy to find. The house was old and rambling and largely unknown to me.

A small Toyota sedan went by in the street, moving

in the direction of the hospital. The man at the wheel looked like Fred Johnson's attorney, Lackner. He stopped up the block, not far from the place where Paul Grimes had been murdered. I heard one of the Toyota's doors open and close quietly, but if anyone got out he was hidden by the trees.

I took the pint of whisky and my gun out of the glove compartment and put them in the pockets of my jacket. Then I crossed the street and knocked on the front door of the Johnson house.

There was a slight noise at the corner of the house. I flattened myself against the wall and made my gun ready to fire. At the end of the porch, the overgrown bushes stirred. Fred Johnson's voice came quietly out of them: "Mr. Archer?"

"Yes."

Fred vaulted over the railing. He moved like a man who had spent his boyhood dodging trouble. His face was pale.

"Where have you been, Fred?"

"At Mr. Lackner's office. He just dropped me off."

"You feel you still need an attorney?"

He ducked his head so that I couldn't read his face. "I suppose I do."

"What for?"

"Mr. Lackner told me not to discuss it with anybody."

"You're going to have to, Fred."

"I know that. Mr. Lackner told me that. But he wants to be present when I do."

"Where did he go?"

"To talk to Captain Mackendrick."

"What about?"

He lowered his voice as if the house might hear him: "I'm not supposed to say."

"You owe me something, Fred. I helped to keep you out of jail. You could be in a cell in Copper City now."

"I owe something to my mother and father, too."

I took hold of him by the shoulders. He was trembling. His mustache drooped across his mouth like an emblem of his limp and injured manhood.

I said as gently as I knew how, "What have your mother and father been doing, Fred?"

"I don't know." He swallowed painfully, and his tongue moved between his lips like a small blind creature searching for a way out.

"Do they have a woman in the house?"

He nodded dismally. "I heard a woman in the attic."

"What was she doing up there?"

"I don't know. My father was up there with her."

"When was this?"

"Early this morning. Before dawn. I guess she's been up there all night."

I shook him. His head bobbed back and forth in meaningless assent. I stopped for fear of breaking his neck.

"Why didn't you tell me that before?"

"I didn't know what was going on up there. I thought I recognized her voice. I didn't know for sure it was Miss Siddon until I went around to the back just now and found her car."

"Who did you think it was?"

"Just some woman he brought in off the street, maybe a woman from the hospital. He used to con them into the house and get them to take off their clothes for him. That was when my mother started to lock him in."

"How bad a mental case is he?"

"I don't know." Fred's eyes had filled with tears and shifted away from my face. "Mr. Lackner thinks he's really dangerous. He thinks the police should take him and put him in a safe place."

So did I, but I didn't trust them to do it with a minimum of danger to others. I wanted Betty, if she was still alive, to survive her rescue.

"Do you have a key to the house, Fred?"

"Yes. I had one made."

"Let me in."

"I'm not supposed to. I'm supposed to wait for Mr. Lackner and the police."

"Okay, wait for them. Just give me the key."

He took it out of his pocket and handed it over, reluctantly, as though he was surrendering some essential part of himself. When he spoke again his voice had deepened, as if the loss of that essential part had somehow been a gain.

"I'll go in with you. You don't know your way around in there like I do."

I gave him back the key and he thrust it into the door. Mrs. Johnson was waiting just inside, standing at the bottom of the stairs. She offered me a ghastly embarrassed smile, the kind you see on dead faces before the undertaker does his work.

"What can I do for you?"

"You can get out of my way. I want your husband."

Her false smile clenched into a fierce grimace, which she turned on Fred. "What have you been telling this man?"

"We have to stop him, Mother."

Her face changed, groping for an expression that could accommodate the doubleness of her life. I thought she might spit at her son, or curse him, then perhaps that she might break down in tears.

"I've never been able to handle that crazy man."

I said, "Will you come up with me and talk to him?"

"I tried that in the course of the night. He said he'd shoot her, and then himself, if I didn't leave them alone."

"He has another gun up there?"

"He always has had. More than one, I think. I've searched the whole place for them when he was blotto, but I've never been able to find them."

"Has he ever used them on anyone?"

"No. He's just a talker." Her face had taken on a frightened questioning look.

"How did he get Miss Siddon to go up there?"

Her heavy dark eyes veered away from mine. "I don't know."

"Did you take her up there?"

"No. I wouldn't do that."

"You did, though," her son said.

"So what if I did? She asked for it. She said she wanted to talk to him, and that was where he was. I'm not responsible for every newspaper reporter that inveigles her way into my house."

I pushed her to one side and went up past her, with Fred at my heels. I paused in the dim upstairs hall, trying to get my bearings. Fred moved past me and turned on the light. The padlock was in place on the attic door.

"Did your mother lock him in?"

"I guess she must have. She has this phobia about his getting away from her, like when he went to British Columbia."

"Go down and get the key from her."

Fred ran downstairs.

Johnson's voice came through the attic door. "Who is that out there?" He sounded hoarse and frightened.

"Archer. I'm a friend of yours."

"I have no friends."

"I brought you some Tennessee walking whisky the other day."

There was a silence. "I could use some of that now. I've been up all night."

Fred came up the stairs two at a time, holding up a small key like a trophy.

"Who is that?" Johnson said.

Fred gave me a look that suggested I do the answering. At the same time, he handed me the padlock key. It gave me a feeling that whatever authority was left in the house was coming to me.

I said, "It's your son, Fred."

"Tell him to go away," Johnson said. "And if you

can let me have a sup of whisky, I'd appreciate it very much."

But it was too late for such amenities. A siren had screamed in the distance, and now I could hear it dying in the street. Acting on strong impulse, I unlocked the padlock and got my gun out and held it cocked.

"What are you doing out there?" Johnson said.

"Bringing you your whisky."

Heavy footsteps were mounting the porch below. I removed the padlock with my left hand and pulled the door open.

Johnson was sitting at the foot of the attic stairs. There was a small revolver, another Saturday-night special, on the wooden step beside him. He was slow in reaching for it.

I stamped on his hand, and scooped up the skittering gun. He put his hurt fingers in his mouth and looked at me as if I had betrayed him.

I pushed him out of the way and went up past him to his makeshift studio in the attic. Betty Siddon was sitting in a plain chair, wearing nothing except the piece of smooth clothesline that held her upright. Her face was pale and dull, her eyes were closed. I thought for a moment that she was dead. The world staggered under my feet like a top that had lost its spin.

But when I kneeled down and cut the ropes, Betty came alive into my arms. I held her close. After a while she stirred and spoke to me.

"You were a long time getting here."

"I was stupid."

"I was the stupid one," she said. "I should never have come here alone. He held a gun on me and made me take off my clothes. Then he tied me into the chair and painted my picture."

The unfinished picture was on a paint-spotted easel facing us. It reminded me of the other pictures I had seen in the last few days, in the art museum, in Mrs. Chantry's house, at Mildred Mead's. Though I found it hard to believe, all the evidence seemed to indicate that the loud complaining drunk whom Mackendrick had just arrested at the foot of the attic stairs was the lost painter Chantry.

While Betty was putting on her clothes, I searched the attic. I found other pictures, most of them pictures of women, in various stages of completion. The last one I found, wrapped in a piece of burlap and covered with an old mattress, was the memory portrait of Mildred Mead that Jack Biemeyer had hired me to reclaim. Under the burlap wrapping was a set of keys which confirmed that Johnson's imprisonment in his house had not been complete.

I carried the picture down the attic stairs and found Fred lingering at their foot.

"Where's your father?"

"If you mean Gerard, Captain Mackendrick took him downstairs. But I don't believe he is my father."

"Who is he, then?"

"That's what I've been trying to find out. I took—I borrowed that picture from the Biemeyer house because I suspected that Gerard had painted it. I wanted to try and determine its age, and also compare it with the Chantrys in the museum."

"It wasn't stolen from the museum, was it?"

"No, sir. I lied about that. He took it from my room here in this house. That's when I suspected that Gerard had painted it. And then I began to suspect that he really was Richard Chantry, and not my father at all."

"Then why did you try to protect him? Because you thought your mother was involved?"

Fred moved restlessly and looked past me up the stairs. Sitting at the top was Betty Siddon, taking penciled notes in a sketch pad held on her knee. My heart jumped. She was incredible. She had been up all night, been threatened and mistreated by a suspected murderer, and all she wanted to do was catch her breaking story as it broke.

"Where is your mother, Fred?"

"Down in the front room with Mr. Lackner and Captain Mackendrick."

The three of us went down the steps. Betty stumbled once, and I felt her weight on my arm. I offered to drive her home. She turned down the offer.

Nothing much was going on in the drab living room. The questioning had reached a near impasse, with both Gerard and Mrs. Johnson refusing to answer Mackendrick's questions and the attorney Lackner reminding them of their rights. They were talking—or, rather, refusing to talk—about the murder of Paul Grimes.

"I have a theory," I said. "By now it's become a little more than a theory. Both Grimes and Jacob Whitmore were killed because they discovered the source of the Biemeyers' missing picture. Which incidentally isn't missing any more." I showed it to them. "I just found it in the attic, where Johnson probably painted it in the first place."

Johnson sat with his head down. Mrs. Johnson gave him a bitter look, at the same time worried and vengeful.

Mackendrick turned to me. "I don't understand what makes the picture so important."

"It seems to be a Chantry, Captain. And Johnson painted it."

Mackendrick got the message by degrees, like a man becoming aware that he has an illness. He turned and looked at Gerard Johnson and his eyes gradually widened.

Gerard returned the captain's look in dim fear and dejection. I tried to penetrate the puffed discolored flesh that overlay the original contours of his face. It was hard to imagine that he had ever been handsome, or that the mind behind his dull reddened eyes had created the world of his paintings. It occurred to me that his essential life might have gone into that world and left him empty.

Still there must have been vestiges of his younger self

in his face, because Mackendrick said, "You're Richard Chantry, aren't you? I recognize you."

"No. My name is Gerard Johnson."

That was all he would say. He stood silent while Mackendrick advised him of his rights and put him under arrest.

Fred and Mrs. Johnson were not arrested but Mackendrick asked them to come to the station for questioning. They crowded into his official car under the eyes of a young detective-sergeant who kept his hand on his gun butt.

Betty and I were left standing on the sidewalk in front of the empty house. I put the Biemeyers' picture in the trunk of my car and opened the front door for her.

She hung back. "Do you know where my car is?"

"Behind the house. Just leave it there for now. I'll drive you home."

"I'm not going home. I have to write my story."

I looked closely into her face. It seemed unnaturally bright, like an electric light that was about to burn out.

"Let's go for a little walk. I've got work to do, too, but it can wait."

She came along with me under the trees, leaning with carefully controlled lightness on my arm. The old street seemed beautiful and formal in the morning light.

I told her a story that I remembered from childhood. There had been a time, it said, when men and women were closer than twins and shared the same mortal body. I told her that when the two of us came together in my motel room, I felt that close to her. And when she dropped out of sight, I felt the loss of part of myself.

She pressed my arm. "I knew you'd find me."

We walked slowly around the block, as if we had inherited the morning and were looking for a place to spend it. Later I drove her downtown and we had lunch together at the Tea Kettle. We were contented and grave, like two people performing a ceremony. I could see the life flowing back into her face and body.

I dropped her off at the newspaper office. She ran up the stairs toward her typewriter.

# XL

I went back to the police station. There was a coroner's wagon in the parking lot, and I ran into Purvis coming out of Mackendrick's office. The young deputy coroner was flushed with excitement.

"I got a positive identification on those bones."

"Where?"

"Skyhill Veterans' Hospital, in the Valley. He was a patient there for several years after the war. His name was Gerard Johnson."

"Please repeat that."

"Gerard Johnson. He was badly wounded in the Pacific. They practically had to rebuild him from the ground up. He was released from Skyhill about twenty-five years ago. He was supposed to go back for regular checks on his condition, but he never did. Now we know why." Purvis drew in a deep satisfied breath. "Incidentally, I have to thank you for helping me with the lead. Remind me to do something for you someday."

"You can do something for me now."

Purvis looked slightly startled. "Okay. Just name it."

"You better write this down."

He got out an official pad and a ball-point pen. "Shoot."

I shot, at a distant target. "Gerard Johnson had a friend in the army named William Mead. Mead was murdered in Arizona in the summer of 1943. Sheriff

Brotherton of Copper City is familiar with the case. He was the one who found Mead's body in the desert and shipped it home to California for burial. I'd like to know where it was shipped to, and where it was buried. It might be a good idea to dig it up and examine it."

Purvis looked up from his pad and squinted into the sun. "Examine it for what?"

"Cause of death. Identity. The works. Also, Mead had a wife. It would help if we could trace her."

"That's a big order."

"It's a big case."

I found Mackendrick alone in his office, looking glum and shaken.

"Where's your prisoner, Captain?"

"The D.A. took him over to the courthouse. Lackner advised him to stand mute. The rest of the family isn't talking either. I was hoping to wrap this up today."

"Maybe we still can. Where are Fred and his mother?"

"I had to let them go home. The D.A. didn't want to bring charges against them, at least not yet. He's fairly new on the job, and still feeling his way. According to him, all we have against the Johnson woman is that she's been living with Richard Chantry and passing him off as her husband, which isn't a felony."

"It is if she was helping him to cover up a murder."

"You mean the murder of the real Gerard Johnson?"

"That's right, Captain. As you know, Purvis has established that the real Johnson was the man in the brown suit whose body was buried in the Chantry greenhouse. It looks as though Chantry murdered Johnson and stole his identity and moved in with Johnson's wife and son."

Mackendrick shook his head ponderously and sadly. "That's what I thought. But I've just got through checking Johnson out with the V.A. and the people at Skyhill Hospital. Johnson wasn't married, and had no son. The whole bloody family is a fake."

"Including Fred?"

"Including Fred." Mackendrick must have seen the pain in my face, because he added, "I know you made an emotional investment in Fred. It'll give you some idea of how I feel about Chantry. I really looked up to that man when I was a young patrolman. The whole town did, even if they never saw him. Now I have to tell them that he's a half-crazy drunk and a killer into the bargain."

"You're absolutely certain that Johnson is Chantry?"

"Absolutely. I knew him personally, remember. I was one of the few who did. He's changed, of course, changed a hell of a lot. But he's the same man. I know him, and he knows I know him. But he isn't admitting anything at all."

"Have you thought of confronting him with his real wife?"

"Naturally I have. I went to her house to talk to her first thing this morning. She'd already flown the coop, probably for keeps. She'd emptied her safe-deposit box and she was last seen headed south on the freeway." Mackendrick gave me a grim look. "You're partly to blame for that, when you took it on yourself to question her prematurely."

"Maybe. I'm also partly to blame for solving your case."

"It isn't solved. Sure, we've got Chantry. But there's a lot left unexplained. Why did he take the name Johnson, the name of the man he killed?"

"To cover up the fact that the real Johnson was missing."

Mackendrick shook his head. "That doesn't make much sense."

"Neither did the murder of Johnson. But he committed it, and the woman knew it. She used the knowledge to take him over completely. He was virtually a prisoner in that house on Olive Street."

"But why did she want him?"

I admitted I didn't know. "There may have been a

previous connection between them. We should look into the possibility."

"That's easier said than done. Johnson's been dead for twenty-five years. The woman isn't talking. Neither is Chantry."

"May I have a try at him?"

"It's out of my hands, Archer. It's a big case, and the D.A. wants all of it. Chantry's the most famous man we ever had in this town." He struck his desk-top with his fist, heavily and repeatedly and slowly, like a dead march. "Jesus, what a comedown that man has had."

I went out to my car and drove the few blocks to the county courthouse. Its square white clock tower was the tallest structure in the downtown area. Above the giant four-sided clock was an observation platform surrounded by a black wrought-iron fence.

There was a family of tourists on the platform, and a little boy chinned himself on the wrought-iron fence and smiled down at me. I smiled back.

That was just about my last smile of the afternoon. I waited for nearly two hours in the outer reaches of the D.A.'s wing. I finally got to see him, but not to talk to. He went out through the waiting room, a bold-eyed young man with dark sweeping mustaches that seemed to bear him along like the wings of his ambition.

I tried to talk my way in to see one of his assistants. They were all busy. I never got past the outer circle of assistant assistants. I finally gave up and went downstairs to the coroner's office.

Purvis was still waiting for a return phone call from Copper City. I sat and helped him wait. Toward the end of the afternoon, he got his call.

He took it at his desk and made notes as he listened. I tried to read them over his shoulder but they were indecipherable.

"Well?" I said when he finally hung up.

"The army assumed the responsibility and expense of shipping Mead's body home from Arizona in 1943. The cadaver was transported in a sealed coffin because it was in bad shape, unfit for viewing. They buried it in a local cemetery."

"A local cemetery where?"

"Right here in Santa Teresa," Purvis said. "This is where Mead lived with his wife. Their address when the army took him was 2136 Los Bagnos Street. She could still be living there, if we're really lucky."

As I followed Purvis's wagon across town into the hospital area, I felt that the thirty-two-year case was completing a long curve back to its source. We drove up Olive Street past the Johnson house, then past the place where I had found Paul Grimes dying.

Los Bagnos Street ran parallel to Olive, a block farther north of the highway. The old stucco house at 2136 had long since been denatured, converted into doctors' offices. On the east it was overshadowed by a tall new medical complex. But on the west there was a prewar frame house with a cardboard "Room to Let" sign in one of the front windows.

Purvis climbed out of his wagon and rattled the rusty screen door of the house with his fist. An old man answered the knock and peered out at us. The pouched and corded neck thrust up from his collarless shirt seemed to throb with suspicion.

"What is it?"

"My name is Purvis. I'm a deputy coroner."

"Nobody died here. Not since my wife died, anyway."

"What about Mr. William Mead? Was he a neighbor of yours?"

"That's right, he was for a little while. He died, too. That was back during the war. Mead got himself murdered in Arizona. I heard that from his wife. I don't take the local paper, I never have. All they ever print in it is bad news." He squinted at us through the screen as if we were carriers of bad news, too. "Is that what you wanted to know?"

"You've been very helpful," Purvis said. "Do you happen to know what happened to Mead's wife?"

"She didn't go far. She eventually remarried and moved to a house over here on Olive Street. But her luck didn't change."

"How do you mean?" Purvis said.

"On her second go-round, she married a drunk. Don't quote me. And she's been working ever since to support his drinking habit."

"Where does she work?"

"In the hospital. She's a nurse."

"Is her husband's name Johnson?"

"That's right. If you know, why ask?"

# XLI

We drove between the dense ranks of the trees that had stood on Olive Street for a century or more. As Purvis and I moved up the walk into the afternoon shadow of the house, I felt the weight of the past like an extra atmosphere constricting my breathing.

The woman who called herself Mrs. Johnson answered the door immediately, as if she had been expecting us. I could feel her somber gaze like a tangible pressure on my face.

"What do you want?"

"May we come in? This is Deputy Coroner Purvis."

"I know." She said to Purvis, "I've seen you at the hospital. I don't know what you want to come in for. There's nobody home but me, and everything's happened that's going to happen." It sounded less like a statement of fact than a dubious hope.

I said, "We want to talk about some of the things that happened in the past. One of them is the death of William Mead."

She answered without blinking: "I never heard of him."

"Let me refresh your recollection," Purvis said quietly and formally. "According to my information, William Mead was your husband. When he was murdered in Arizona in 1943, his body was shipped back here for burial. Is my information incorrect?"

Her black gaze didn't waver. "I guess I kind of forgot all that. I always had a pretty good forgettery. And these awful things that I've been living through sort of wiped out everything, you know?"

"May we come in and sit down with you," Purvis said, "and talk about it?"

"I guess so."

She moved to one side and let us enter the narrow hallway. There was a large worn canvas suitcase standing at the foot of the stairs. I lifted it. It was heavy.

"Leave that alone," she said.

I set it down again. "Are you planning to leave town?"

"What if I am? I haven't done anything wrong. I'm still a free agent. I can go where I like, and I might as well. There's nobody left here but me. My husband's gone, and Fred's moving out."

"Where is Fred going?"

"He won't even tell me. Off with that girl of his, probably. After all the work I've put into this house, twenty-five years of hard work, I end up all alone in it. Alone and without a nickel and owing money. Why shouldn't I get out?"

I said, "Because you're under suspicion. Any move you make is likely to trigger your arrest."

"What am I under suspicion for? I didn't kill Will Mead. It happened in Arizona. I was nursing here in Santa Teresa at the time. When they told me he was dead, it was the biggest shock of my life. I haven't got over it yet. I'll never get over it. And when they buried him out in the cemetery, I wanted to crawl in with him."

I felt a twinge of compassion for the woman but kept it under control. "Mead isn't the only one who's been killed. There are also Paul Grimes and Jacob Whitmore, men that you and your husband were doing business with. Grimes was killed here in your street. Whitmore may have been drowned in your bathtub."

She gave me a sudden shocked look. "I don't know what you're talking about."

"I'll be glad to explain. It may take a little time. Could we go into the living room and sit down?"

"No," she said. "I don't want to. They've been firing questions at me most of the day. Mr. Lackner advised me not to do any more talking."

Purvis spoke up in a dubious voice: "I'd better give her her rights, don't you think, Archer?"

His nervousness encouraged her, and she turned on him. "I know my rights. I don't have to talk to you or anybody else. Speaking of rights, you have no right to force your way into my house like this."

"No force was employed, ma'am. You invited us in."

"I certainly did not. You invited yourself. You bullied your way in."

Purvis turned to me. He had gone pale with the bureaucratic terror of making an attributable mistake.

"We better leave it for now, Archer. Questioning witnesses isn't my field anyway. For all I know, the D.A. will want to grant her immunity. I wouldn't want to ruin the case by making a mistake at this late date."

"What case?" she said with renewed vigor. "There is no case. You have no right to come here hustling me and harrying me. Just because I'm a poor woman without any friends and a mentally ill husband who doesn't even know who he is, he's so far gone."

"Who is he?" I said.

She gave me a startled look, and fell silent.

I said, "Incidentally, why do you call yourself Mrs. Johnson? Were you ever married to Gerard Johnson? Or did Chantry simply change his name to Johnson after he murdered the real Gerard?"

"I'm not talking," she repeated. "You two get out of here now."

Purvis was already out on the porch, dissociating himself from my unorthodox questioning. I followed him out and we parted on the sidewalk.

I sat in my car in the failing afternoon and tried to straighten out the case in my mind. It had started with the trouble between two brothers, Richard Chantry and his illegitimate half brother, William Mead. It appeared that Richard had stolen William's work and William's girl and eventually murdered him, leaving his body in the Arizona desert.

Richard came to Santa Teresa with the girls and, despite the fact that murder was an extraditable offense, was never brought back to Arizona for questioning. He prospered in California and, as if his talent had fed on William's death, developed in just seven years into an important painter. Then his world collapsed. An army friend of William's, Gerard Johnson, got out of the veterans' hospital and came to visit Richard.

Gerard made two visits to Richard, the second accompanied by William's widow and son. That was Gerard's last visit to anyone. Richard killed him and buried him in his own greenhouse. Then, as if in penance, Richard stepped down from his own place in the world and took Gerald's name and William's place. He had come to this house on Olive Street and lived as a drunken recluse for twenty-five years.

In the first years, before he put on the disguises of age and alcoholism, he must have lived in close confinement, like an insane relative in a nineteenth-century attic. But he hadn't been able to stay away from painting. In the end the persistence of his talent had helped to destroy him.

Fred must have become aware of his father's secret life as a painter and taken the first unconscious steps toward identifying him with the lost painter Chantry. This would explain Fred's overpowering interest in Chantry's work, culminating in his theft or borrowing of the Biemeyers' painting. When Fred brought that painting home to study it, his father took it from Fred's room and hid it in his own—the attic where he had painted it in the first place.

The missing painting was in the trunk of my car. Chantry was in jail. I should be feeling happy and successful but I wasn't. The case hung heavy on my hands and stillborn in my mind. It kept me sitting there under the olive trees as the afternoon slowly faded.

I told myself that I was waiting for the woman to come out. But I doubted that she would as long as I was parked there. Twice I saw her face at the living-room window. The first time she looked frightened. The second time she was angry, and shook her fist at me. I smiled at her reassuringly. She pulled down the frayed blind.

I sat there trying to imagine the life of the couple who had lived in the gabled house for twenty-five years. Chantry had been a moral prisoner as well as a physical one. The woman he had been living with under the name of Johnson must have known that he had killed the original Johnson. She probably knew that he had killed her legal husband, Mead, as well. Their cohabitation was more like a prison sentence than any kind of marriage.

Their secret, their multiple guilty secret, had been guarded by further crimes. Paul Grimes had been beaten to death in the street, and Jacob Whitmore probably drowned in this house, simply in order to preserve Chantry's cover. It was hard for me to sit still with such knowledge. But I felt that I had to wait.

Behind the rooftops to the west, the sun had died and suffused the sky with red. Now even that was fading, and the first gray chill of night was coming on.

A yellow cab pulled up behind my car. Betty Siddon got out. She said as she paid the driver, "Do you mind waiting for a minute? I want to be sure my car is where I think it is."

The driver said he would wait if she didn't take too

long. Without noticing me, or looking in my direction, she started to wade through the weeds toward the back of the house. She seemed a little unsteady on her feet. So far as I knew, she hadn't slept since she had slept with me. The memory hit me like an arrow that had been in the air since then.

I followed her around to the back of the house. She was bent over at the door of her car, trying to unlock it. The Johnson woman was watching her from the kitchen window.

Betty stood up and leaned on the car door. She greeted me without animation: "Hello, Lew."

"How are you, Betty?"

"Tired. I've been writing all day, to no avail. The publisher wanted to cut my story down to nothing, for legal reasons. So I walked out."

"Where are you going now?"

"I'm on a mission," she said with faint irony. "But I can't seem to get this car door open."

I took the keys from her hand and opened the door. "You were using the wrong key."

Being able to correct her on this point made me happy, for some reason.

It made Betty more tired. Her face was pale and heavy-eyed, half dissolved in twilight.

"What kind of a mission?" I asked her.

"Sorry, it's top secret, Lew."

The Johnson woman opened the back door and stepped outside. Her voice rose like a stormy wind: "You two get out of here. You've got no right to harass me. I'm an innocent woman who took up with the wrong man. I should have left him years ago and I would have, too, if it hadn't been for the boy. I've lived with a crazy drunk for twenty-five years. If you think it's easy, try it sometimes."

Betty cut her off. "Shut up. You knew I was in your attic last night. You talked me into going up there yourself. You let me stay there all night with him, and you didn't lift a finger to help me. So shut up."

Mrs. Johnson's face began to twist and work like some amorphous sea creature trying to dodge an enemy, perhaps evade reality itself. She turned and went back into the kitchen, closing the door behind her carefully.

Betty yawned profoundly, her eyes streaming.

I put my arm around her shoulders. "Are you all right?"

"I will be in a minute." She yawned again, and waited, and yawned again. "It did me good to tell that woman off. She's one of those wives who can watch a man commit murder and feel nothing. Nothing but her own moral superiority. Her whole life's been devoted to covering up. Her motto is save the surface and you save all. But nothing got saved. The whole thing went to rot, and people got killed while she stood by and let it happen. I almost got killed myself."

"By Chantry?"

She nodded. "That woman doesn't have the nerve to act out her own fantasies. She stands to one side and lets the man do it for her, so she can have her dim little sadistic orgasms."

"You really hate her, don't you?"

"Yes. I do. Because I'm a woman, too."

"But you don't hate Chantry, after what he did to you?"

She shook her head, and her short hair blurred in the twilight. "The point is that he didn't do it. He was thinking about killing me. He even talked about it. But then he changed his mind. He painted my picture instead. I'm grateful to him—for not killing me, and for painting my picture."

"So am I."

I tried to put both arms around her. But she wasn't ready for that.

"Do you know why he took pity on me? Naturally you don't. Remember the time I told you about, when my father took me to visit Chantry? When I was just a little girl?"

"I remember."

"Well, he remembered, too. I didn't have to remind him. He actually remembered me from the time I was a child. He said my eyes hadn't changed since then."

"I'm afraid he has."

"Has he not. Don't worry, Lew, I'm not getting sentimental about Chantry. I'm simply glad to be alive. Very glad."

I said that I was glad she was alive, too.

"There's only one thing I'm sorry about," she added. "All through this thing, I've kept hoping that somehow it would turn out that he wasn't Chantry. You know? That it had all been a horrible mistake. But it wasn't. The man who painted those pictures is a murderer."

"I know."

# XLII

Betty's cabdriver appeared at the corner of the house, looking unhappy. "You've kept me waiting a long time, Miss, I'm going to have to charge you."

Betty paid him off. But when she got into her own car it wouldn't start. I tried it. The engine didn't turn over for me either.

I lifted the hood. The battery was gone.

"What am I going to do now? I have to go on an errand."

"I'll be glad to drive you."

"But I have to go by myself. I promised I would."

"Who did you promise?"

"I can't tell you. I'm sorry."

She seemed to be drawing away from me. I stepped closer and looked at her face. It was scarcely more than a pale oval now, dark-eyed, dark-mouthed. Night was flowing between the high old houses like a turbid river. I was afraid she would be swept away, this time beyond my reach.

She touched my arm. "Will you lend me your car, Lew?"

"For how long?"

"Overnight."

"For what purpose?"

"You don't have to cross-question me. Just give me a yes or no."

"All right. The answer is no."

"Please. This is important to me."

"The answer is still no. I'm not going through another night like last night, wondering what's happened to you."

"All right. I'll find someone who is willing to help me."

She started to walk toward the street, stumbling a little among the weeds. I was shaken by the idea that I might lose her and went after her.

She turned at the sidewalk. "Are you going to lend me your car?"

"No. I'm not letting you out of my sight. If you rent a car or borrow one, I'll follow you."

"You can't bear to see me get ahead of you, is that it?"

"No. You were way ahead of me last night. You put yourself in an exposed position. I don't want that to happen again. There's such a thing as having too much nerve." I took a deep breath. "Have you had any rest today?"

She answered evasively, "I forget."

"That means you haven't. You can't take a long night drive without any sleep. God knows what you might run into at the far end."

"God and Archer," she said bitterly, "they know everything. Don't you and God ever make a mistake?"

"God did. He left off Eve's testicles."

Betty let out a cry of pure sharp female rage, which

somehow diminuendoed into mirth. She finally settled for both the car and me, on condition that she be allowed to do at least half the driving. I opted for the first shift.

"Where are we going?" I said as I started the engine.

"Long Beach. I assume you know where that is."

"I ought to. I was born there. What's in Long Beach?"

"I promised not to tell anyone."

"Promised who?" I said. "Mrs. Chantry?"

"Since you know everything," Betty said clearly and carefully, "it would seem superfluous to answer any of your questions."

"So it's Francine Chantry. What is she doing in Long Beach?"

"Apparently she had a car accident."

"Is she in the hospital?"

"No. She's at a place called the Gilded Galleon."

"That's a waterfront bar. What's she doing there?"

"I think she's drinking. I've never known her to drink much, but she seems to be breaking down."

"Why did she call you?"

"She said she needed my advice and help. We're not really close but I suppose I'm as close to her as anyone is. She wants my advice in a public-relations capacity, she said. Which probably means that she wants me to help her out of the mess she's got herself into by running away."

"Did she say why she did that?"

"She simply panicked."

I thought as I turned onto the freeway that Francine Chantry had some reason to panic. She had guilty knowledge of the death of Gerard Johnson, and possibly of the death of William Mead.

I drove hard. Betty slept against my shoulder. The combination of the speeding car and the sleeping woman made me feel almost young, as if my life might have a new beginning after all.

In spite of the early-evening traffic, we were in Long

Beach in two hours. It was my home territory, as I had
said, and the lights along the waterfront shone with remembered promise, even if all it had led to was the present.

I remembered the Galleon from the days when my
marriage had been breaking up and I was looking for
ways to pass the long nights. The place had changed
surprisingly little since then, much less than I had. It
was what was known as a family tavern, which meant
that it accommodated drunks of all ages and sexes. I
stood just inside the door, washed by waves of human
sound, while Betty made her way around the horseshoe-
shaped bar. Everybody seemed to be talking at once,
including the barmaids. I could understand why the
loud factitious family atmosphere might appeal to a
woman as lonely as Francine Chantry probably was.

I saw her at the far end of the bar, sitting with her
silver head drooping over an empty glass. She seemed
to be slow in recognizing Betty. Then she threw her
arms around her, and Betty responded. Though I felt
some sympathy for Mrs. Chantry, and some pleasure in
Betty's warmth, I didn't like to see the two women embracing. Betty was young and clean. Francine Chantry
had been living for decades deep in the knowledge of
murder.

It was beginning to show in her face and body, reaching up for her from the earth like gravity. She stumbled
before she got to me, and had to be supported by the
younger woman. She had a cut on her forehead. Her
jaw was slack and grim, her eyes dull. But she held on
to her bag the way a plunging fullback holds the ball.

"Where's your car, Mrs. Chantry?"

She roused herself from her apathy. "The garageman
said it was totaled. I think that means that it isn't worth
repairing. I doubt that I am, either."

"Were you in an accident?"

"I don't really know what happened. I was trying to
get off the freeway, and things went out of control all of

a sudden. That seems to be the story of my life." Her laughter was like a dry compulsive cough.

"I'm interested in the story of your life."

"I know you are." She turned to Betty. "Why did you have to bring *him* along? I thought we could have a constructive talk about the future. I thought you and I were good friends."

"I hope we are," Betty said. "But I didn't think I could handle this by myself."

"Handle what? I'm no problem."

But there was a note of terror in Francine Chantry's voice. She sounded like a woman who had stepped off the edge of the world and discovered too late that she could never step back. When we got into my car and entered the freeway, the sense of moving through empty space stayed with me. We seemed to be flying above the rooftops of the tract houses that lined the freeway on both sides.

Betty was driving too fast, but I was content to have her do her stint. She had had some recent sleep; and I wanted a chance to talk to Francine Chantry.

"Speaking of your future," I said, "your husband may be hard to convict."

"My husband?" She sounded confused.

"Richard Chantry alias Gerard or Jerry Johnson. It may not be too easy to pin these murders on him. I gather he isn't talking. And so much of it happened so long ago. I wouldn't be surprised if the prosecutor was willing to make a deal with you. I doubt that he'll want to bring any major charges. Of course that depends on him, and on what you have to offer."

She let out another burst of dry laughter. "My dead body? Would he accept my dead body?"

"He'll want you alive and talking. You know more about this case than anyone."

She was silent for a minute. "If I do, it's not by choice."

"So you were telling me the other night. But you really made your choices long ago. When you dropped

William Mead and took up with his half brother Chantry. When you left Arizona with Chantry, even though you must have known that he was a major suspect in the murder of William Mead. Seven years later, you made a final choice, when you decided to cover up the murder of Gerard Johnson."

"Who?"

"Gerard Johnson. The man in the brown suit. It turns out he was a friend of William Mead's. He'd just got out of five years in a veterans' hospital when he came to Santa Teresa to see your husband. I think he had evidence involving Chantry in William Mead's death."

"How?"

"Perhaps William Mead had been threatened by Chantry and they had quarreled over you, or over Mead's pictures, which Chantry stole. And Mead told his army buddy Gerard about it some time before Chantry killed him. When Gerard Johnson turned up in Santa Teresa with William's widow and little boy, it marked the end of Chantry's freedom. He killed Gerard in an effort to stay free, but it only made him more completely unfree. It was a final choice for Chantry as well as you."

"I had no part in the choice," she said.

"You went along with it. You let a man be killed in your house and buried there, and you kept quiet. It was a bad choice for you and your husband. He's been living out its consequences. The murder of Gerard Johnson put him in the hands of William Mead's widow, the woman who calls herself Mrs. Johnson. I don't know why she wanted him. There may have been something between them in the past. Or perhaps the Johnson woman was simply interested in driving a hard primitive bargain with Chantry. He'd killed her husband, now he had to take her husband's place. I don't know why Chantry accepted the bargain, do you?"

Francine Chantry was slow in answering. Finally she said, "I don't know anything about it. I've had no idea that Richard was living in town. I didn't even know if he was alive. I didn't hear from him once in twenty-five years."

"Have you seen him recently?"

"No. I have no desire to see him."

"You're going to have to. They'll be wanting you to identify him. Not that there's much doubt about who he is. He's deteriorated physically and mentally. I think he must have had an emotional breakdown after he murdered Johnson, perhaps before. But he can still paint. His paintings may not be as good as they were, but nobody else could have painted them."

She said with some irony, "Apparently you're an art critic as well as a detective."

"Hardly. But I do have one of his recent paintings in the trunk of my car. And I'm not the only one who thinks that it's a Chantry."

"Are you talking about the painting of Mildred Mead?"

"Yes. I found it this morning in Johnson's attic, where it originated. Where the whole current case originated. That picture seems to be the central thing in the case. Certainly it brought me into it. And it was the painting of it that got Chantry into his present trouble and led him to commit these new murders."

"I don't quite follow that," Francine Chantry said. But she sounded interested, as if this talk of her husband's work had acted on her like a stimulant.

"It's a fairly complex chain of events," I said. "The woman he's been living with on Olive Street—call her Mrs. Johnson—sold the painting to the artist-dealer Jacob Whitmore. That blew Chantry's cover. Whitmore sold the painting to Paul Grimes, and that blew it wider.

"Grimes recognized it as Chantry's work and evidently used the knowledge to blackmail Mrs. Johnson into stealing drugs for him. And he probably demanded more new pictures from Chantry. Grimes had sold the picture of Mildred Mead to Ruth Biemeyer, who had her own reasons for being interested in Mildred. As you probably know, Mildred was Jack Biemeyer's mistress."

"Everybody in Arizona knew it," Francine Chantry said. "What wasn't so generally known was that Ruth Biemeyer had a crush on Richard when they were both young. I think that's the essential reason why she talked Jack into moving to Santa Teresa."

"That's what he says, anyway. It made for a tight family situation which was made still tighter when Mildred Mead came to town. I think Chantry may have seen Mildred some time in the last few months and been moved to paint that memory picture of her."

"I wouldn't know."

"Haven't you seen him recently?"

"No. Certainly not." She didn't look at me. She was peering through the windshield into the broken darkness. "I haven't seen Richard, or heard from him, in twenty-five years. I had no idea that he was living in town."

"Not even when you got a phone call from the woman he was living with?"

"She didn't mention him. She said something about the—the burial in the greenhouse, and she let me know that she needed money. She said if I would help her out she'd go on keeping the whole thing quiet. Otherwise she'd tell the world the real reason for my husband's disappearance."

"Did you give her money?"

"No. I wish now I had. And I very much wish he had never painted that memory portrait of Mildred. You'd almost think he was trying to be found out."

"Perhaps he was, unconsciously," I said. "Certainly Fred was doing his best to find him out. No doubt Fred borrowed the painting from the Biemeyers partly for professional reasons. He wanted to establish whether it really could be a Chantry. But he had personal reasons, too. I think he may have connected it with pictures he had seen in the past in the Johnson house on Olive Street. But he failed to make the final conscious connection between his foster father, Johnson, and the painter Chantry. Before he could do that, Johnson-Chantry took the painting from Fred's bedroom. And the Biemeyers hired me to get it back for them."

Betty tapped the horn. We were moving down the long inland slope behind Camarillo. There were no cars immediately ahead of us. I looked at her and she looked back. She raised her right hand from the wheel and touched her mouth. I got the message. I had talked more than enough, and I subsided.

A few minutes later, Mrs. Chantry said, "It wasn't his first memory picture of Mildred. He painted several others, long ago, in our days together. One of them was a pietà."

She was silent for a long time, until we were on the outskirts of Santa Teresa. Then I heard her crying softly. There was no way to tell if she was crying for Chantry or herself, or perhaps for the long-dead partnership that had held their young lives together and spawned his work. When I looked sideways at her face, I could see the bright tears on it.

"Where do we go from here?" Betty said.

"The police station."

Francine Chantry let out a cry that subsided into a groan. "Can't I even spend the night in my own house?"

"You can go back there and pack a bag if you want to. Then I think you should go to the police, with your lawyer."

Much later, in the pre-dawn chill, I woke in a dark bed. I could feel Betty's heart and hear her breathing like the quiet susurrus of a summer ocean.

A harsher bedroom scene came into my mind. I had last seen Francine Chantry in a hospital room with specially screened windows and an armed guard outside the door. And just outside the half-open door of my partly sleeping mind another woman seemed to be waiting, a short lame white-haired woman who had been beautiful.

The word "pietà" came back into my mind. I woke Betty up with my hand on the curve on her hip. She sighed and turned over.

"Lew?"

"What's a pietà?"

She yawned deeply. "You ask the darnedest questions at the darnedest times."

"Does that mean you don't know?"

"Of course I know what a pietà is. It's a traditional picture of the Virgin Mary mourning over the body of her son. Why?"

"Francine Chantry said her husband painted one of Mildred Mead. I assume she was Mary."

"Yes. I've seen the picture. They have it in the local gallery, but they don't exhibit it publicly. It's slightly embarrassing, or so some people think. Chantry painted the dead man as a self-portrait."

Betty yawned and went to sleep again. I lay awake and watched her face emerging in the slow dawn. After a while I could see the steady blue pulse in her temple, the beating of the silent hammer that meant that she was alive. I hoped that the blue hammer would never stop.

# XLIII

When I woke up a second time, Betty had gone out. She had left four things for me on the kitchenette table: a carton of granola, a bottle of milk, a safety razor, and a cryptic note, which said: "Had funny dream—Mildred Mead Chantry's mother—is this possible??"

I ate my breakfast food and drove across town to Magnolia Court. Mildred Mead failed to answer my repeated knocking on her door. An old man came out of the next cottage and looked me over from the distance of a generation. Eventually he volunteered the information that Mrs. Mead, as he called her, had gone out.

"Do you know where she went?"

"She told the taxi-driver to take her to the courthouse."

I followed Mildred there, but she wasn't easy to find. The courthouse and its landscaped grounds occupied a city block. I soon decided that I was wasting my time walking up and down its graveled paths and tiled corridors looking for a small old limping woman.

I checked in at the coroner's suite of offices and found Henry Purvis there. Mildred had come to his office within the past half-hour.

"What did she want from you?"

"Information about William Mead. He was her natural son, apparently. I told her he was buried in the Santa Teresa cemetery, and I offered to take her out to visit his grave. She didn't seem interested in that. She got off on the subject of Richard Chantry. She claimed she had been his model at one time, and she wanted to get in to see him. I told her it simply wasn't possible."

"Where is Chantry being held?"

"District Attorney Lansing has him here in a special cell with round-the-clock guards. I couldn't even get in there myself—not that I particularly want to. Apparently he's gone completely off the rails. They have to sedate him to keep him quiet."

"What happened to Mildred?"

"She walked out. I sort of hated to let her go. She seemed pretty upset, and she'd been drinking. But I had no reason to hold her."

I went outside and made another circuit of the grounds and courtyards. No Mildred. I was getting nervous. Whether or not there was truth in Betty's dream, I felt that Mildred was in some way central to the case. But I was losing her, and losing the morning.

I looked up at the four-sided clock on the courthouse tower. It was ten. There was only one person visible on the observation platform, a white-headed woman whose rather clumsy movements caught my eye. Mildred. She paused and turned and gripped the black iron fence. It was almost up to her chin. She peered over it, down into the stone-paved courtyard.

She was extraordinarily still. She looked like a woman staring down into her grave. The life of the city seemed to freeze in widening circles around her.

I was nearly a hundred yards away and a hundred feet below. If I raised an alarm, it might only trigger the action she seemed to have in mind. I walked to the nearest door and took the tower elevator up.

When I stepped out on the observation platform, she had turned to face me, her back against the iron fence. She turned again and tried to clamber over the fence into empty space. Her lame old body failed in the attempt.

I put my arms around her and held her securely. She was breathing as if she had climbed the tower hand over hand. The frozen life of the city resumed, and I began to hear its sounds again.

She struggled in my arms. "Let me go."

"I don't think so, Mildred. Those flagstones are a long way down and I wouldn't want you to take a fall on them. You're too pretty."

"I'm the hag of the universe." But she gave me an up-from-under look, the automatic mannerism of a woman who had once been small and beautiful and was still handsome. "Will you give me a break?"

"If I can."

"Just take me down and turn me loose. I won't do anything—not to myself or anybody else."

"I can't take a chance on that."

I could feel the heat of her body through her clothes. Sweat gathered on her upper lip and in the blued hollows of her eyes.

"Tell me about your son William."

She didn't answer me. Her makeup was eroding, and her gray face peered at me through it like a death mask.

"Did you trade in your son's dead body on that big

house in Chantry Canyon? Or was it somebody else's dead body?"

She spat in my face. Then she went into a fit of passionate weeping. Then she was still. She didn't speak as I took her down in the elevator, or when I handed her over to the D.A.'s men and women.

I told them that she should be carefully searched and kept under observation as a determined potential suicide. It was just as well I did. District Attorney Lansing told me later that the woman who searched her found a brightly honed stiletto wrapped in a silk stocking and tucked under her girdle.

"Did they find out what she was carrying it for?"

The D.A. shook his head. "Presumably," he said, "she intended to use it on Chantry."

"What was her motive?"

Lansing pulled alternately at the ends of his handlebar mustaches, as if he were using them to steer his mind through the complexities of the case. "This isn't generally known, and I'll have to ask you to keep it to yourself. Chantry seems to have murdered Miss Mead's son in Arizona, thirty years ago. To give credit where credit is due, I got that from Captain Mackendrick. He's been doing some excellent spadework in this case. I think he'll be our next chief of police."

"Good for him. But how does the revenge theory fit in with her suicide attempt?"

"Are you certain it was a real attempt?"

"It looked real to me. Mildred wanted out, and the only thing that stopped her was that iron fence. That and the fact that I happened to see her up there."

"Well, it's not inconsistent with the revenge motif. She was thwarted in her attempt at revenge, so she turned her anger against herself."

"I don't quite follow that, Mr. D.A."

"No? You're probably not as familiar as some of us are with recent developments in criminal psychology." There was an edge on his smile.

I gave him a soft answer because I wanted something from him. "It's true I never went to law school."

"But you've been of real assistance in spite of that," he said reassuringly. "And we're certainly grateful for your suggestions."

His eyes went distant on me, and he stood up behind his desk. I stood up, too. I had a nightmare vision of my case moving inexorably away from me.

"Could I possibly have a minute with your prisoner, Mr. D.A.?"

"Which one?"

"Chantry. I want to ask him a couple of questions."

"He isn't answering questions. The public defender has advised him not to."

"The questions I have in mind aren't connected with these murders, at least not directly."

"What are they?" Lansing said.

"I want to ask him what his real name is, and get his reaction. And I want to ask him why Mildred Mead tried to kill herself."

"We don't really know that she did."

"I know that she did, and I want to know why."

"What makes you so sure that Chantry might possess the information?"

"I think he and Mildred are closely connected. Incidentally, I feel sure that Jack Biemeyer will be interested. Biemeyer hired me, you know."

Lansing said in a voice that seemed to be testing itself for firmness, "If Mr. Biemeyer has any suggestions, or any questions, I think he should communicate them to me directly."

"I'll tell him that."

The Biemeyer house had a deserted look, like a public building that had been emptied by a bomb scare. I got the painting of Mildred Mead out of the trunk of my car and carried it up the flagstone walk to the front door. Just before I got to it, Ruth Biemeyer came out. She put a finger to her lips.

"My husband is very tired. I've been trying to get him to rest."

"I'm afraid I have to talk to him, Mrs. Biemeyer."

She turned toward the door, but all she did was pull it closed. "You can talk freely to me. I'm really your principal in this case. The picture that was stolen belongs to me. That is my picture that you have there, isn't it?"

"Yes. I wouldn't say it was stolen, though. Let's say Fred borrowed it, for scientific and biographical purposes. He wanted to establish who painted it, and when, and who the subject was. It's true the answers to these questions had personal meaning for Fred. But that doesn't make him a criminal exactly."

She nodded. Her hair shifted in the wind and made her suddenly prettier, as if light had blown into her head.

"I can understand why Fred did what he did."

"You should be able to. You had your own personal reasons for buying the painting. Mildred Mead had moved to town, and your husband was seeing her again. Didn't that have something to do with your hanging that picture of her in your house? As a reproach to him, perhaps, or a kind of threat?"

She frowned. The light in her eyes shifted, turning inward like a flashlight exploring a dark room.

"I don't know why I bought it. I didn't even realize at the time that it was Mildred."

"Your husband must have."

There was a silence between us. I could hear the sea marking time far down at the foot of the hill.

"My husband isn't in very good shape. He's aged in the last few days. If all this got out it would destroy his reputation. And maybe destroy him."

"He assumed that risk when he did what he did a long time ago."

"Exactly what did he do?"

"I think he made the Chantry imposture possible."

"The Chantry imposture? What do you mean by that?"

"I think you know what I mean. But I'd rather discuss it with your husband."

She bit her lower lip. With her incisors bared, she looked a little like a watchdog at the door. Then she picked up the painting and led me through the house to her husband's study.

He was sitting in front of the photograph of his copper mine. His face had come apart. He pulled it together and smiled uncertainly with one side of his mouth.

"What do you want from me? More money?"

"More information. This case started in 1943. It's time it was closed."

Ruth Biemeyer turned to me. "Exactly what happened in 1943?"

"I can't tell you all of it. I think it started when William Mead went home to Arizona on leave from the army. Home isn't exactly the word. Mead had a young wife and an infant son waiting for him here in Santa Teresa. But his mother was still living in Arizona. Where exactly was Mildred living, Mr. Biemeyer?"

He pretended not to hear me. His wife answered for him. "She was living in Tucson but spending the weekends in the mountains with my husband."

Biemeyer gave her a shocked look. It made me wonder if his affair with Mildred had ever been directly spoken of till now. I said:

"That probably came as no surprise to William. His mother had lived with other men, notably the painter Lashman. Lashman had been a father to him, and taught him to paint. When William came home to Arizona on leave he found that his so-called half brother, Richard, had taken some of his work and assumed the credit for it. The Chantry imposture really started with Richard Chantry himself, when he stole William's paintings and drawings, and incidentally married William's girl Francine.

"The two young men had a fight over these matters. They fought to the death. William killed Richard and left his body in the desert, dressed in William's own army uniform. He was an illegitimate son who had probably dreamed all his life of taking Richard's place. This was his chance to do it, and incidentally to get out of the army and out of a forced marriage.

"But he couldn't have done it without the help of other people, three other people to be exact. First he had the help of Francine Chantry. She was obviously in love with him in spite of his marriage to Sarah and his killing of Francine's husband. She may even have incited that killing. In any case it didn't prevent her from coming to Santa Teresa with him and living here as his wife for seven years.

"I don't know why he took the risk of coming back here. Perhaps he had some idea of keeping an eye on his son. But so far as I can tell, he didn't see Fred in all that time. It may be that his living here, so close to his wife and son but invisible to them, was part of the game of doubleness he was playing. He may have needed that kind of tension to keep him in orbit and sustain the Chantry illusion and his art.

"The main thing was to get out of Arizona free and clear, and it was his mother who made that possible for him. What Mildred did was probably the most difficult thing of all. She looked at young Richard Chantry's dead body and identified it as the body of her own son, William. It was a bold action, and not her last. She loved her bastard son, no matter what he was guilty of. But it was a fierce and tragic love she had for him. This morning she tried to reach him with a stiletto."

"To kill him?" Ruth Biemeyer said.

"Or to let him kill himself. I don't think it would have made much difference to Mildred. Her own life is pretty well finished."

Jack Biemeyer let out an involuntary sigh.

His wife turned to me. "You said William had help from three people."

"At least three."

"Who was the third?"

"I think you know. William Mead never would have gotten out of Arizona, or succeeded in staying out, without some help. Somebody had to turn off Sheriff Brotherton's investigation and see that the case was closed."

Ruth Biemeyer and I looked at her husband. He lifted his heavy arms as though our eyes were guns.

"I wouldn't do a thing like that."

"You would if she told you to," his wife said. "She's been telling you what to do ever since I can remember. You'll be going down to the county jail to ask her what to do next. And she'll tell you to spend a fortune defending her murdering son, and you'll do it for her."

"Maybe I will at that."

He was watching her face. She looked at him in surprise and sudden fear.

Biemeyer stood up slowly, as if he was lifting a great weight on his shoulders. "Will you drive me down there, Archer? I'm feeling a bit shaky."

I said I would. Biemeyer started out of the room ahead of me. He turned at the open door and faced his wife.

"There's something you need to know, Ruth. William is my son, too. My illegitimate son by Mildred. I was just a kid in my teens when he was born."

Desolation crept over her face. "Why didn't you tell me before? It's too late now."

She looked at her husband as if she was seeing him for the last time. He took me out through the empty echoing spaces of the house. He walked uncertainly, staggering a little. I helped him into my car and started down the hill.

"It was an accident," he said, "just one of those accidents that happen to people. I met Mildred after a high-school football game. Old Felix Chantry threw a party in his mountain house. I was invited because my mother was his cousin. You know, a poor relation."

He sat for a while with his head down, then spoke in a stronger voice. "I scored three touchdowns that day, four if you count Mildred. I was seventeen when William was conceived, eighteen when he was born. There wasn't much I could do for him. I had no money. I was trying to make it through college. Mildred told Felix Chantry that the child was his, and he believed her. He let the boy use his name and gave her money for the boy's support until she broke with him and went to Simon Lashman.

"She did what she could for me, too. She helped me get a football scholarship and when I graduated she saw that Felix gave me a job at the smelter. She helped me up the ladder. I owe her a great deal."

But there was no warmth of gratitude in his voice. Perhaps he sensed that his life had been mislaid when he was young, and even in his age was still loose in his grasp. He peered out at the city we were driving through as though its shadowed streets were alien.

I felt the strangeness, too. The halls of the courthouse were like catacombs. After an elaborate proceeding that reminded me of the initiation rite into a tribe of aborigines, the D.A.'s men ushered us into the presence of the man I had taken.

He didn't look like a mass murderer, in spite of the armed guards who stood one on each side of him. He looked pale and weak and worried, as violent men so often do after the event.

"William?" I said.

He nodded once. Tears had begun to form in his eyes and run down his cheeks, slowly, like the sparse blood from stiletto wounds.

Jack Biemeyer stepped forward and touched his son's wet face.

# ABOUT THE AUTHOR

ROSS MACDONALD was born near San Francisco in 1915. He was educated in Canadian schools, traveled widely in Europe, and acquired advanced degrees and a Phi Beta Kappa key at the University of Michigan. In 1938 he married a Canadian girl who is now well known as the novelist Margaret Millar. Mr. Macdonald (Kenneth Millar in private life) taught school and later college, and served as communications officer aboard an escort carrier in the Pacific. For over twenty years he lived in Santa Barbara and wrote mystery novels about the fascinating and changing society of his native state. Among his leading interests are conservation and politics. He is a past president of the Mystery Writers of America. In 1964 his novel *The Chill* was given a Silver Dagger award by the Crime Writers' Association of Great Britain. Mr. Macdonald's *The Far Side of the Dollar* was named the best crime novel of 1965 by the same organization. Recently, he was presented with the Mystery Writers of America's Grand Master Award. *The Moving Target* was made into the highly successful movie *Harper* in 1966. *The Goodbye Look* (1969), *The Underground Man* (1971), *Sleeping Beauty* (1973) and *The Blue Hammer* (1976) were all national bestsellers. Ross Macdonald died in 1983.

# THE THRILLING AND MASTERFUL NOVELS OF ROSS MACDONALD

Winner of the Mystery Writers of America Grand Master Award, Ross Macdonald is acknowledged around the world as one of the greatest mystery writers of our time. *The New York Times* has called his books featuring private investigator Lew Archer "the finest series of detective novels ever written by an American."

Now, Bantam Books is reissuing Macdonald's finest work in handsome new paperback editions. Look for these books (a new title will be published every month) wherever paperbacks are sold or use the handy coupon below for ordering: